Comments: If Dr. Gordon doesn't stop thinking about Ms. Serenov and start concentrating on his book, he is liable to have the time of his life.

MEN at WORK

MEN at WORK
JANICE KAISER
BODY AND SOUL

TALL, DARK
AND SMART
E=MC²

Harlequin Books

TORONTO · NEW YORK · LONDON
AMSTERDAM · PARIS · SYDNEY · HAMBURG
STOCKHOLM · ATHENS · TOKYO · MILAN
MADRID · WARSAW · BUDAPEST · AUCKLAND

HARLEQUIN BOOKS
225 Duncan Mill Road, Don Mills,
Ontario, Canada M3B 3K9

ISBN 0-373-81019-9

BODY AND SOUL

Dear Reader,

Vacations are very special times. They give people a chance to back away from life—to renew themselves. Sometimes vacations are quiet; sometimes vacations are filled with action and adventure. And once in a great while, if they are lucky, they will find true love in an unexpected place.

In *Body and Soul*, when Professor Derek Gordon goes to a sleepy little Northern California town for his sabbatical, his goal is to get away from his problems for a while and finish his book. The last thing he expects is to wind up embroiled in Lara Serenov's life. But the beautiful poet not only brings excitement to Derek's sabbatical, she brings him a sense of hope—hope that Derek can find a way to discover life...and true love...again.

Janice Kaiser

For Ruth & Al Kaiser
On their Golden Wedding Anniversary

CHAPTER ONE

HE BRUSHED AWAY a cobweb and peered through the windowpane. Across the cove breakers were slamming into the sea cliff, sending a fan of spray over the rocks. Derek Gordon contemplated the scene. Already he had a sense of the isolation of the place. That pleased him. He was looking forward to spending a number of months alone.

A gull soared above the rocks, the stiff breeze holding it aloft. The bird seemed indifferent to all but the sea. It was the way Derek wanted to feel himself. He wanted to forget everything and everyone but his work. That was, after all, what had brought him to this remote stretch of coastline. But he knew he wouldn't succeed—not completely.

Outside, a truck door slammed. Derek turned around as Mark appeared at the door of the cottage. The young man leaned against the doorjamb. They looked at each other.

"That's the last of it," Mark said, nodding toward the boxes of books on the floor. "You need anything else?"

"No, you've been a big help."

The younger man looked around the room. "This place needs a good dusting."

"The owner said someone would be by this afternoon to clean it up. It's been vacant since last fall."

"It looks it."

Derek slid his hands into the pockets of his cords and gave Mark a faint smile. "My needs are simple. A comfortable chair, a good reading light, a place for my type-writer, a bed, some food…and peace and quiet.''

Mark's expression was vaguely sarcastic, and critical—always critical. It had been since Derek announced he was going away. ''You're a regular Buddhist monk.''

''Yeah, I suppose.''

They looked into each other's eyes. Certain things hadn't been said, and Derek wanted to clear the air before Mark left. But it was hard to talk about Margaret. It was painful for them both. They each loved her, and yet each of them suffered alone. In so many other ways they were close, able to share their feelings. But as Margaret's condition grew worse, her illness separated them rather than drawing them closer. Derek knew, though, he had to say something.

''You resent the fact that I'm leaving her, don't you?''

''Mom? She won't know the difference.''

''But you will.''

''You aren't married to me.''

''You're my stepson. It matters what you think.''

''It shouldn't.''

''Well, it does.''

Mark looked annoyed. ''What do you want me to do about it, Derek?''

''You can't change your feelings, I understand that,'' he said. ''But I'd feel better knowing you at least recognize my motives.''

''Hey, you're married to a vegetable. What else needs to be said?''

''Your mother's not a vegetable, and it doesn't help to talk about her that way.'' Their eyes met and the tension between them became palpable. Derek was angry, with himself as much as Mark. He turned to the window, hoping his emotion would abate.

The breakers were still crashing against the rocks. Nothing had changed, except there were two gulls instead of one, hovering mindlessly over the surf.

"I plan on driving down at least once a month to visit," Derek said without turning. "Since that means I won't be seeing her as often as before, you may feel the burden is falling to you. That's not my intention. I want you to know that."

"Don't worry about me. My mother is my mother, whether you exist or not."

Derek turned around. The words had stung, but Mark didn't look as though he had any regret. "I've always thought of us as a family," Derek said. "I've known you and loved you since you were a boy."

"Look, there's no need to get sentimental. Let's each do our thing, and let the chips fall where they may. I'm not living my life for you, and I can't expect you to live yours for me—or Mom, either, for that matter."

Derek took a deep breath. "I love your mother," he said, his voice thick with emotion.

"Yeah, and so do I."

They stared at each other, two bull moose, one beginning to age some, the other young and green and a little reckless with emotion. The tension could last for years, Derek could see that now. As long as Margaret lived, she would cast a shadow over their lives.

Mark drew himself up. "Well, I've got a long drive back. I'd better get going."

"Thanks again for all you've done," Derek said. "I appreciate the help. Especially under the circumstances."

Mark nodded slowly and went out the door. Derek followed him onto the porch. He watched as Mark opened the door of the truck and climbed in. He was so much like his mother. They had the same auburn hair, high cheekbones and narrow straight nose.

Derek had always been glad the boy didn't have much of his father in him—it had been easier to love Mark as a son, thinking of him as his wife's alone. Even though there was only eighteen years difference in their ages, the boy really had been like his own child. He hoped one day they could become close again.

Mark rolled down the window as though he might want to say something. Derek waited. The steady breeze off the Pacific blew through the cypress, fluttering his dark hair, tinged at the temples with gray. There was a pungent salty smell to the air that was invigorating.

Mark leaned out the window. "Mind if I ask you something personal?"

"Of course not." Derek stepped off the porch and went to the truck.

Mark's eyes grew distant, uncertain. "Have you ever considered getting a divorce?"

The question was unexpected. "No I haven't."

"Maybe you should."

"Why?"

"Isn't it pretty obvious? You're only…what…thirty-eight? And you're married to someone who's been in a nursing home for five years now, somebody who's been sick for more than seven years."

"Margaret's my wife. You don't stop loving someone simply because they're ill."

"I know. But she's not going to get better."

"You want me to divorce your mother? Is that what you're saying?"

"I'm saying that ignoring the facts is as bad as lying." He started the engine.

"Look, Mark, if it's permission you're trying to give me, fine. I appreciate it. If for some reason you think that I, or your mother, or you would be better off if I divorced her, then I'll be blunt and tell you I have no intention of doing so. For whatever reason.''

''What if there was someone else?''

''There isn't.''

''But what if there were?''

''Then I'd deal with that at the time.''

Neither said anything more. The surf beat against the rocks below the house. In the distance the gulls called, and the wind continued to blow steadily.

Mark put the truck in reverse. He tried to smile. ''All right, professor. Guess I'll be seeing you, then.''

Derek nodded and smiled back, knowing a truce was the best he could hope for. ''Take it easy driving home.''

The truck backed around. It climbed the drive to the highway. Derek watched until it was out of sight. Then he went inside, looking this time at the familiar boxes containing his research materials, books and manuscripts. He had come to the Mendocino coast to work, all right. But it was also a self-imposed exile. Over the past few years he had come to know loneliness, but after a year in splendid isolation Derek Gordon figured he'd know it even better.

SHE PUSHED THE BUTTON on her tape recorder, then moved across the deck to the railing. Leaning on it, she looked out over the sea of pines toward the ocean, a ribbon of blue green in the distance. Her own voice came from the machine, behind her.

Lara closed her eyes and listened carefully to the sound, her mind following the rhythm and cadence of each phrase. For a long time she concentrated on her voice, letting herself drift with the emotion evoked by the lines, letting herself relive the feelings that had prompted her to put them on paper in the first place.

Overhead the pines encircling her retreat moaned in the

breeze that flowed up the mountainside from the narrow valley below. The rich, dry air kissed her skin, causing her to shiver slightly, despite its warmth. Lara loved to work outside. She loved the clean, verdant smell of the woods—the solitude, the independence, the poetic nature of her existence.

She pushed the rewind button, then picked up her notepad. Scanning the written text, she toyed mentally with a word that had jumped out at her like the caw of a jay in the quiet morning air.

Then, behind her, a man said, "Where's your friend?"

Lara jumped, then spun around. He was peering through the railing at the side of the deck. The face was familiar. It was a face from the past, from a different age, a different life.

"Steve, what are you doing here?" She put her hand to her chest. "You scared me to death."

He grinned. "I heard voices when I was coming around the house. I thought you was having a party with some of your writer friends or something."

She stared, wide-eyed, still not believing he was there. Over the past few years she had seen Steve Adamson a time or two, but they hadn't spoken. Not in a long time.

"Surprised to see me, huh?"

"To be honest, yes."

"Just thought I'd pay a social call. Anything wrong with that?" He let his eyes trail down her bare legs in an obvious, possessive way. Then he smiled.

"We've lived within twenty miles of each other for ten years. You've never paid a social call before."

"Then it's about time I did." He put a hand on the rail. "Mind if I come up on the deck?"

"Look," she replied, gesturing toward the tape recorder, "I'm working. I don't want to socialize."

"Why so unfriendly?"

"Steve, it was a long time ago. I'd just as soon forget we ever met."

"Met? Is that what you call it, Lara?"

"You know what I mean."

Steve Adamson looked at her legs again, and Lara suddenly became very conscious of what she was wearing. She wore shorts and a filmy muslin blouse and she was braless. She'd washed her tawny-blond hair, and it was hanging past her shoulder in ringlets. It wasn't the way Steve, or any man, should see her. She put down her pad and folded her arms over her breasts, giving him a hard look.

But he either misread her expression or ignored the hint. He took hold of the railing and climbed over, bounding onto the deck with booted feet.

Lara faced him. Steve was bigger than she recalled. He still had the body of the football player he'd been in high school, but his face had weathered and matured in a rugged, even handsome sort of way. Gone was the callow look of the boy who'd once been her husband.

He was gazing at her with fascination, perhaps remembering her as she had been. The corner of his mouth curled in silent amusement. He parted his lips slightly and his tongue flicked at the inner edges of them. It was hard to tell whether the gesture was a conscious one, but it was clearly suggestive. Lara didn't like it. And she didn't appreciate his unexpected visit, either.

"What do you want, Steve? Why are you here?"

He responded with another smile. Then he moved past her to the tape recorder and pushed the play button. Lara's taped voice broke the silence, sounding curiously formal, considering the circumstances. Steve listened to several lines of the poem before pushing the stop button, his finger lingering on the machine almost affectionately.

"I always liked your voice. It was sexy, even when you was a kid." He hadn't looked at her. He was still toying with the tape recorder. "Remember how you used to sit up writing poems at night when I was already in bed, horny as hell? For a long time I thought you did it to get me hot and bothered, so it'd be fantastic when we got it on."

"Steve..."

"But that wasn't why you did it, was it?" He turned to her finally. "You cared more about writing poems than making love."

Her eyes flashed. "I don't appreciate that kind of talk. You're out of line."

His response was a grin.

"Where's your wife?" she asked.

"Mary Beth and me split up a while back." Steve acted as though his announcement explained everything she needed to know. He ambled over to a canvas director's chair and defiantly sat down. He stretched out his jeans-clad legs. "Be honest, Lara, isn't even a part of you glad to see me?"

"No."

His expression turned thoughtful. "You know, I never figured that out. Why the hell did you marry me, anyway?"

"Steve, that was thirteen years ago. We were kids. Children. Who we were then has nothing to do with who we are now."

"Bull. People are people. I'm the guy you married. A little older. Been around more. That's all."

"I don't want to talk about this."

"Things weren't so bad in those days—once you put your poems away and came to bed," he said, ignoring her. "I think you gave me up too soon, Lara." His look was very suggestive.

She gazed at him incredulously. It was still hard for her

to believe this was happening. Steve Adamson had practically ceased to exist in her mind. It seemed absurd to think they'd once been married. She had been only eighteen at the time and the marriage hadn't lasted six months. It had hardly been more than an interlude in her life, a game. Children playing grown-ups. She'd married for reasons having little to do with him, and yet he'd had no idea. Not then. And evidently not now.

Steve didn't move. His large hands were folded over his chest as he stared at her. He was looking at her body, a menacing expression on his face. It frightened her, bringing back the horror of their last weeks together. He had practically raped her when she'd refused to make love.

Of course, people didn't call it rape back then. He was just another demanding husband asserting his conjugal rights. Lara's bitterness, long repressed, returned. Steve Adamson wasn't a part of her life—he hadn't been for a long time. But seeing him face-to-face, feeling his leer, brought back some things she'd half forgotten and never thought about.

"Go, Steve. Leave. It's the last time I ask."

He frowned. "Why are you so unfriendly? I haven't been drinking. There's no reason to be afraid."

"I'm not afraid. I'm annoyed." But she was frightened. Her heart was pounding. "We've got nothing to talk about."

"You know, Lara, people say some pretty strange things about you. There are guys who think you're gay because you hang out all by yourself in this cabin, never going out."

"I don't care what people think."

"Of course, I know you're straight." He grinned wryly. "You and me had some pretty good times together, didn't we?"

"I have no wish to discuss this with you. As far as I'm

concerned, you're the same as dead. And I'd like to leave it that way. Now go, before I call the sheriff."

Steve stood, drawing up his large frame. "It's a shame you feel that way, Lara. I came by because I thought maybe we could be friends again. You've been alone for a long time, living like a nun up here. And I'm alone now, too. I thought it would be kind of nice if we was to get together again."

"I'm not interested."

His eyes trailed down her. "Damned shame. You and me could have some fun." He puffed out his chest.

Steve was strong and rough-hewn, a man of thirty-one, Lara's age. She knew little about his life except that he worked in and around the lumber industry, mostly driving logging trucks. He had blond hair and a heavy beard that seemed too dark for his coloring, though he was always clean shaven. Some women might consider him attractive—she had once, though that wasn't the reason she married him.

"Cute outfit, by the way," he said, gesturing with his hand. "But how come you're holding your arms like that?" He laughed. "Covering something up?"

"Needless to say, I didn't expect you."

He walked over and blatantly looked down at her folded arms. She felt her muscles tense, remembering his strength and his anger.

"Be honest. Don't you get horny now and then?"

"My sex life is none of your business. If you aren't off this deck in thirty seconds, I'll be on the phone to the sheriff."

"All right. I'm out of here. But let me put it to you straight. I still got a thing for you, Lara. Even when I was with Mary Beth I'd think about you sometimes...how it would be if you and me was still married. If you want to hate me for that, go ahead. But it's true."

Lara swallowed hard. She still couldn't believe the words she was hearing. "You're wasting your time, Steve."

"If you're making me go, I'm walking out of here like a man. Through the front door."

Lara considered the wisdom of letting him into the house, but her place was so isolated the danger inside or out was probably the same. She decided to let him save face.

Turning, she opened the slider. Behind her, she heard the thump of his boots on the wooden planks. She proceeded through the living room, knowing he was right behind her. Her place was scarcely more than a cabin, consisting of three rooms below and a sleeping loft above the main room. She opened the front door, then turned to him. As she stepped aside to let him pass, he stopped to look down at her breasts.

"Damn, if you don't have the sweetest pair," he said under his breath. "You always had a nice set."

Instinctively she started to cover herself, but Steve grasped her arms, digging his fingers into her flesh.

"Let go," she snapped, clenching her teeth.

"I've thought about these little beauties, remembering the things we used to do," he said in a low voice.

"I said, let go!" Her voice was shrill, almost a scream.

Then, with great strength, he virtually lifted her off the floor, pulling her slowly toward him until her breasts touched his chest. Their faces were inches apart. Raw terror welled within her like a sickness. She looked into his eyes, dreading what she would see.

Without changing his expression, Steve raised and lowered her, rubbing her breasts against the front of him while his eyes bored into hers. "Next time you're alone in bed," he whispered, "think of this." The corner of his mouth twisted. "I'll be at my place. Call me any time you want. It can be just like before, Lara. You and me."

"Get out of here," she spit.

His expression didn't change. He slowly released her. Once free, Lara backed away. Steve stared a moment longer, then turned and walked across the porch and down the steps.

She slammed the door after him, throwing the dead bolt and falling against the heavy wood with a cry of anger. Then she thumped the door with her fists as the tears started streaming down her cheeks.

DEREK GORDON PARKED across from McGaffy's General Store in Mendocino. It didn't appear to be the sort of place you could buy a lot of food, but he decided to have a look inside so that he'd know what was available. After locking the door of his BMW he walked over to the store, amused by the movie-set look of the place with its wood plank sidewalk that ran the length of the building, and beyond. The windows were full of museum pieces rather than merchandise. He was immediately dubious about the prices he'd likely find.

Mendocino was an intriguing place, despite having been overtaken by tourism. Derek had heard that except in summer, most visitors came on weekends. He'd already decided to make a point of avoiding coming to town then.

As he reached for the handle of the glass-paned door, it opened. He stepped back, but a woman came hurrying out so quickly that they collided and the paper sack she was carrying fell to the sidewalk with a thud.

Noticing that the contents had spilled, Derek bent over to help her retrieve everything. He was surprised to see a small pistol and rounds of ammunition among the items spread out on the planks.

"Sorry," she said, "that was clumsy of me." She stooped, too, and helped shove the shells into the sack.

Derek glanced up at her, seeing a surprisingly lovely face. Her blue-green eyes flickered over him with embarrassment.

"I trust you didn't just rob the place," he joked.

She laughed, and they stood up. He handed her the sack. Their eyes lingered for a moment and she brushed back her disheveled blond-streaked hair. "Not robbery. Self-protection," she said.

"You must run the local chapter of the National Rifle Association."

Her expression changed from embarrassment to mild annoyance. "No. I live alone." But she finished the statement with a faint smile. After another silent look she left him, walking across the street toward a four-wheel-drive vehicle parked in front of his BMW.

Derek watched her go. Her legs were bare, long and shapely. The red flannel shirt she wore hung loosely—nearly to the bottom of her shorts. He started to go inside, but noticed two rounds of ammunition that had rolled against the building. Picking them up, he turned and called to the woman, who was just closing the door of the Jeep. She leaned out the window as he walked across the street, holding up the rounds for her to see. "Two more," he said.

She held out her palm, and he handed her the bullets. "Thanks."

She had a nice smile, but there was more distance than warmth in it. "I hope I didn't offend you with my NRA remark," he said, resting his hand on the door of the Jeep.

She looked surprised. "No. I'm not political."

"Just into self-preservation?"

She nodded. Derek didn't sense a particular eagerness to talk. But her eyes fascinated him. Something powerful was fulminating under her cool veneer, and it bothered him a bit that she should intrigue him so. "My name is Gordon, by the way. Derek Gordon. I'm new in town."

She stuck her hand out the window of the Jeep. "Lara Serenov," she said perfunctorily. "Welcome."

Derek took her hand. It was thin, the fingers long. She seemed eager to go, so he made no attempt to prolong the encounter. There was no point. "Nice to know you," he said.

"Yes," she said. "Nice to know you, too." She turned the ignition key, starting the engine. "Thanks for retrieving my ammunition."

"Pleasure." He stepped back. Lara smiled at him with the same distance as before.

She pulled away, and he headed back toward the store, wondering why he'd let himself behave like a teenage boy.

Inside the door he came face-to-face with a man with a bushy mustache. He was in his forties and wore a wool shirt and jeans. He was grinning.

"Nice legs, eh?" the man said, holding his smile.

Derek glanced back out the door. "You mean..."

"Lara Serenov. I saw you talking to her."

"An unexpected encounter with an armed woman," Derek said wryly. "I take it she was a customer, not a bandit."

"A longtime customer."

"A local then."

"Lara's a native. Born and raised on the coast. She's been coming here since I bought this place, and before that from what I understand."

"You're the proprietor, apparently."

"Yes. George Krumholtz is my name." He extended his hand.

"Derek Gordon."

"Up for the weekend?"

"Up for the year. I'm renting a place down below Albion."

"A year, huh? You an artist, a writer, a craftsman or a cultist? Seems like everyone that comes up here these days is one or the other."

"A professor at Cal, so I guess that makes me a little of each. Actually, I'm on sabbatical and came up to write the definitive work on theology and political philosophy."

"Afraid I won't be buying it, even if it makes paperback," Krumholtz said with a laugh. "I don't get much past Stephen King these days."

Derek smiled. "That's all right. Not many people will read it beside my students, and they don't have any choice."

The man grinned. "I guess college hasn't changed since I was in school. Seemed like every third book you read was by one of your professors."

Derek nodded. "It's our racket."

"Well, Professor, anything I can find for you?"

He looked around. "Just dropped by to see what you've got."

"Help yourself, then." Krumholtz turned and went toward the counter at the back of the store.

Derek roamed around for a few minutes. The stock appeared to be half hardware and dry goods, and half tourist junk and things that would appeal to the artsy, organic crowd. On the counter near the cash register there was a small stack of booklets. The author's name, Lara Serenov, caught his eye. Picking up one of the books, he saw it was a volume of poems. He glanced over at George Krumholtz, who was now staring out the front windows of the store.

"Lara Serenov is a poet, I see," Derek said offhandedly.

"Yes, a local celebrity of sorts. I keep those here because I know her. Sell a few, too."

"Is she good?"

"I'm not into poetry myself, but the people who know seem to think she is. I like her and consider her a friend. She'll autograph a volume for purchasers if they leave it here." He reached under the counter and held up a copy of the book. "She signed one for somebody when she was in just now."

Derek paged through the copy in his hands, stopping to read a few lines now and then. The themes seemed to favor nature and attendant emotions, but then that struck him as fairly typical of poetry. "I don't know much about it, either," he said, "but maybe I'll buy a copy and decide for myself." He moved to the cash register and took out his wallet.

"Seeing her didn't hurt, I imagine," Krumholtz said with a smile. "I told Lara she made a mistake not putting her picture on the book. She'd sell a lot more. That's for sure."

"She's not married, I take it."

"No, not anymore. Been living alone back up in the hills for years. A regular hermit. Her father has a ranch over by Willits somewhere, but they aren't very close from what I hear. She's a real loner."

"Hence the gun and ammunition."

"That's new. Some guy's started bothering her, I guess. Lara didn't say much, but must be bad enough she feels she needs protection."

"That's a shame." Derek put a ten dollar bill on the counter.

"Price a woman pays, living on her own. It is too bad, though." Krumholtz rang up the sale and counted out his change as Derek stared at the book.

"She's stuck in your mind, eh?"

Derek started to deny it, but wondered if there might not be some truth to the suggestion. "She is…an unusual woman, isn't she."

"Well, Lara's a strange duck, even if she is attractive as the dickens."

Derek took the change Krumholtz had given him and put it in his pocket, then picked up the small paper sack containing the book. "Why do you say she's a strange duck?"

"Lara's…I don't know…I guess you'd say independent. She was married to a local fellow years ago. That went sour and…well…she's not shown a lot of interest in men ever since, notwithstanding the fact that half the male population's been in love with her at one time or another."

"That's too bad."

"She seems happy enough, though. Has a cabin up in the woods, on a mountaintop off Flat Pine Road."

"She must have friends."

"Oh, sure. Lara's not antisocial. Her thing's the local Literary Guild. She and Calle Bianco kind of run it. They're close."

"The Literary Guild, huh?"

"I don't know if your kind of writing fits in, but if you're interested, you might give Lara or Calle a call. Don't know their numbers offhand, but you can get them off the bulletin board down at the end of the street. You'll find everything you could possibly want on it, legal and illegal."

"I might do that." Derek wondered whether the notion was totally inconsistent with the isolation he'd planned for himself.

"It's those legs, Professor," Krumholtz said with a laugh. "And that face of hers. Lara will do that to a man. I've seen it before."

Derek shook his head. "No, George, I'm not looking for

that." He held up the sack with the book inside. "I'm curious about her work. Besides, I'm married."

Krumholtz shrugged. "Well, a guy can fantasize once in a while. I'll admit that I do."

Derek nodded. "I suppose a little of that is good for the soul." He winked. "Nice meeting you, George. Thanks for the book, and the conversation."

"You don't want to leave it to have Lara autograph it for you?"

"No. Not now. I think I'll read it first."

Krumholtz saluted him. "Come in again, Professor."

Derek Gordon said goodbye, went out and got in his car. On his way out of town he noticed the bulletin board the storekeeper had mentioned. He started to drive on, but changed his mind, pulling over at the last minute. Without pausing long to think about it, he got out of the car and went over and jotted down Lara Serenov's phone number.

CHAPTER TWO

BY THE TIME Derek got back to the house the cleaning woman had already gone. His boxes were stacked neatly in the corner, his suitcases were lined up in the bedroom. The cottage was scrubbed clean. He put the groceries he had bought in the kitchen then returned to the living room.

The cottage was pleasant, a place he could live and work in equally well. The main room would also serve as his study. It contained a desk, an easy chair and a small couch. In addition to windows that afforded a view of the cove, there were French doors leading to a patio facing the point. Opposite the French doors was a stone fireplace that would be nice in the winter when an icy wind was whistling around the eaves.

Derek eyed the boxes of books, but decided not to unpack and set up his study until the next day. He would start fresh, beginning the long process that would culminate in the completion of his book sometime the following summer, if everything went according to plan.

Instead he picked up the sack from McGaffy's that contained Lara Serenov's volume of poems, and settled into the easy chair. He studied her name on the cover of the book, enjoying the impression of her that still lingered in his mind. It was a strange sensation.

Derek never had this kind of feeling toward women anymore. He had been faithful to Margaret over the years, even in her illness, and his steadfastness had made any attraction he felt toward other women superficial and transitory. That didn't prevent him from noticing women, of course, but he couldn't remember ever being quite so aware of someone after such a brief encounter.

Derek read the first three or four poems in the volume. He was hardly a critic, but he found the mood and rhythm of the lines appealing. They elicited a *tristesse*, the elusive feeling of sadness he had sensed in the woman herself. Or was he imagining it?

Derek closed the book, wondering if his loneliness was catching up with him. Perhaps something had been shaken loose by what Mark had said earlier.

Putting the book aside, he went to the French doors and looked out at the cypress trees on the point, bent and molded by the wind into artistic configurations. The sun was getting low in the sky and the scene seemed pleasant, so he went outside and strolled toward the outcrop of rock.

It was an idyllic spot, and Derek imagined that until the weather changed at the end of fall he would be spending a lot of time out there, watching the ocean. Grasping the gnarled old trunk of a cypress, he braced himself against the strong breeze and watched a fishing boat moving south, a mile or so out to sea.

But in looking at the blue-green water, he saw Lara Serenov's eyes and felt a strange yearning to see them again. He could understand how so many men might have been entranced by her. She was coolly—and a touch mysteriously—alluring.

Derek inhaled the salt air, contemplating his reaction to Lara and finding it a bit unsettling, if only because he could tell she wouldn't be easy to forget. He sensed in her a need, a need he wanted to fulfill.

It was probably the teacher in him. He had exchanged

only a few words with Lara, yet he wanted to help her, to sympathize, to be her friend.

Derek had a history of doing that sort of thing. In a way it had been like that with his wife. Margaret had been a widow with a small child, seven years older than he when they met. His mother had tried to tell him that he felt sorry for her, that he was letting his compassion rule his heart. It wasn't true. He had loved Margaret. He still did, though circumstances had taken her from him, leaving him virtually a widower, and alone.

Many people thought him a saint for staying by her, when disease had destroyed her body and affected her mind. But he could never regard his loyalty as duty or sacrifice. Margaret was his wife, and he honestly didn't see how ill fortune could change that.

Yet now he had met a woman who had captured his imagination. Noticing her, even feeling drawn to her, was natural enough, he knew. Still, it hadn't happened before. Why now?

He craned his neck to see the fishing boat that had moved far down the coast. Again he pictured Lara Serenov's face—her eyes and wide, sensuous mouth. Wanting to escape the memory, he turned and looked at the house, resting his back against the rough trunk of the cypress. He thought about his work, envisioning a year alone in contemplation, deeply engaged in the creative process. But the diversion didn't succeed for long. Lara—the tangle of her blond hair, her mouth, her lovely eyes—crept back into his mind.

Feeling a twinge of frustration, he picked up a stone from the ground and tossed it into the waters of the cove. It made an ineffectual splash between two swells, making him think about the proverbial drop of water in the ocean. Out of the billions of living things out there, he wondered if his stone falling into the sea had been noticed by half a dozen—or even one.

THE JEEP BOUNCED ALONG the twisting drive leading to the cabin. Lara peered ahead through the trees, feeling apprehensive.

She pulled into the carport alongside the house and got out. After buying the gun and ammunition at McGaffy's, Lara had driven into Fort Bragg to do her monthly grocery shopping, figuring since she was out, she might as well kill two birds with one stone.

As she walked around the back of the vehicle to unload her groceries, she noticed something lying on the porch at the front door. It appeared to be wrapped in tissue paper. Curious, she went over, discovering that the bundle was flowers—a half dozen wilted yellow roses that looked as though they had been lying there for several hours. The note tucked in the blossoms read:

Lara,
Sorry if I scared you this morning. I guess I got out of line. But you ought to feel complimented knowing you can turn a guy on so easy. I really have been thinking about you a whole lot. Maybe I even have a thing for you again.

If you'd just forget about the past, maybe we can try and be friends, if you know what I mean. Maybe we made a mistake when we split up, and I think it's worth finding out. I bet we'd like it.

This is no joke. Please give me a chance.

Steve

Lara's stomach dropped as she stuffed the note back in among the blossoms. She opened the door and carried the flowers into the kitchen, where she put them on the counter. The buds looked pathetic. She felt sorry for Steve, but she also felt a strange kind of horror, as though a bad dream had sprung to life.

She began unloading the groceries from the Jeep, glancing uneasily down the drive each time she went in and out the front door. He might be out there somewhere, watching her. It made her crave the safety of the cabin. All she wanted was to get inside and bolt the door.

After she had put the food away, she placed the gun she had bought at McGaffy's in the tea towel drawer. Then she picked up the flowers. She pictured Steve's face as he had sat defiantly on the deck, ogling her body.

And she remembered him as he had been years earlier, before she had left him. One night he had come into their small living room wearing nothing but his jockey shorts. She was in her nightgown, reading. She could tell at once he was angry that she had stayed up.

"Quit reading those damned poems!" he'd roared. "Come to bed."

"I don't want to make love, Steve," she'd said.

"Well, I do!"

When she didn't move from the couch, he glared at her. Then he lifted her gown, eyeing her like a hungry beast. They were just children in adult bodies at the time, but that didn't reduce the horror of what he did next.

He tried to pull her panties off. When she resisted he fell on her, pinning her arms with one strong hand while he ripped off her nightclothes with the other. She struggled, but he became more forceful, taking her finally on the couch. When he finished, he left her soaked with the sweat of their struggle, her body bruised and sore. She never slept with him again after that.

Lara shivered at the recollection and dropped the roses

heads first into the garbage sack next to the counter. Then she went out on the deck, sat down and tried to calm herself. The sun was setting over the Pacific, leaving an orange glow in the western sky. But even the beauty of the vista she loved so didn't soothe her.

Steve's visit didn't mean anything, she told herself again. It would blow over. It would pass just as their marriage had all those years ago.

There was a sound behind her at the side of the deck and Lara jumped, expecting to see Steve. But it was only a squirrel playing with a dead branch. Being jittery wasn't like her. She'd let Steve get to her, and that wasn't good.

Lara closed her eyes and took a deep breath. Thank heavens, she thought, she'd had the sense to end the marriage when she did. Their time together had been brief, but it had been hell. Steve's interest in her had been glandular. Her interest in him had been not much better.

After Lara's mother died and her father remarried, her life had seemed to fall apart. She and her stepmother didn't get along and, since she'd never been very close to her father, Steve provided the excuse she needed to slip away from the nest.

In high school she had managed to resist the temptation to find substitute affection from boys. In her senior year Steve Adamson came along and managed to crack her fragile shell. The night of the senior dance he'd taken her virginity. In desperation and shortsighted immaturity, she had used Steve to escape from her home and wreak revenge on a parent who didn't seem to care.

But why was she dredging up all that again? The marriage had been laid to rest years ago, and here she was, trembling as though it had been yesterday. Lara admonished herself. She had to get control of her emotions.

What she needed, she decided, was a nice hot soak in

the tub to help her relax. Going inside, she locked the slider and went to the bath. She had just stripped down when the telephone rang, giving her a momentary start.

Lara wondered who it could be, worrying immediately that it might be Steve. Slipping on a T-shirt and panties, she went to the phone in the kitchen. She picked up the receiver, listening with uncertainty before saying hello.

The man's voice on the other end was unfamiliar, and it took her a moment to realize from his explanation that it was Derek Gordon, the fellow she'd run into at McGaffy's Store.

"I hope I'm not calling at a bad time," he said, probably sensing the disorientation in her voice.

"No. It's all right."

"George Krumholtz told me you were the person to call about the Literary Guild," he explained, "and I got your number off the bulletin board in town. I wanted to inquire about the organization."

"Oh. Sure," she said, collecting herself. "What can I tell you?"

"Are there qualifications for membership, or is it the sort of thing anyone can participate in?"

"We're not restrictive. All you need is an interest in literature. Do you write?"

"I write, but not literature, I'm afraid. I'm a college professor, and I'm doing a book on political philosophy."

"If poets and essayists and fiction writers wouldn't bore you, you're more than welcome to join us. I believe our next meeting is coming up soon. If you'd like to hold on, I'll check my calendar." Lara put down the phone and started looking for her appointment book. As she did, she heard the sound of a vehicle out front.

"Oh, Lord," she mumbled, and went to the window to

look through the curtains. Dusk was falling, but she recognized Steve Adamson's truck.

A cry of panic passed her lips. *The gun.* She needed her gun. She went to the drawer and removed the pistol. Her hand was trembling. Then she saw the telephone receiver lying on the counter. She'd forgotten about the caller. She picked up the phone.

"Look, Mr. Gordon, I'm afraid I can't talk anymore," she said, hearing the panic in her own voice. "An emergency has come up."

"Are you all right?"

"Yes. Well…it's somebody who's just driven up. A guy. Someone who's been bothering me." She tried to stay calm, but fear had gripped her.

"Do you want me to call the police?"

"No. It's all right. I'll call the sheriff, if I have to."

There was a knock at the door.

"I can't talk now. He's at the door. I have to go. I'm sorry."

"Shall I call back later?"

"No…I mean yes. If you want. But I have to hang up now." Lara put the receiver back on the hook.

There was another knock on the door. Feeling the skimpy T-shirt covering her bare flesh, Lara stole silently into the hallway. When she saw she had remembered to lock the door, she sighed with relief. Steve knocked again, but she kept quiet, hoping he would go away.

"Lara," he called through the door. "I know you're in there. Your damn car's sitting right here in the carport. Let's talk, all right?"

Her stomach clenched. Her grip tightened on the gun. "No, this is not a good time."

"Come on, Lara. I drove all the way up here. Didn't you get my flowers?"

"Yes, but you're still wasting your time, Steve. I'm not interested. Please, go away."

He didn't respond. A moment later she heard him walking across the porch, but she didn't hear the door to his truck open or the engine start. What was he up to?

Lara was still at the entry when she heard something in back, on the deck. Through the glass spanning the rear of the cabin she saw him. Terror seized her, but she didn't cry out. She stood motionless in the darkened hallway, trying to maintain control.

Steve peered into the dim interior, looking for her. In his hand was a can of beer. She stood in shadows and he hadn't yet spotted her. As she watched, he tried the door, but thankfully it was locked.

There were no drapes across the back. Considering the isolation of the cabin, Lara had assumed she wouldn't need them. Now she saw that had been a mistake. Wearing nothing but a T-shirt, she felt as exposed as a fish in a bowl.

Steve spotted her, then rapped on the glass. "Come on, Lara, for Chrissake! I'm not going to hurt you."

She clenched the pistol, then slowly moved it behind her thigh to keep it from his sight, deciding to threaten him only if absolutely necessary. Having a weapon did give her courage, though she'd always felt guns were a blight on civilization. Slowly she moved toward Steve, trying not to let her fear show.

He grinned, apparently enjoying the way she looked. He lifted the beer can. "I've got a six-pack in the truck. Let me bring it in. We can talk...just like the old days."

Her face was a mask of hostility. "Damn you, Steve Adamson!" she screamed through the glass. "Get off my property! This is the last time I warn you. Stay away from me!"

His expression turned dark. By his eyes she could see

that he was already half-drunk. He pressed his large palm against the glass and glared at her. Lara didn't know what she should do, except that she had to be firm.

Finally Steve spun around and heaved the beer can off the deck and into the falling darkness. Then he slipped through the railing and went around the house. Lara waited until she heard the truck door open, then let out a sigh of relief. But she knew she wouldn't be able to relax until she heard the engine start. She waited, but nothing happened.

Returning to the kitchen window, she saw Steve sitting in the passenger seat of the truck with the door open. He had opened another can of beer and was swilling it. Then, taking the rest of the six-pack, he went back around the cabin, appearing several moments later on the deck. Lara groaned as he sat down in one of the chairs, propped a booted foot on the rail and began to drink.

She knew she had to be firm, but she was hardly intimidating dressed as she was. Quietly mounting the stairs, she found her terry-cloth bathrobe and put it on, cinching the tie tightly about her waist. After slipping the gun into her pocket, she went downstairs again and marched over to the window. She rapped on the glass. For a moment Steve ignored her, but finally glanced in her direction.

"Steve, get out of here. I'm warning you."

He ignored her, tilting his head back and draining the rest of the beer. After tossing the empty over the railing, he took another can.

Furious, Lara went into the kitchen and dialed the sheriff. She explained the problem to the dispatcher, who asked if Steve had threatened her or tried to force an entry.

"No, not exactly," Lara replied.

"Well," the woman said, "I'll try and get a deputy up there as soon as possible. My problem is two personal injury accidents, a bar brawl, and no spare patrol cars in the west county area at the moment. Try to hold on. It might be a while before we can respond. Chances are he'll get tired and go home. But if he shows signs of violence, call back and we'll spin somebody off.''

Lara hung up in frustration. She didn't blame them for tending to those with a greater need, but it seemed a woman had to be raped before people took a man's threats against her seriously. She peeked out the kitchen door and saw Steve still sitting on the deck, drinking. She wasn't sure what she should do now. Was it safer to ignore him, and hope he would cool off and go away, or would he become more dangerous if she let him stay and get drunk?

Her only real leverage was her gun. If she threatened him with it, and he didn't take her seriously, she might be forced to use it. And despite her fear, Lara wasn't sure she could do that. She elected to lie low instead, sitting at the table in the kitchen where he couldn't see her.

The minutes seemed to drag by interminably as she sat on the edge of the chair, her knees clenched, her flesh chilled despite the warmth of the air. Every once in a while she went to the kitchen door and looked out at the deck, but Steve was always there, either sitting or standing at the rail, a can of beer in his hand.

It was almost dark outside when she again went to the doorway and stared out at him. Steve was only a shadowy figure, but she could see him pacing, like a caged animal. As she watched, he went to the sliding door and peered in, slamming the glass in frustration with his open palm.

"Damn it, Lara!" he shouted drunkenly through the glass. She flinched at the angry sound of his voice. "Open up and talk to me. I've been nice to you. I even brought you flowers, damn it!" He hit the glass again, this time so hard the whole side of the house seemed to shake.

He was very drunk now. That could mean real trouble.

Steve Adamson had been a mean drunk when they were married, and from the gossip she'd heard in town he hadn't changed. Lara took the pistol out of her pocket.

Just then she heard something out front and saw the lights of a vehicle coming up the drive. *The sheriff!* Lara couldn't remember ever having felt so glad to see a peace officer.

She ran to the front door as the vehicle stopped directly in front of the cabin, its high beams bathing her in a sea of light. The driver's door opened, and a figure stepped out.

"Miss Serenov, are you all right?"

The voice was vaguely familiar, but didn't have the ring of authority one associated with a police officer. Lara scrutinized the car, realizing it wasn't a cruiser at all. The man reached in and extinguished the lights. As he approached, she saw that it was the man who had called earlier, the professor.

"I was worried," he said, coming up on the porch, "and thought I ought to make sure you were all right."

Lara was so surprised she didn't know what to say. In a way she was disappointed, but in another way she was happy for any friendly and protective male figure, stranger or not.

Derek Gordon gestured toward the pickup truck. "Does that belong to the fellow who's been bothering you?"

"Yes, he's out back on my deck," she managed to say. "He's drunk and won't leave."

"Did you call the police?"

He had a stern expression on his face that Lara found comforting. Someone had finally taken her problem seriously, and she felt overwhelmed with gratitude. "Yes," she said, wanting to clutch his arm the way a child might pull at her mother's skirt when frightened.

He hesitated, glancing down at her bathrobe for the first

time. "If you think it would help, I'll talk to him," he said calmly.

"I don't know what to do."

"Let me have a word with him." Derek gestured toward the door and Lara stepped inside the dark house. She turned on the hall light and locked the door behind them. The living room was dark, too, so she turned on a lamp and the outdoor light, which illuminated the deck. Steve stood in the middle of it, appearing a bit dazed by the sudden light and the sight of another person inside.

"What's his name?" Derek asked.

"Steve. Steve Adamson."

Derek went to the slider and opened it, stepping out onto the deck. "What seems to be the trouble, Steve?" she heard him say.

"Who the hell are you?" Steve said, his voice reflecting his intoxication.

"I'm a friend of Lara's."

"A friend?" Steve said with a hoot. Then he peered through the glass at her. "This is a friend of yours? Somebody you let walk right in your living room while I have to cool my heels on this stinking deck?"

"Look, Steve," Derek said, "this isn't helping matters. I think you'd better go."

"Yeah?" Steve said, turning surly. "Because you say so?"

"Because Lara doesn't want you here. I think that's pretty obvious. Now why don't you get in your truck and move on out before there's trouble?"

Steve pulled himself up to his full height. "There's going to be trouble all right, buddy. Nobody tells me to go if I don't want to. And that includes you."

"The police are on their way up. You're lucky I got here

before they did. Now I suggest you get going before they drag you off to jail.''

''The hell with you!'' Steve clenched his fists. His face turned redder than it already was.

Lara knew trouble was imminent. Steve was beyond reason. And while the professor lacked neither courage nor strength, she judged that he'd be no match for the burly truck driver. But before she could do anything, Steve made a move toward Derek. The professor slipped to the side, tripping the intoxicated giant and shoving him to the deck, where he sprawled face down.

Enraged, Steve scrambled to his feet. Before he could get to Derek, Lara stepped out onto the deck and screamed at him to stop, her gun pointed directly at him.

''Jeez, Lara!'' he said, his eyes rounding with surprise. ''What the hell are you doing?''

''I'm about ready to shoot you, I'm so mad. And if you don't get off of my property right now, I will!''

Steve sobered somewhat. He looked at Derek, and he glanced at the gun in Lara's hand. ''Well, I guess the odds are about even now,'' he said snidely. Then he pushed past Derek, giving him a little shove as he went to the edge of the deck.

''I'll be back. I won't give up,'' he shouted as he slipped through the railing.

Lara and Derek exchanged looks as Steve disappeared around the house. Her arm holding the gun fell limp, and she felt as though she would burst into tears.

''Come on,'' Derek said, leading her inside. He put his hand on her shoulder reassuringly as her eyes filled.

Out front the truck's engine roared to life. The tires spun, kicking gravel against the side of the cabin as Steve took off. Lara was trembling and Derek, in a comforting gesture, put his arms around her. She was on the verge of crying.

As Derek stroked her head, Lara became aware of the warmth of his hand through her robe. She noticed his unfamiliar but pleasant scent. Looking into his face, she felt both self-conscious and embarrassed.

Derek smiled. "I guess I owe you a debt of gratitude," he said gamely. "Your friend, Steve, didn't seem too pleased with my interference."

She laughed miserably, moving away from him a little. "I should thank you. It was just a matter of time before he would have decided to come through the glass."

Derek nodded toward the gun still in Lara's hand. "You look like you were ready for him."

"I tried to talk tough, but I don't know if I could have pulled the trigger." She backed toward the stairway leading to the loft. "I was caught by surprise when he came, as you can see. If you'll excuse me a moment, I'll get some clothes on."

Without waiting for a reply Lara scurried up the stairs. She took off her terry robe and put on jeans and a shirt, feeling a good deal more comfortable.

Derek was perusing the books on her shelves when Lara got to the bottom of the stairway. She paused, then went over to where he stood.

"You said on the phone you're a college professor. Where do you teach?"

"At Cal, Berkeley."

"Oh? You have quite a commute, don't you?"

He grinned. "I'm on a sabbatical at the moment. I've rented a cottage on the ocean."

Derek Gordon had an intelligent, sensitive look about him that appealed to Lara. And he was attractive, in a professorial sort of way. She rarely reacted positively to men, but there was something kind, thoughtful and caring about this man that put her at ease. She liked that.

"By the way," she asked, "how did you know how to find me?"

"It wasn't easy. George Krumholtz said you lived on a mountain off Flat Pine Road, so I followed the road up and starting checking the mailboxes when I got near the top."

"I'm lucky you did. It's awfully generous of you to put yourself out like this. If I had to rely on the sheriff, there's no telling what would have happened."

"You took care of yourself rather well. And me, too, for that matter."

Lara smiled, still a little embarrassed.

"Anyway," Derek added, "I had an ulterior motive. I bought a book of your poems and thought I might get it autographed."

She laughed. "Seriously?"

"Yes. It's in the car."

"Maybe getting that published was worthwhile, after all." She was smiling, surprised and pleased that the emotional trauma of a few minutes ago had already passed.

"I'll go out and get it, if you don't mind." Derek left the house and returned a minute later. "There's somebody coming up the drive," he said. "You might want to retrieve your gun, in case it's Steve returning for another round."

Lara got the weapon, but Derek, who had gone back outside, called to her that it was a patrol car. Putting the pistol in the kitchen drawer, she joined Derek at the door. A deputy was getting out of his car when she got there. They watched him come up onto the porch. He was a big man, even larger than Steve Adamson.

"Lara Serenov?"

"Yes, I'm she."

"Deputy Stiles. We had a report of a disturbance. Is this the man?"

"No, this is Derek Gordon, a friend. I was talking to him on the phone when Steve arrived."

"Steve?"

"Steve Adamson," Lara said. "He's my former husband. For some reason, he's started coming around. Tonight he was drunk, banging on the door. I was scared to death."

"She ran him off, though," Derek said. "I tried to talk to him, but the guy was beyond reason."

"Forgive my bluntness," the deputy said, looking back and forth between them, "but was this a jealousy thing, ex-husband versus new boyfriend?"

"No," Lara assured him, "Steve never laid eyes on Derek until today." She couldn't help smiling. "To be honest, I hadn't either."

"We're recent friends," Derek said with a smile.

The deputy grinned. "Whatever you say. Mind if we go inside?"

Lara led the way into the living room. The deputy took a chair and she and Derek sat on the couch together. She felt even more comfortable with the professor's presence than she had before. She glanced at him curiously from the corner of her eye.

Deputy Stiles asked for the details, and Lara recounted what had happened that day, starting with Steve's unexpected visit that morning. The officer listened. After she had described the brief scuffle, and Steve's retreat in the face of the gun, Stiles rubbed his chin.

"I take it you don't want Adamson coming around anymore," he said.

"Exactly. Whatever it takes to make sure he stays away."

"You've got a couple of choices. You can come in and swear out a complaint. He trespassed, and taking hold of you this afternoon was a kind of assault. But I doubt the

DA will want to go very far with it. There's a lot of folks that really should be behind bars that she's got on her mind these days.''

"I know it doesn't seem serious to you, Deputy Stiles, but—''

"No, no. That wasn't what I was saying at all. Don't get me wrong.''

"You're saying if he raped me, it might be more worthwhile investigating.''

"No, I'm not saying that, either. It's just that I've got to look at this from a practical perspective, and you should, too. These things between a man and a woman are awfully hard to prosecute, short of there being physical violence. Even in rape cases it comes down to one person's word against another's.''

"You want me to arrange for witnesses if he attacks me, is that it?''

"No, Miss Serenov. And I wish you wouldn't take what I'm saying as being unsympathetic. If you were my sister or daughter, I'd be fighting mad. But you're a citizen, Steve Adamson's a citizen, and we're public servants. I've got to look at this dispassionately. If you want my honest opinion, you might be best off to see a lawyer. A restraining order, or even a suit for damages, might squelch the fellow's romantic ideas.''

"Then you won't do anything?'' she said, glancing at Derek.

"No, there is something I can do, short of arresting him. I don't know Adamson personally, though I've heard of him. I can go see him and have a little talk. I won't guarantee the results, but sometimes when a badge lays a hand on a fellow's shoulder, he'll sit up and take notice. That may do more to cool him down than all the cold showers in the world.''

Lara felt somewhat mollified. "All right, Officer. I appreciate anything you can do."

"One other thing, Miss Serenov. Be careful with that peashooter of yours. If we come up here and find Adamson lying on your porch with a bullet between his eyes, I'd like a little more than this conversation to make out a case of self-defense. What I'm saying is, don't pull the trigger too lightly."

"Thanks for the advice."

"I guess I don't have to tell you, your situation here is pretty inviting for a guy like Adamson. It might be a good idea to spend a few days with friends or relatives until we get a feel for his mood."

Lara groaned.

"The decision's yours, of course. But speaking from experience, that's my advice."

Lara nodded, and the deputy got up to leave. She walked him to the door. When she returned to the living room, Derek Gordon was glancing through her book of poems. She sat in the chair Deputy Stiles had been in.

"I'd better be going myself," Derek said. "But if you're planning on leaving for the night, I'd be glad to stay with you until you're ready to go."

"That's awfully kind of you, but I wouldn't want to impose. You've done so much already—practically getting into a fight with a strange man for my sake."

"Fortunately things worked out all right."

They looked at each other, feeling the awkwardness of the situation.

"You were really married to Steve?" Derek asked.

"A lifetime ago. It was one of those childhood mistakes."

"And he's just started bothering you again?"

"Steve hasn't grown up, as you could easily see. He's

recently broken up with his second wife, and I guess he had an urge to look to the past. Today was the first time we've spoken in thirteen years.''

Derek shook his head sympathetically. "What an unpleasant surprise." Remembering the book in his hand, he handed it to Lara. "Maybe I can get your autograph, since I'm here."

She smiled. "Of course. Let me get a pen." She went to the kitchen and returned a moment later.

"I like your work, by the way," he said. "I've only read a few of the poems, but I've enjoyed them."

"It's a labor of love, not profit."

"That's true of most worthwhile things."

Lara was writing on the flyleaf, and only nodded. She signed her name, then glanced over the brief inscription—"To Derek Gordon, my champion and newfound friend." She handed him the book.

Derek read what she had written and thanked her. When he looked into her eyes he saw a different woman than the one he'd seen in town that afternoon. Granted, they had a bit of a history now, but there was more to it than that. There was an unspoken acceptance that heartened him.

"What do you plan to do tonight?" he asked. "Go to a friend's?"

"I don't know," Lara said, running her fingers through her wavy blond hair. "I feel fine now. But once you've gone, I'm sure every sound I hear outside will be Steve." She bit her lip thinking. "Maybe I'll give a friend a call and see if I can stay with her."

"I'll follow you as far as the highway, if you like."

"Thanks, but it's not necessary."

Lara sensed a curious ambivalence on Derek's part. He almost seemed reluctant to leave. Strangely, she shared the feeling, finding comfort in his presence. But he got up to leave. Lara rose, too. She was sorry now she hadn't accepted his offer to stay until she was ready to go. Then she remembered the reason he had phoned her.

"You know, in all the excitement, I forgot to get the date of the next Literary Guild meeting. Let me check." Lara went into the kitchen, finally finding her calendar in her business drawer. She returned to the living room. "Next Friday, at three," she said. "At Calle Bianco's house."

"That's nearby, obviously."

"She lives just outside of Mendocino. I'll write down the address." She copied it down on a slip of notepaper and handed it to him.

He studied the paper.

"It's not difficult to find," she explained. "South half a mile or so on the Coast Highway toward Albion, then left on her road to the third or fourth house. You'll see all the cars."

Derek nodded, then went outside.

"It was an eventful evening," she said.

He looked into her eyes. "Well, I got my book autographed anyway."

"And you saved my tail feathers."

He extended his hand. "It wasn't a wasted evening. We can say that."

Lara took his hand. His flesh felt warm. "No. It could have turned out much worse."

Laughing good-naturedly, Derek Gordon pulled her toward him, giving her a friendly hug. To her surprise, she liked the feeling, his warmth.

He went to his car. The porch light illuminated the immediate area, but the halo of darkness in the surrounding trees seemed foreboding. She was really sorry now that he was leaving.

When he was gone Lara closed the front door and locked

it. Then she leaned against the wall and thought about what had happened. Fortunately Derek Gordon's kindness mitigated somewhat the terror Steve had evoked.

Gathering herself, she decided to call Calle right away. She was eager to get out of the cabin. The isolation scared her. Lara needed to be around people, and Calle's houseful of kids would certainly fill that need.

"Sure," her friend said over the sound of a screaming child in the background, "come and stay as long as you like."

"It's really all right?"

"Of course. If you can stand the rollaway, there's no problem."

Lara didn't explain what had happened, saying she'd tell Calle everything when she got there. After hanging up, she went to the loft, threw some things into an overnight bag and hurried out the cabin and to her Jeep.

Moments later, as she drove along the road, she wondered how different her life might have been if, the first time around, she'd meet someone like Derek Gordon instead of Steve. She wouldn't be fleeing in the middle of the night to the home of a friend, that much was for sure.

What terrified her most wasn't what had happened. Rather it was the uncertainty, the not knowing whether the danger was over, or whether she would have to face Steve again and again.

CHAPTER THREE

THURSDAY WAS Calle Bianco's night with the kids. Her husband, Tony, bowled that evening each week, and he always stayed out late with his friends. "The little monsters," as Calle called them, had been fed by the time Lara arrived and were watching television. Calle led Lara into the kitchen and poured two full glasses of wine from the gallon jug she kept in the pantry. A brief glance told her Lara's tale would be an emotional one.

Calle listened, her chin resting on her pudgy hand. She shook her head and uttered words of dismay and sympathy at all the appropriate places, getting up from the table occasionally to check the chili she was warming for Lara's dinner.

Calle Bianco was the only person in whom Lara confided her innermost thoughts and fears. Outwardly, the two women couldn't have been more different. Calle was an Earth Mother figure—half literary being, half rural housewife. She was big, dark-haired, with a round pretty face. Unlike Tony, she had a college education. She loved to write, bringing in almost as much money doing free-lance articles as her husband did as a pipe fitter.

When Lara had finished her story, Calle reached over and patted her hand. "You don't deserve this, kiddo. I'm so sorry."

"I just wish when I wake up tomorrow it would be all

over. I'm afraid it won't be, though. I have a feeling Steve's not going to give up easily.''

"Maybe the sheriff's talk with him will help. I mean, the guy can't be completely stupid. At some point he's got to get bored, and want to go on to someone else more promising.''

"Well, I certainly didn't give him any encouragement.''

"Tell me more about this professor. He sounds like a nice guy.''

"He was very kind.''

"What did he look like? Old, young, what?''

"Oh, he's quite nice-looking. Handsome. Dark-haired. Intelligent, sensitive.''

Calle smiled. "Young then?''

"I don't know. Late thirties, I suppose.''

Calle poked her friend in the arm, beaming. She didn't need to say anything. Lara knew exactly what she was thinking.

"Calle, it wasn't like that at all.''

"Weren't you attracted to him?''

"Are you kidding? With what was going on? It didn't even cross my mind.''

"Come on. You might be closed down, but you're not dead.''

Lara sipped her wine. "In that sense I am, yes.''

"You're in the guy's arms. You had to be aware. He had to notice you, for heaven's sake!''

"I wasn't thinking about that. Really.''

"Lara!'' It was Calle's "mother'' voice. She resorted to it whenever she wanted to express utter dismay. "How did he act toward you?''

"Nice.''

"Yeah, but did he act interested?''

"Calle, I told you I don't think in those terms. I saw him as a human being. That's all."

"He wanted to come to the meeting of the Literary Guild. That's a good sign."

Lara gave her a look.

"I take it he was single."

"I don't know. I didn't ask."

"Was he wearing a ring? Did he look married? It's usually written all over their faces."

"If so, it was written in code. It was enough for me that he showed up when I needed help. That was it."

Calle let out a long sigh. "You know, I thought I'd never survive Jodie's bed-wetting, but I'm beginning to think your catatonia's going to do me in for sure."

"Didn't one of Tony's cousins become a nun?" Lara teased. "Think of me that way. Blissfully in poetry heaven."

Calle groaned and got up to check the chili again. She wasn't a gourmet, but she did do first-class home cooking. "This is ready," she said, stirring the contents of the pot with a wooden spoon. "Get yourself some more wine, if you want it."

Lara poured herself some and, as she began eating, Calle went off to mediate a fight between her oldest daughter, Jodie, and her son, Tony Two, as they called him. The time alone gave Lara a welcome chance to assimilate everything that had happened.

She felt chastened by her friend's words of admonishment, though she had answered Calle honestly. Lara truly didn't have designs on the professor, though maybe she had noticed him, and his reaction to her, a bit more than she had let on. Still, her habit of indifference to the opposite sex was ingrained.

Calle returned, mumbling something about motherhood,

though any displeasure she felt with her children was always brief. She was the consummate parent—engaged, interested, steadfast. Probably sensing the conversation regarding Derek Gordon had pretty much run its course, Calle started talking about an article she was doing on the early Chinese of Mendocino County.

Lara liked Calle's mind. She was bright, and never boring. Intelligence in a person was always so appealing. Maybe that was one of the things about Derek Gordon she had liked. They hadn't really talked about intellectual subjects but, being a professor at Cal, he had to be bright. And she had noticed an unmistakable glint of intelligence in his eyes.

Lara realized she hadn't even asked him about his work. It would have been the polite thing to do, though admittedly there hadn't been much of an opportunity. Maybe, if he came to the meeting next week, she could engage him in conversation.

"I'm having the same problem I usually run into," Calle was saying. "I dig up so darn much information, I start losing the forest among the trees. I can't come up with a theme."

"What do you mean by a theme?"

"Good nonfiction writing has to have a central message. It's not enough simply to inform. It's the same in writing a poem, isn't it?"

"In a way. But you don't usually set out to convey a particular message. It just flows naturally from what you're feeling."

"I'm much too logical to write poetry. My brain insists on working from evidence to a conclusion." She shrugged. "So how's your writing going? Any scintillating poems lately?"

Lara told her about the piece she had been working on,

though it only brought Steve to mind. She forced her thoughts away from her ex-husband and tried to give Calle a feel for the mood of the poem. "It was inspired by a jay that's been hanging around my deck recently."

"A talking bird, perchance?" Calle laughed, and Lara playfully slapped her arm.

Little Theresa, Calle's three-year-old, came wandering into the kitchen just then. By the sleepy look on her face, she was ready for bed.

"Look who's here," Lara said, picking her up and holding her on her lap. She loved the feel of the child's pudgy body.

Combing Theresa's hair back with her fingers, Lara almost regretted that she would never have a little one of her own. It was one of those trade-offs in life. Though she loved children, she had long since decided it was not reason enough to change her philosophy about getting involved again.

She talked to the child for a few minutes, but Theresa was tired and soon lost the desire for further socializing. So Lara gave her to Calle, who threw her over her shoulder and headed off to begin the bedtime ritual.

While Calle put Theresa and the other two children to bed, Lara finished her wine. She pondered Calle's comments about Derek Gordon, wondering if what he had done was proof of some sort of interest in her. He had been a gentleman, but there had been a sensual awareness in his eyes. She wasn't too jaded to have noticed that.

She wouldn't tell Calle about it, however. It didn't necessarily mean anything. And besides, she much preferred to think of Derek as a Good Samaritan, and a friend.

Calle returned to the kitchen just as Tony Bianco arrived home. He put his bowling ball down by the refrigerator, kissed his wife and greeted Lara warmly. Calle told him

Lara would be staying the night, and gave him a brief rundown of Steve's visit.

Tony, who was a big man without being fat, nodded as though he'd just figured something out. He scratched his practically bald pate. "That would explain it," he said.

"Explain what?" his wife asked.

"When I drove in, I saw Steve Adamson's truck parked up the road. Soon as I pulled into the drive, he headed off toward the highway."

Lara looked at Calle with horror. "Oh, damn him," she said, biting her lip. "All the time we were sitting here talking he was right outside!"

Calle reached over and put an arm around her shoulder. "Don't worry, honey. You're safe with us."

"I know," Lara said, her eyes glistening. "But what about tomorrow?"

STEVE ADAMSON OPENED the kitchen cupboard. It was bare except for some cups and saucers and a couple of juice glasses. He banged the door shut and looked at the kitchen sink, which was heaped with dirty dishes. He'd have to wash them if he wanted to eat lunch off a clean plate.

Cursing Mary Beth again, he peered down at the mess, hating the thought of having to wash up. Unable to find the sink stopper, he ended up using a saucer, which he placed upside down over the drain. Then he turned on the tap and squeezed a healthy slug of liquid detergent into the mess. Since he hadn't washed a dish in as long as he could remember, he wasn't sure how much soap was needed. Noticing the liquid had the consistency of maple syrup, he used about the same amount that he normally put on his pancakes.

Bubbles and steam were soon welling up in the sink.

He'd apparently overdone the soap. He turned off the tap, deciding to let the entire mess soak awhile.

On the table were several skin magazines he'd gotten in Fort Bragg a few days earlier. He picked up one and stared vacantly at the naked women. The pictures only reminded him how deprived he was. His sex life had been reduced to looking at photographs of women. Angrily he threw the magazine against the wall, cursing Lara and Mary Beth equally.

But it was Lara who made him the most angry. There was no good reason for her to treat him the way she had. He'd tried to be nice. Seeing her in that sheer blouse had made him want to get it on with her the way they had when they were first married.

Lara hadn't forgiven him for what had happened years ago, that was plain. Deep inside she had to be craving a man, though. She had to be! So far as he knew, no one had gotten to her since him.

Of course, maybe she'd had some recently, and the story hadn't gotten around. Maybe the guy who showed up was making it with her. But Steve didn't know who he was. And anyway, he might just have been a friend. No, chances were Lara was ready for some good rowdy sex, even if she didn't know it.

And if she didn't, Steve was determined to help her learn. She owed it to him. She'd broken up their marriage without really giving him a chance. Mary Beth had been good to him for quite a while after they got married, but Lara hadn't been. She'd never appreciated what he had to offer.

Just thinking about Lara, and picturing her in that see-through blouse, made him want her real bad. Steve thumped his fist on the table. Everything had been going wrong lately. First there was Mary Beth leaving, then he'd been laid off from his job, then Lara acting so uppity, like he was trash or something.

Steve swore softly. He wanted a woman, and he was hungry. What a hell of a mess.

He got up and went to look at the dishes. The bubbles were still all over the place, but the water had mostly drained away. He pulled out a plate, almost dropping it because it was so hot. It was still dirty, but the soap and water had softened the crud. He managed to wipe most of it off with the dish brush, and the rest with a tea towel.

While he dumped the stew from the open can onto the plate, he wondered whether he ought to spring for twenty bucks and have that Mexican maid at the motel come and clean up for him, like she had before. Money would be tight for a while, but the mess in the house was getting to him again.

Steve put the plate in the microwave and watched it cook through the window. When steam started coming off the stew he decided it was done. He took his last beer from the refrigerator and had just sat down when he heard a vehicle out front.

Through the window, he saw a sheriff's car and cursed under his breath. *Don't tell me that broad's brought charges against me,* he thought.

Steve recognized the deputy getting out of the cruiser. His name was Stiles, a big mother who didn't hesitate to knock heads together if a fellow got out of line. He doubted he would be coming alone to make an arrest, though. Usually at least two deputies came for that.

Stiles knocked on the door, and Steve went to the front room to open it. He looked at the officer though the screen door. "Yeah?"

The deputy's aviator shades hid his eyes. He didn't smile, and he didn't exactly frown. "Afternoon, Adamson,'' he said. ''I've got a little problem I want to talk to you about.''

''What kind of problem?''

''All right if I come in?''

Steve thought for a moment, but couldn't see any reason why not. ''I guess so.'' He pushed the screen door open and turned to look at the mess. He kicked aside some clothes on the floor, then cleared off an easy chair.

Stiles stood in the middle of the room, big as a moose, taking off his glasses and hat. When Steve went to the couch, the deputy sat in the chair.

''Wife out of town?''

Steve gave him a crooked grin. ''Yeah. How could you tell?''

''Looks like a prime example of male housekeeping.''

''Mary Beth went back to her ma's up in Crescent City. I figure she'll be back before long. If not, who gives a damn? Huh?''

''Looks like she didn't train you very well.''

''That what you came to see me about—how I'm doing with my chores?''

Stiles gave a little laugh. ''No, Adamson, it's a bit more serious than that. There's a lady up on Flat Pine Road you seem to have inconvenienced some yesterday. I came by to make sure it wouldn't be happening again.''

''You here to arrest me?''

''No, just to have a friendly chat.''

''I didn't break no laws.''

''Well, technically you did, but at my suggestion Miss Serenov decided not to bring charges.''

''What for? Littering?''

Stiles's expression hardened. ''You don't seem to be taking this as seriously as I'd hoped.''

''I didn't do nothing.''

"You were right on the edge of something pretty serious. And if you don't back off, you're going to be in a hell of a mess."

"That a threat?"

"Let me put it this way. If that woman gets hurt, Adamson, I might be tempted to grind my boots in your face in the process of arresting you."

"Then it is a threat."

"A word to the wise."

"I'm a citizen, and just because you've got a badge you don't have no right to tell me where I can go, or who I can talk to."

"That's true. But if Miss Serenov doesn't want you bothering her, the law will see that you don't."

"A judge maybe, but not you."

"I'm here to save you and everybody else a lot of trouble," Stiles said. "Sometimes an informal approach works best. I'm hoping you have the sense to hear what I'm saying and act accordingly."

"Fine. You said it. I heard it. So if that's all you came for, I'd just as soon you go so I can eat my lunch."

The deputy got to his feet. "All right. I won't trouble you more than I have, friend."

Steve got up, too.

"But think about what I've said, Adamson. For your own good."

"Lara's my ex, you know. And it just might be she likes me more than she's letting on."

"I doubt it."

Steve grinned. "Well, I guess we'll see, won't we, Sheriff?"

"So long as nobody gets hurt in the process."

Steve shrugged and the deputy went to the door.

"Afternoon, Mr. Adamson," Stiles said, without turning

around. He put his hat and glasses on and returned to his car.

Steve watched him through the screen door, hating the guy's swagger. It ticked him off, being threatened that way. He had half a mind to find Lara right then and show her what a real man could do.

DEREK GORDON SAT on the rocks out on the point, staring at the sea. He had been thinking about yesterday's rather dramatic events. It bothered him that Lara Serenov was so intriguing to him, but she was. He had been trying to come to terms with that, wondering how much of what he felt was due to her neediness and how much of it was simple attraction. He did want to protect her, but there was something else, too, something that left him feeling very uncomfortable.

When he'd gotten home the night before he'd read every one of her poems. It was a way of trying to deal with growing obsession. He craved knowledge of her, and reading her work was a way of peering into her soul.

That morning he had disciplined himself enough to unpack his things and get his office set up. But when he sat down to work, his mind kept turning to Lara's hauntingly beautiful face and the fear that he sensed dwelled deep within her.

Derek watched the waves crashing against the rocks on the other side of the cove. There was a struggle starting to build within him, and he didn't like it. He sensed he'd be at war with himself before long.

When he'd been living a more normal life with Margaret, an attractive woman had come along from time to time, but he'd never had any trouble handling it. Temptation had never been one of his problems.

Once an associate professor in the sociology department,

a spicy and energetic little redhead, had propositioned him. He had declined as kindly and considerately as he could. Not that he didn't find her attractive. The fact was, he simply wasn't interested. There wasn't room in his life for anyone but his wife.

He couldn't say that anymore. There *was* room in his life for someone else, if not an actual need. Yet if his marriage was to mean anything, how could he behave differently simply because the woman he loved was incapacitated? His commitment to Margaret had to mean more than that. Maybe this infatuation would pass. With luck, Lara Serenov's magic would vanish like the morning fog.

Rousing himself, Derek left his scenic spot and returned to the cottage. He had come to like the place.

The volume of Lara's poems on the table by his reading chair drew his eye like a magnet as he entered the living room. He wanted to go over and take it in his hand. It seemed silly, more appropriate behavior for one of his love-struck students than for him. And yet what he felt for her was so real. Was he falling in love again?

The thought, phrased that way, seem ludicrous. It was Margaret he loved. He always had.

On an impulse Derek went to the phone and dialed the number of the nursing home in Berkeley. In the early days he'd called once or twice a day to check on her, and would visit nearly as often. At first he could speak with her, though real communication had been difficult. But they hadn't even been able to talk for a couple of years now. When he phoned he'd discuss her with the staff. Eventually it became clear that the calls were a burden to the nurses, who really had nothing new to tell him anyway. So he phoned less and less frequently.

The call was answered by the head nurse, a longtime

employee at the home. She knew Derek well and recognized his voice immediately.

"I understand you've left us for a while, Professor Gordon," she said amiably.

"Not in spirit," he said, feeling a bit disingenuous in his choice of phrase. "How's Margaret?"

"Nothing to tell you, I'm afraid. Her condition just doesn't change. Not so that you would notice, anyway."

Derek was more disappointed than usual. He would have liked to hear something encouraging—any little piece of information that hinted that the woman he loved was still alive in that poor frail body of hers. "Has Dr. Duckett seen her recently?"

"I'm sure he was in for his usual visit, Professor Gordon. But I wasn't here at the time, so I couldn't tell you what he said. There's nothing on the chart, though. Your wife's condition is unchanged. That's really all I can tell you."

Derek knew he was taking up the woman's time to satisfy his own emotional need. It wasn't fair, and it really did no good. Thanking her, he hung up.

After the call, he moved around the room, trying to fight his anxiety. In his more lucid moments he realized he was being a lot more emotional about things than common sense and good judgment dictated. What he needed to do was get his mind off Lara Serenov, and even off Margaret, for that matter. He needed to concentrate on his work.

Feeling a sudden resolve, Derek decided he would dedicate himself to his book. He would start fresh the next day. As far as the evening was concerned, he would drive into town and buy himself a good dinner someplace. Having people around would probably help. Then he would come home, get a good night's sleep and begin his life anew in the morning.

Glancing again at Lara's book of poems, he resisted the

temptation to thumb through it. Instead, he took the volume over to the bookshelf he'd set up that morning and slipped it inconspicuously between two ponderous treatises on political theory. He hoped he could deal with his thoughts of Lara Serenov in a similar fashion.

IT WAS LATE AFTERNOON when Lara drove up Flat Pine Road toward her cabin. She glanced in her rearview mirror to make sure Tony Bianco was still there. The ancient Chevrolet he drove mostly to work and back seemed to labor on the grade, and she didn't want to leave him behind.

Lara had spent the day with Calle, but knew she couldn't stay with the Biancos indefinitely. Besides, with the passage of time her fear had abated. She had her gun and the telephone, neither of which would be necessary if the deputy had managed to talk some sense into Steve. And she was determined not to let her ex-husband force a change in her life.

Still she had agreed to let Tony follow her home, to make sure everything there was all right. Once safely inside, she was confident she would be okay.

They came to Lara's drive and she turned in, going slowly through the woods so as not to kick up too much dust in Tony's face. When they arrived at the cabin, everything seemed to be in order. There were no flowers on the porch. The windows and doors were all intact. Tony waited while she went inside and took a quick look around. The place was as she had left it.

Coming back out onto the porch, she nodded to her friend's husband. "Not a thing wrong, Tony," she called to him.

"You'll be all right, then?" he said.

"Fine. Thanks an awful lot for following me up here. It was really sweet of you."

"No problem. Glad to help." He waved to her. "You take care of yourself. Call us if you need anything."

"I will."

Tony left and Lara went inside. It was good to be home, even though she knew her free life-style would have to be modified somewhat. The first thing she would have to do was order some drapes. And she would be a little more careful what she wore out on the deck in the future, too— at least until this business with Steve had blown over.

Although she was glad to be back in her own nest, the day with Calle had been pleasant. They hadn't been together for that long in months. When she'd told Calle so, her friend suggested Lara was probably spending too much time alone.

That comment had led to a brief discussion about Derek Gordon, which Calle was soon made to realize was not overly appreciated. Lara didn't mind the subject matter so much as the fact that she felt Calle was pushing. Why was it so important to her that something come of this nascent friendship Lara had forged with the professor?

The incident with Derek, and her conversation with Calle, did convince Lara that she might have been playing the Robinson Crusoe role to excess. It probably was time to come out of her shell, if only so that she appeared less needy to perverse would-be saviors like Steve.

Although she hadn't said anything to Calle, Lara had decided to start on her new social regimen immediately. She would drive into town after dinner, maybe browse through the bookstore or have coffee with someone if a likely friend showed up. It wasn't much. Still, it was more than she'd been doing recently. Feeling a good deal better for having planned positive action of some kind, Lara went happily off to the kitchen to fix herself dinner.

She had just finished eating when she heard a vehicle

coming up the drive. She hurried to the window and was relieved to see it was a sheriff's cruiser. She met Wally Stiles at the door.

"I had a talk with your ex-husband this afternoon," he said, "and wanted to tell you about it."

"Come in, please."

They went into the living room. Lara could tell from the deputy's expression the news wasn't good. "I take it the conversation didn't go well."

"I'm not convinced he's persuaded to stay away. Let me put it like that."

"What did he say?"

"He wasn't pleased with my visit, and even less with my suggestion he leave you alone. He knew there wasn't much I could do but talk, and he as good as told me so."

"So...it didn't do any good."

"I don't know about that. Just the fact that we're aware of him might cause him to think twice. But there's no guarantee. That's mainly what I wanted you to know...so that you don't let your guard down."

"No, I won't. I'm going to be careful. He doesn't give me much choice."

"I wish there was more that I could do. Of course, if he bothers you again, call us immediately."

Lara nodded wearily. "I will." She shook her head. "It's a damn shame someone can get away with upsetting your life this way."

"Hopefully it'll pass soon, Miss Serenov, and he'll move on to something or someone else."

"I wouldn't wish him on any woman."

The man grinned and got to his feet. "Well, my purpose in coming was to let you know what happened."

Lara got up, too. "Thanks."

After she'd seen the officer out she returned to the

kitchen and began clearing away her dinner dishes. She brooded for a while, but decided nothing had changed. Steve couldn't win unless she gave in to him. She would go ahead with her evening as she had planned.

DEREK WALKED OUT of the Mendocino Hotel and into the evening air, which he inhaled with pleasure. He had had a demicarafe of wine with his meal and was feeling pleasantly high. Knowing he shouldn't drive, he decided to walk around for half an hour or so, until his head cleared.

His wanderings took him out of the small business district and along the residential streets. The houses were mostly old weathered clapboard painted white or gray. They were separated from one another by hedges or rickety fences. Though the trees and structures had endured for a long time, there was a fragility about the town that struck him. Places of human habitation dominated by nature were like that.

It was twilight, and lights were coming on in many of the homes. The people seemed to be settling down for the night, though the wind was light and not particularly threatening. As he walked, he again savored the salt air.

Derek soon found himself on Little Lake Street, which led out to the point. He followed it, passing the Mendocino Art Center. Ahead, beyond land's end, was the sea and the luminescent sky. The last rays of the sunset were fading into darkness. A low band of deep purple clouds masked the horizon, separating the sky from the sea.

He could see where the street ended at the tip of the point. The barren spot of land was a mere shadow, though as he drew closer he could make out the shape of a vehicle on the promontory. Even before he was close enough to tell, he began suspecting it was the Jeep, her Jeep.

As he descended the last bit of road, Derek could see a

figure perched on the hood of the vehicle, like a figurehead on the prow of a ship. It was a woman. Her hair was blowing in the breeze. She was sitting erect, facing out to sea. It was Lara.

Derek stopped perhaps twenty yards from where she sat. His dilemma was apparent. Should he speak to her? Her book of poems—telling her how much he enjoyed it—was reason enough. But something held him back. It was fear. Fear of the attraction he felt.

The image she presented in the half-light, sitting with her arms wrapped about her knees, was the most powerful yet. He was unable to take his eyes off her.

She hadn't moved. She was sitting perfectly still. Why was she there, and what was she thinking? he wondered. He wanted to know the answer badly, but he had resolved not to subject himself to the temptation of Lara Serenov. To taste more of her would only make his hunger worse. For that was what it was—hunger. Obsession.

He knew he should leave, yet he wanted to share the beauty of the moment a bit longer. He looked out to sea at the dying light. But her presence was too strong. It called to him. He watched the wind blowing her hair like streamers.

Finally he forced his eyes from her. He stared down the coast toward Albion. A few scattered lights were visible on the dark mass of land. One hundred and fifty miles away was San Francisco, and across the inland bay was Berkeley and the home he had shared with Margaret.

His other life seemed so far away. The innocence and purity of what he and Margaret had shared seemed remote, too—a different time, a different place entirely. Much more real was this longing, this desire for the unknown, virtually mystical creature nearby. In a strange way that he was only beginning to appreciate, she possessed him.

It was fantasy, he knew. A trick. He had deceived himself about his needs, and now his mind was taking its revenge. If he were to master this, he'd have to begin now, while he still could.

Turning, Derek walked up the dark road toward the town. He didn't look back. He knew he couldn't. He was afraid his desire was stronger than he.

CHAPTER FOUR

THE DAY OF the Literary Guild meeting, Lara drove to Calle's early to help with the preparations. Since school hadn't started yet, Jodie and Tony Two had been sent up the road to a neighbor's. Little Theresa wasn't feeling well so her mother kept her at home, hoping she might nap during the meeting.

Lara arrived to find things already pretty well organized. Calle was in the kitchen. When Lara asked what she could do to help, her friend said, "Entertain Theresa."

So Lara sat in the living room with the child on her lap. Theresa was quite listless, though she did seem interested in the attention. So the two of them sat quietly, the girl with her head resting contentedly on Lara's breast.

Lara hummed a lullaby, as her mother had for her as a child when she wasn't feeling well. She stroked Theresa's head and they both looked out the window at the trees swaying in the wind.

The week had been strangely quiescent, though in the sense of the lull before the storm. Steve Adamson hadn't actually put in an appearance, though there had been a few not so subtle hints of his presence.

One afternoon Lara had taken her tape machine down into the narrow valley below her cabin where she frequently went to write. After several productive hours in the lush nature she so dearly loved, she returned home to find six empty beer cans neatly lined up on the railing of her deck.

There was no other sign of his presence. No note, no flowers. No indication of an attempt to enter the cabin. It was a reminder, a message, that he hadn't forgotten her.

And then, late one night, she had thought she heard someone out on the deck. It could have been an animal or her imagination. Her new drapes, which she'd paid a premium price for in order to get an early delivery, had been hung that day, so she couldn't see out. The privacy made her feel more secure, even if it did enable Steve to climb onto the deck unseen.

More than once during the week she had thought of Derek Gordon, wondering, despite herself, whether she would see him again. Calle's curiosity had sparked her own interest, though she couldn't actually say she thought in terms of anything but friendship. Still, because of him, she had looked forward to Friday with greater anticipation than the Guild meetings usually evoked.

Calle came out of the kitchen for a moment and stood with her hands on her hips, smiling at Lara and Theresa. "Well, if you aren't the picture of motherhood," she said warmly. "You look as natural as can be."

Lara glanced down at Theresa, who'd practically dozed off. "I guess we're special friends."

"It looks that way."

"How's everything going?" Lara asked.

"I'm about finished. Didn't have to fix nearly so much as last time. There were a lot of cancellations. The Labor Day weekend. We forgot all about that when we set the date. A lot of people wanted to go away, I guess."

"How many are you expecting?"

"Six or eight, counting your professor."

"He's not mine, Calle."

"Well, he certainly isn't mine!"

"All right. I invited him, so he's mine."

Calle smiled broadly. "I'm dying to see what he looks like."

"I hope he shows up, so that you'll be able to. Then maybe you'll finally let go of the subject."

Calle looked hurt.

"I'm sorry," Lara quickly said. "That was unkind. I shouldn't have been critical."

"That's all right. I know what you're going through." Calle returned to the kitchen, and Lara sang some more to Theresa, stroking her head. When Leonard Keyes arrived several minutes later, Calle came in to take the girl to her room.

Leonard, a wizened little man who looked older than his sixty years, wrote historical novels about obscure times and places, mostly set in Asia and the Middle East. His plots invariably involved tyrannical warlords and their attempted exploitation of innocent young peasant girls. The books' strength, it seemed, was the rich historical detail that the author wove into the tale, though they never sold particularly well.

Mary Ailes and Trudy Simon arrived next. Both were middle-aged. Mary wrote children's stories. Trudy was a reporter for the paper in Fort Bragg. Hardy Kline, a merchant in Ukiah and the author of numerous unpublished short stories and poems, came next, followed by Shirley Wilsey, who, like Calle, wrote articles for periodicals.

Leonard Keyes took center stage, telling the others the news of his latest sale, which he hoped would be a breakthrough book for him. As he related the story Lara found herself looking out the window, wondering if Derek Gordon would come.

After Leonard finished his discourse, they broke into smaller conversation groups. Shirley was telling Lara of her decision to quit her insurance office job so she could write full-time when Lara noticed a car slowly going by out front.

A minute or so later she saw Derek come up onto the porch, and was surprised at how glad she was to see him. He knocked, and Calle went to the door. The conversation stopped when everyone saw the newcomer. Derek introduced himself to Calle, who glanced over at Lara, her eyes rounding slightly as a signal of satisfaction with what she saw. Calle took him by the arm then, and brought him into the crowded living room.

She immediately began the introductions, going around the room. When he got to Lara, she said, "And of course you know Lara Serenov."

Derek said, "Hi, Lara," smiling as a friend would, though he had scanned the room for her the moment he came in the door.

Calle finished the introductions, then got a chair for Derek. Judging by the way Calle studied the crowded room, Lara could tell she wanted to place the chair near her, but the best Calle could do was wedge it on the other side of Shirley Wilsey, who was sitting beside Lara.

Derek took his seat, smiling again at Lara, who for some reason felt her heart beating nervously in her breast. She was wearing a white skirt and a turquoise cotton sweater and had put her hair up for the occasion. She'd wanted to look nice.

Derek looked even more handsome than she had remembered, in a charcoal sweater and black cords. The gray at his temples was highlighted by the sweater, which made him seem distinguished, yet casual.

Hardy inquired what kind of writing Derek did, and seemed relieved to learn that he didn't publish short stories or novels by the dozens. Mary Ailes asked Derek to tell them about his book, which he did in a few brief sentences. Lara was impressed by his modesty.

"We've never had a genuine scholar in the group," Trudy said with evident admiration.

"That's not true," Leonard Keyes protested. "You have to know your history to write historical novels."

Lara glanced at Calle as the conversation continued. Her friend's expression all but screamed, "Grab this one, honey!"

Uncharacteristically, Lara blushed. Then she remembered Calle's question about whether Derek was single. She was sure he was. But when she glanced over and saw that he had on a wedding band, her heart dropped. She was genuinely disappointed, much more than she would have thought.

She caught Calle's eye again and pointed to her own ring finger, then tilted her head slightly in Derek's direction. The expression on Calle's face turned dour as she confirmed the sighting. Lara shrugged in response to Calle's pout.

The interplay between them went unseen by Derek, who was busy getting acquainted with the rest of the group. Lara watched him out of the corner of her eye, actually permitting herself to speculate secretly on what might have been. It was an unusual game for her, and harmless enough, even though she never did that kind of thing.

Then, her voice rising over the rest of the group, Calle drew Derek's attention with a question. "How long will you be in Mendocino, Professor Gordon?" she asked.

"I have a year's lease on the house I'm living in and have to be back on the campus next fall," he replied.

"Is your wife with you, then?"

Lara waited for his answer, watching with a mixture of sadness and morbid amusement.

"No, Margaret is in a nursing home in Berkeley. She has myasthenia gravis, a muscle disease."

There were murmurs of sympathy.

"I'm so sorry to hear that," Calle said. "I take it, it's a serious illness."

"Unfortunately, yes. She's been in the home for about five years."

"How terrible."

Others shook their heads sympathetically.

He looked around the group, his eyes lingering briefly on Lara. "It's something we live with," he said, with a let's-change-the-subject tone. "No point in dwelling on an unfortunate situation."

"You have our sympathy," Calle said, speaking for the group. "If there's anything we can do, don't hesitate to call on us. It must be difficult for you, being alone. You're always welcome here, if you'd like a home-cooked meal."

"Thank you," Derek said, obviously embarrassed. "Thank you."

Lara knew that Calle was sincere. She was genuinely a good-hearted person, and had been caught off balance by Derek's revelation. Lara had been, as well. She glanced at Derek. He was looking at her as though he would like to say something. Perhaps he had intended to tell her about his wife and was sorry the information had come out publicly.

"Well, ladies and gentlemen," Calle said to the entire group. "I've made plenty of cake and other goodies. Everything's on the dining room table. It's buffet style, so come in when you're ready and serve yourself."

Calle's baking was widely appreciated, and the announcement was greeted with pleasure. Several people got up immediately, including Shirley Wilsey. Derek took the opportunity to slide over onto her vacant chair. He extended his hand to Lara.

"I didn't get to say a personal hello," she said, smiling warmly.

"How's everything going? Any more trouble with Steve?"

"Not really. Hopefully, that's behind me."

They were practically alone in the room. Voices and the sound of dishes and silver clattering were coming from the adjacent dining room.

"You know," she said, "I had no idea about your wife. I'm very sorry."

He accepted her expression of sympathy with a nod, but didn't comment.

"Is she all right mentally? I really don't know anything about the disease."

"In Margaret's case, myasthenia only affects the throat and face, and sometimes her lungs. But about five years ago she had a serious attack. She stopped breathing entirely. They did an emergency tracheostomy and barely managed to save her. The doctor thinks there may have been some brain damage, but it's difficult to tell. She hasn't been able to speak for a couple of years."

"How sad. Poor thing. Is there any hope at all of recovery?"

Derek shook his head. "She'll never get better. Her condition is fragile, and there's always the danger of infection. How long she survives, the doctor tells me, depends mostly on the quality of her care."

Lara shook her head. "I'm sure your wife is suffering, but it has to be terribly hard for you, too."

"I try not to dwell on it."

Lara could see it was something he didn't want to talk about, and she understood. Everything about him suddenly fell into place. He was married, but he was very much alone. His wife and his marriage were important to him, though, she could tell that.

The others were beginning to come back into the living room, a plate in one hand, a cup of tea or coffee in the other. "It'll be all gone, if you don't hurry," Hardy Kline said.

Derek winked at Lara. "We'd better get going, then, hadn't we?"

They went into the dining room, falling into line behind the last person. Calle was behind the table, pouring coffee and tea. Lara was very much aware of Derek beside her, particularly under Calle's watchful eye. She was conscious of his after-shave, his calm, scholarly aura.

She wouldn't have thought, by the way she was feeling, that she'd just learned he was married. Yet she felt strangely relaxed. Perhaps knowing he was unavailable had taken the threat of possible involvement away. She could relate to him as a friend, which was what she had truly wanted from the beginning.

"It's so nice having you in the group, Professor Gordon," Calle said, looking at Lara for a reaction.

"Thank you, but I'm only Professor Gordon in Berkeley. Here I'm just plain Derek."

"Oh, but 'Professor Gordon' sounds so…academic," Calle enthused. "When I was a coed, I adored my professors—especially the good-looking ones. The other girls were into rock stars, but I was into teachers."

Derek laughed. "Encountering an admiring student happens to all of us occasionally."

Calle handed him a cup of coffee. "I bet you're no stranger to it. You must be besieged by love-struck coeds." She looked pointedly at Lara. "Wouldn't you be enamored, if you sat for an hour listening to this man talk about Thomas Aquinas or Sir Thomas More?''

She couldn't help smiling. ''I suppose I would—despite the subject matter.''

Derek grinned. ''Thank you, but honestly, my life is a good deal more pedestrian than you're suggesting.''

''I don't believe it for a minute,'' Calle said.

They went back into the living room and Lara couldn't help wondering why Calle was still pushing things. If anyone had ever been a champion of the institution of marriage, it was Calle Bianco. Besides, there wasn't any percentage in getting involved with a married man...that was a sure road to heartache, if ever there was one!

Shirley Wilsey, who seemed charmed by Derek, too, engaged him in conversation as soon as they sat down. Judging by Shirley's tone, the remark about love-struck coeds might be equally applied to single young female writers in Mendocino.

Lara chose to ignore Shirley and Derek and turned to Leonard Keyes. A question or two produced a flood of conversation, for Leonard was known for his willingness to talk about his own work.

As was their custom, the group held a brief reading and critique session after everyone had finished their food and drink. Hardy Kline started things with one of his ponderous poems. Mary read a few pages of her new juvenile mystery, which produced some enthusiastic and favorable comments.

Out of curiosity, Lara glanced at Derek from time to time to see whether he was bored. He seemed to be listening politely and with interest. She couldn't help admiring his attractive, yet sympathetic, demeanor. There was something about him that was both provocative and calming. How could a man excite and soothe at the same time?

At the moment Calle was asking for comments and suggestions on her article about the early Chinese of Mendocino County. Shirley suggested a good reference source, and Derek mentioned that the library at Berkeley had an excellent collection of reference material on California history.

Lara was staring at Derek when Hardy asked her if she had brought a poem. The question jarred her into awareness. Fumbling, she replied that she didn't have anything ready. The truth was, she had brought her latest poem with the intention of reading it, but Derek's presence inhibited her.

After a last cup of coffee the gathering began to break up. Lara intended to help clean up, but Calle made a point of telling her that she could easily handle things. Lara carried a tray of cups and saucers into the kitchen anyway, and by the time she returned to the front room the group had dispersed. Except for Derek. He seemed to be hanging back.

Calle was talking to him. "Well, did we make you feel at home?" she asked.

"I'm overwhelmed," he said pleasantly.

"I meant what I said about you coming for dinner. You're always welcome."

"That's very kind."

"And I want to thank you," she went on, "for saving Lara the other day. She's my best friend and I would have died if something had happened to her." Calle put her arm around Lara, who had come up to them.

Derek chuckled. "She saved me as much as I saved her."

Lara lowered her eyes in embarrassment. "It was a team effort."

Calle looked at them benevolently, as though bestowing

her blessing. Derek turned to Lara. "Can I walk you to your car?"

Lara gave her friend a plaintive look. "Are you sure I can't help clean up?"

"Absolutely not."

Lara shrugged. "I guess I'm being tossed out."

"Then you're a captive audience," he said, taking her by the arm.

They said their goodbyes and went out into the breezy air. "Quite a group," he said as they strolled toward the gate.

"I hope it wasn't too tedious for you."

"To the contrary. I enjoyed it. And I'd like to come next month, if you wouldn't mind."

"Of course I wouldn't mind," she said with genuine surprise. "You're more than welcome. Everybody seemed to like you."

"That's nice, but I wasn't worried about them. I was thinking more about you," he said, stopping at the gate.

"Me?"

"I feel badly how the fact that I'm married came out. I'd intended to tell you about Margaret privately."

Lara read a lot in his eyes and it made her uncomfortable. "Why would that be important?"

"I didn't want you to have the wrong impression about my going to your house last week."

She tried to scoff. "Is it a requirement that a man be single to help a woman in distress?"

"No, perhaps not." Derek glanced around and spotted her Jeep a few steps up the road. They walked toward it.

"If you're thinking I misread your intentions, Derek, I didn't. So don't worry."

"I was hoping we could be friends."

"I thought we already were."

They were at her Jeep, and he turned to her. "I read all your poems, by the way."

"Oh?"

"After I got home from your place that evening."

She wasn't sure what he was trying to say. "Did you like them?"

"Very much. I studied them, actually."

"Studied them?"

"Getting to know the author through her work."

The comment disturbed her. There was something in his tone of voice, an intimacy. Lara reached for the door handle, unsure what to say. She was about to tell him goodbye when Calle called to them from her porch. She made her way out to the road.

"Tony just called," she said, coming up to them. "He won a hundred dollars on a lottery ticket and told me he's buying some steaks and a bottle of wine and to invite you two for dinner. I told my husband about you, Derek, and he said I should be sure and include you."

"That's very kind, but I—"

"Tony wouldn't let me take no for an answer," she interrupted. "That's one area he always has his way. He loves playing the role of the good host." She looked at Lara. "What do you say?"

"I've thawed a chicken breast."

"It'll keep."

Lara glanced at Derek.

"I have a feeling we're staying for dinner," he said affably.

"I told you I meant to have you over," Calle said. "The invitation came a little sooner than I expected, that's all." She took them each by the arm. "Come on, Tony's excited. He wants to pour wine for guests and be effusive."

STEVE ADAMSON TURNED OFF the Coast Highway and headed for the Bianco place. He hadn't gone far before he saw Lara's Jeep in the beams of his headlights. "Bingo!" he said aloud, and hooted.

But his joy abated when he saw the BMW that belonged to that friend of hers, the guy who'd tripped him on her deck, the guy who looked like a lawyer or an accountant or something. Steve cruised past. Lights shone from the house, and a bunch of people were sitting at a table. Steve knew he couldn't stop to check things out, so he continued up the road.

A hundred yards away there was a vacant house with a For Sale sign out by the mailbox. Steve pulled into the driveway and walked back along the dark road. When he reached the front of the Bianco place, he could see that Lara was there all right, along with Tony, Calle and that guy from the other night.

Steve slipped through the bushes to get closer to the window. From his vantage point, he had a good view of Lara. Her hair was up and she looked real pretty—so damned pretty it made him sort of ache in the loins.

Inside the four of them were laughing and talking. The guy kept looking at Lara. Even though he was being cool about it, Steve could tell he was hot for her body. A man would have to be half-dead not to be turned on by Lara Serenov.

It was hard to tell if she liked the guy, but Steve did notice her glancing at him every once in a while. And her cheeks looked very pink, like she was embarrassed or something. Of course, it could have been the wine.

As Steve watched, Tony filled Lara's and Calle's glasses. When Lara lifted the wineglass to her lips, he stared at her mouth, thinking how it would taste to kiss her. The thought made him want her so bad he'd probably have squeezed her to death if he'd had her alone. Damn, he was horny!

One thing was sure. He wasn't going to quit until he had her. He was going to get Lara Serenov between the sheets again if it was the very last thing he ever did. Even if she was getting it on with this joker in the meantime, sooner or later he'd get her. It'd serve them both right.

Steve glared at the guy, wondering if he gushed over Lara's poetry, if that was why she ran around with him. It burned him but good the way she acted—like she was too good to spit on him—but at the same time she was flirting with this snooty lawyer, or whatever he was.

Steve felt his temper starting to build and he knew he had to leave before he did something stupid. There'd be time to take care of Lara later. It would be easy enough. All he had to do was catch her alone, without her gun.

AFTER DINNER LARA HELPED Calle clear the dishes while Tony and Derek went into the living room. Though the men were as different as night and day, they quickly developed a rapport. Tony wasn't well educated, but he had an engaging mind and was at peace with himself, qualities that enabled him to talk to almost anyone.

Lara glanced in at the men from the kitchen. "It was sweet to invite us to dinner," she said, moving close to Calle, "but I hope you aren't getting any ideas."

"What ideas?"

"About me and Derek. He's married, and I'm not interested right now, anyway. You know that."

"I know you've been in your shell too long."

"Yes, but trying to promote something with Derek is hardly the thing to do, even if I were interested in accommodating you, which I'm not."

Calle looked at her. "I know that. I'm doing this because

he's safe, and you're friends anyway. A woman shouldn't cut herself off from men entirely. Besides, the practice will do you good. I'm thinking of the guys down the line.''

"I wish you'd let me worry about my future,'' Lara said with thinly disguised annoyance. Calle was taking things a bit too far. "At times during dinner, the way you were talking, he had to assume you were playing matchmaker. I could have slugged you when you made that comment about me being too reclusive.''

"I'm sorry, but motherhood has a way of stripping away one's subtlety. I'll try to be more careful.''

"Just let go of this matchmaking obsession.''

"All right, but you loosen up, too! You aren't a nun, Lara Serenov. You only like to think you are.''

Lara glared at her. "If you weren't my best friend, I'd pop you one!''

"Go ahead, it might make you feel better.''

They stared at each other, their sober expressions slowly turning to smiles. Calle dried her hands on a towel and they embraced. Lara almost felt like crying.

"Come on,'' Calle said, "Let's go in and join the men.''

The four of them sat and talked for a while, Lara glancing at Derek every so often, seeing him, despite herself, through Calle's eyes. There was a definite current flowing between herself and Derek. She felt it every time their eyes met. But he wasn't coming on to her. She could feel him holding back. And it wasn't hard to guess why.

After a polite interval Lara announced that she had to go home. Tony asked if she felt okay about returning to her place alone, or if she'd prefer to have him follow.

"I'm okay,'' she replied. "I think the problem with Steve has blown over.''

"Knock on wood,'' Calle said.

They all got up. "If you're feeling at all uneasy, it

wouldn't be any problem for me to make sure you get home all right," Derek said.

"Thanks," she replied, "but I can't be mollycoddled the rest of my life."

"No, but it wouldn't hurt for a week or two," he replied.

"I agree," Calle chimed in.

"All right," Lara said, giving her friend a telling look. "Tonight I've been outvoted."

They said goodbye to the Biancos on the porch, and Derek went with Lara to her Jeep. "This really isn't necessary," she said.

"It'll make me feel better," Derek said, "not to mention Calle."

Lara looked at him in the dim light coming from the Biancos' porch. He was awfully good-looking, and his kindness and gentle manner only added to his attractiveness. She felt drawn to him, though she didn't want to admit it.

Lara got in her vehicle and Derek went to his car. They drove up the highway and then east along Flat Pine Road. She glanced at the impersonal headlights in her rearview mirror, but thought about Derek Gordon. She was glad he was escorting her home, glad he'd wanted to. Despite the surprise of the day—the fact that he was indeed married—she had a very warm feeling for him.

They soon left the road and made their way up the long drive through the woods to Lara's cabin. There was a glow of light coming from within—the living room lamp on the timer. Everything appeared to be normal. After she parked in the carport, Lara got out of her Jeep and headed for the porch. Derek followed her.

"Shall I have a look around?" he asked, as she began searching her purse for her key.

"It's not necessary."

Lara fished out her key ring. In doing so, she dropped the folded piece of paper on which she had typed the poem she'd planned to read at the meeting. Derek picked it up. She unlocked the door and, by the light coming from within, he saw what was on the paper before handing it back.

"Why didn't you read this?"

"I don't know. I was inhibited, I guess."

"Why?"

"Because of you," she replied honestly. She stuffed the paper back into her purse, and looked at Derek uneasily.

"I can see I've been a problem," he said without the slightest trace of self-pity, "and I'm sorry about that." He studied her face in the dim light. "Your friend, Calle, hasn't made it any easier, either."

"She's crazy, but I love her." Lara looked into his eyes, feeling a connection between them. Emotion was evident on his face, and she felt it as well.

Then he said, "I haven't told you yet about the woman I saw in your poems. She was really quite lovely. Sensitive, perceptive and a touch sad. I liked her. I understood her. Maybe I even felt I had a lot in common with her."

Lara looked down, unable to hear those things and still meet his gaze.

"But I want to tell you something," he said. "I wasn't going to come to the meeting today. I'd decided against it."

"Why?"

"Let's just say I thought it would be better for both of us if I didn't."

Lara knew exactly what he meant. It was a strangely frank admission. "So, why did you come?" she asked, without engaging his eyes.

"I thought we might be friends. Real friends."

She felt her heart start to pick up its beat. She didn't know why. Something in his tone of voice perhaps. She looked at him in the faint light, seeing not just a man who was appealing, but someone who was different, someone who affected her in a way she wasn't used to.

In the ensuing silence they stared at each other. Lara's eyes glossed with tears.

Derek reached over and touched her cheek with his fingertips. Then, as though it were the most natural thing in the world, he leaned forward and kissed the corner of her mouth. It was a friendly caress.

Lara stood still. His gesture didn't frighten her, it actually moved her. But the feeling was deep inside, far below the outward layers of calm.

Derek pulled back and gazed into her eyes. It was such a quiet, unthreatening look he gave her. But there was tenderness in it and, beneath the surface, a whisper of longing.

He was poised on the point of turning to go, but for some reason he didn't. Lara hadn't budged, perhaps hadn't even breathed. She didn't know why, but she was paralyzed.

It was then he moved back toward her, his mouth descending again. As their lips touched, his arms slipped around her waist and his body came up against her. She didn't stiffen, but neither did she kiss him back. Her lips slowly softened, though, and as her breathing returned her lungs began to fill with his scent. Her lips parted slightly and she experienced the taste of him.

The kiss was tender, but there was an underlying forcefulness about it, demanding a response. Lara didn't think about what was happening. Though she might have been shocked, she wasn't. She was curious. She was trapped in the sensation.

Then the kiss deepened. His tongue traversed her lips, finding her teeth and the tip of her tongue. He pulled her body more firmly against him and she yielded to his strength, finding herself beginning to kiss him back. Slowly the pressure subsided. His grasp slackened, his lips softened, lingering momentarily near hers. His breath washed over her.

He retreated then, in the same gradual way he had assailed her, his hands finally slipping free. There was question in his eyes, perhaps disbelief and apology as well. But he didn't say anything. He did touch her face a final time, though, before he went down the steps and to his car.

CHAPTER FIVE

DEREK DROVE through the inland valley, its golden hills rising on either side above the vineyards and orchards. The morning sun slanted in the windshield, forcing him to shade his eyes with the visor. He had been up since before dawn, had drunk a cup of coffee as he watched the sea slowly emerge from the obscurity of night.

He hadn't slept well. Kissing Lara had been as wrong as it had been inevitable. Now he had to do something about it.

The place for it wasn't in Mendocino. It was at home in Berkeley, with Margaret and with Mark. He wasn't exactly sure what he would do when he got there, except that he would see them both. Maybe it was time to find out what really mattered to him.

As the countryside rolled by and the sun gradually rose, Derek stared up the road, thinking of Lara. He remembered her as she had been that first time he saw her outside McGaffy's General Store. He pictured her in her bathrobe the night of his confrontation with Steve, frightened as he held her in his arms. He saw her on the hood of her Jeep, hugging her long legs as she stared out to sea. He saw her at Calle's, her tawny hair piled on her head, her blue-green eyes watching him with curiosity and suspicion. And he especially remembered her sensuous mouth just before he kissed her.

But as much as the physical woman, it was her inner

being that touched him—Lara drew him, inveigled him without intending to, which only made her allure more enticing. He desired her physically, but he craved her even more spiritually. He wanted her, body and soul.

Derek drove along the highway in a detached, yet uneasy state of mind. Still the time passed quickly. There was little traffic before Santa Rosa, and most of it was outbound—the mass exodus for the Labor Day weekend. Others were escaping while Derek was making his pilgrimage home.

In Marin he took the Richmond–San Rafael Bridge to the East Bay, then drove south to Berkeley. It was a hazy warm day, hotter than the Bay Area usually was, even in the summer.

Once he was in the familiar urban environment, the rustic Mendocino coast seemed to fade from his consciousness. Driving up University Avenue, past the fast food places, motels and funky shops, he had a sense of the isolation he'd been in the past few weeks. Nothing had changed in Berkeley; everything was as he had left it.

He drove toward the campus nestled against the side of the Berkeley hills, then followed the familiar route through the twisting streets of Northside, coming eventually to the nursing home where Margaret had spent the past five years. As usual, there was no place to park. Derek had to circle the block until he finally found a spot.

He walked back to the hospital in the hot still air on a sidewalk pitched here and there by the roots of the great shade trees lining the street. The large old shingled houses with broad porches looked familiar but stolid compared to the white clapboard homes of Mendocino. How frail in comparison those coastal dwellings seemed, sitting on their high point of land above the ocean, leaning into the unrelenting wind.

As he approached the entrance to the home, Derek decided he had to put Lara and Mendocino out of his mind for a while and concentrate on Margaret. He mounted the steps and went inside. The receptionist recognized him and smiled, greeting him as she had on dozens of other occasions.

"We haven't see you for a while, Professor Gordon," she said, intending the words as conversation, not chastisement.

"I've been away," he replied, realizing she wasn't aware of his sabbatical. He leaned against the counter and looked at the woman purposefully. "How's Margaret?"

"Nothing to report that I know of," she replied. "But you might want to talk with Miss Quinn. She's on duty now."

Derek went down the familiar hall to the nursing station, passing a few patients sitting at their doors in wheelchairs, or moving along the corridor. He greeted an elderly woman patient whom he'd seen many times before.

The duty nurse, Miss Quinn, was sitting at her desk studying charts when he came up. She was young, heavyset and obdurate in her professionalism. "Oh, Professor Gordon," she said, looking up, "I didn't expect to see you."

"Came home for Labor Day weekend."

The nurse's slight smile signaled acknowledgement, but nothing more. Approval or disapproval wasn't an issue for her. "I was in to see Mrs. Gordon a few minutes ago," the woman said, "and she was sleeping. But you can look in and check. Sometimes she just dozes for a few minutes, as you know."

Derek nodded. "How has she been?"

"The same."

He turned and went down the side hall to the first doorway, Margaret's room. Pausing, he looked in and saw her lying in bed, her head and shoulders elevated by a pillow.

She was asleep, her expression tranquil to the point of being slack. She was bathed in the indirect light coming from the window by her bed, which gave her skin a pallid appearance.

Seeing her familiar profile he felt a pang of sadness go through him, followed by guilt. It was the first unequivocal feeling of guilt he'd had since meeting Lara. Slowly he moved into the room, expecting to discover something, though he wasn't sure what. Insight? Understanding?

But Margaret was truly unchanged—familiar, dear, a tragic figure. The reality of her condition—and his—struck Derek heavily as he gazed at her. He sat on the edge of the bed, hoping that her eyes might open and she would look at him. Even if she did, he couldn't be sure there would be recognition. Still it would be contact, contact that in the past he had lived for.

But Margaret didn't move. She showed no sign of life, save for the slow rise and fall of her chest.

Derek took her hand, which lay limply at her side. Her flesh was cool, lifeless. There was no response to his touch. He stroked her hand, squeezing it lightly as he always had. It was instinctual when he was with her. She was his wife. And he did love her.

He reached up and caressed her face, pushing back the strands of auburn hair lying against her temple. There were many white hairs among the brown, more than he had remembered. The thought struck him that she was aging without being aware of it, unable even to fret about the process or make the little jokes people make in coping with their mortality. Moisture filled his eyes.

Then, almost miraculously, Margaret opened her eyes. For an instant he thought he saw recognition, but he couldn't be sure. Whispering a greeting, he leaned close and kissed her cheek. Margaret gave no response, but the contact did spur him on. He began talking, trying to reach out to her.

He spoke about the past, the outings they'd shared on previous Labor Day weekends, their camping trips with Mark when he was a boy. When he stopped long enough to collect himself, and to let Margaret respond, he saw that she couldn't, that she might not have understood anything he said. Her face was expressionless. The eye contact might not have been contact at all. She seemed to be looking through him, not at him.

During the brief silence in which he questioned her with his eyes, her lids slid closed and she returned to wherever it was she had been. Derek sat silently for a long time, rubbing her hand. When he finally laid it down at her side he realized that nothing, really, had changed. Margaret was the same as when he had entered the room.

He got up then, and went to the chair next to the window. Sitting there, he was able to see her face. Sounds of staff and patients came from the hallway outside, but the room was silent. Even Margaret's breath slipped silently in and out of her lungs. Time meant nothing.

Thoughts of Lara did not come easily to him, but he made himself consider her because that was one of the things he had come to do. He tried to put her into the perspective of his life—life with an incapacitated wife he had once loved without qualification, and still did.

But Lara did not willingly intrude. His images of her would not cooperate. Did that mean that there wasn't room for both women in his heart? Or did his subconscious know something about Lara that his conscious mind didn't?

Still, Derek coaxed her image into his mind. He pictured her lovely face—the hair, the eyes, the mouth. He asked himself what his feelings for her were and how they compared to what he felt for Margaret. It was a horrible game that couldn't be played anywhere but in his heart. And yet he had to do it.

Soon he realized there were neither answers nor profit in the exercise. Margaret couldn't help him, though perhaps that was in itself worth knowing. After a long period of contemplation, Derek finally got up to leave. He went to his wife's bedside, touched her cheek with his fingertips, then left the nursing home to find his stepson.

MARK LOOKED OVER THE TOP of his book at Marcy, who was lying on his bed, acting as though she were oblivious to him. In those tight shorts she wore, she had to know he couldn't easily ignore her. It still seemed odd to have a girl in his room. Once or twice while he was in high school he'd sneaked his girlfriend in for fooling around, but this was different.

After two years in a frat house, he was back home and free to do pretty much as he wished. Of course, Derek had told him to use his good judgment before having any parties, but the principal condition was that the master bedroom was off limits.

Even with the freedom he had, Mark had been living pretty quietly. He'd been going out with Marcy Brandt for only two weeks, though they'd seen each other practically every day. She had spent the night twice. As he continued admiring her figure, Marcy turned her head, catching him.

"Hey, Gordon, if you don't get that book read, we'll end up spending the entire weekend indoors," she said.

"I can think of worse fates," he replied, giving her a crooked grin.

Marcy, a leggy blonde with short, spiky hair, turned to hide her smile. "Is that all you ever think about?"

"Just about."

"Sex is not worth flunking out of school," she said without looking at him.

"Who said they're mutually exclusive?"

The girl rolled onto her side so that her firm little breasts poked in his direction from under her T-shirt. Her head rested on her hand. "Haven't you ever heard of deferred pleasure? Think of sex as something you have to earn."

Mark shook his head. "Remind me never to go out with a business major again. Who wants his carnal desires quantified?"

"I can go home if you don't like my philosophy," Marcy said in a tone somewhere between provocative and threatening.

"No," he said, poking his tongue into his cheek, "I'm on my last chapter. Think what a waste of capital it would be to close down operations now. You've almost got me where you want me."

The girl grimaced. "Remind me never to go out with a psychology major again. Who wants his motivations analyzed every two minutes? Anyway, we're going on a picnic when we're through studying. Remember?"

Mark was about to ask why there wasn't time to make love *and* have a picnic, but he heard a car in the drive. They both turned toward the window.

"I wonder who that could be?" he said, rousing himself.

"One of your prior investments, maybe?" Marcy said with a laugh.

Mark was at the window, looking down into the street. In the drive was Derek's BMW. "Damn, it's my stepfather."

Marcy bolted upright. "What's he doing here? I thought he was off on a sabbatical somewhere."

"He's supposed to be." Mark tucked in his shirttail and

slipped on his sneakers. "I'll go down and see what he wants."

"Shall I leave?"

"No," Mark said, waving his hand, "he's already figured out I'm past puberty. Derek's cool. Don't worry. If he's staying, just come down acting like you belong here."

Mark went out the door and bounded down the stairs. Through the curtain of the front door he could see his stepfather putting his key in the lock. Despite the intrusion, he was almost glad to see him. Mark opened the door.

"Hi! Sorry to drop in unannounced," Derek said, "but on a whim I came down to see your mother, and thought I'd swing by and say hello."

"No problem," Mark said, stepping back so that Derek could enter. "A friend of mine and I were upstairs studying."

Derek grinned. "A *friend*?"

"Yeah, the kind you're thinking."

Derek chuckled. "This is a new situation for us, isn't it? Maybe we'll have to arrange some kind of a system of signals whenever I come by, so I'll know if the coast is clear."

Mark laughed. "Like one if by land, two if by sea?"

"Something like that." Derek glanced up the staircase, then at his stepson. "Do you have a few minutes to talk, or is this a really bad time?"

Mark shrugged. "We can talk. Just let me tell Marcy I'll be tied up for a while." He headed for the stairs.

"Sure it's okay?" Derek called after him.

"Yeah," Mark said. "I'll let her know everything's cool."

He found Marcy sitting on his bed. She seemed worried. "What's the matter?" he teased. "You look like you got caught with your hand in the cookie jar."

She wrinkled her nose. "It's *his* house, isn't it? What did he say?"

"Nothing. I told him you're here. It's no big deal. He wants to talk about something. Probably about my mother. You want to come down and meet him?"

"Do you think I should?"

"Doesn't matter either way."

Marcy threw herself back onto the bed. "Maybe I'll just ride things out up here."

Mark laughed. "You white-collar criminals are all alike."

The girl buried her head in his pillow. "Shut up, Gordon."

Mark went back downstairs. Derek was standing by the windows in the living room, looking out at the street. "So what's up?" Mark said.

Derek turned around. "You still upset?"

For a while Mark had almost forgotten about the tension between them in Mendocino. He wished that somehow the problem would go away, that they could be as comfortable with each other as they used to be. But that was about as stupid as wishing his mother would miraculously recover, though there had been a time when he used to dream about that, too. He plopped onto a chair. "What do you mean...upset?"

Derek studied him for a moment, seeming to censor one thought after the other. Finally he said, "It's pretty obvious you don't approve of my leaving Berkeley...and your mother."

"I told you that's your business."

Derek hesitated. "Well, there's no point in beating that dead horse anymore. I'd rather deal with what's happening now."

"What *is* happening?"

"I've been over to see your mother...."

"She's all right, isn't she?"

"Yes. It's not that."

"What, then?"

Derek walked across the room slowly and turned to face him. "Remember when you asked why I didn't have another relationship, and I told you because I hadn't met anyone I cared about? I said that I loved your mother, and no one else."

"Yes..." Mark could tell by the ring in Derek's voice what was coming.

"Well, what I said was true. And I still love your mother. That hasn't changed."

"But you've connected with somebody." His voice was flat.

"I've met a woman I'm very fond of. I consider her a friend."

Mark felt the air going right out of him. He'd known this would happen eventually, but knowing it and dealing with it weren't quite the same. Both hurt and anger filled him. "Congratulations."

Derek grimaced. "It doesn't call for congratulations. That's not why I told you."

"Then why *did* you tell me?" Mark felt a surge of adrenaline. There hadn't been many times in his life when he'd been in an adversarial position with his stepfather. They'd always gotten along so well. But this was different. Derek had betrayed his mother. And in doing so, he was betraying him.

"I don't know. I wanted to tell you. I guess I would have told your mother, if there'd been a way."

Mark shook his head. "No, not that. It wouldn't have been right. It would have killed her."

"I don't mean like that," Derek said. "What I mean to

say is, I'd deal with Margaret honestly. Under the circumstances, though, there's nothing I can do."

"So you're telling me, because you can't tell her." Mark heard the accusation in his voice.

"I'm not trying to burden you, Mark. It's just that we did talk about it, and I thought you'd understand."

Mark put his feet on the coffee table. In the past his parents had admonished him for that sort of thing, but Derek didn't say a word, and Mark didn't care right now anyway. "Who is she, anyway?"

"Her name's Lara Serenov. She lives up in Mendocino...in the mountains outside of town. She writes poetry."

Mark could see that telling him wasn't easy for Derek, but that didn't inspire his respect. "So, what are you going to do?"

"Nothing's happened, Mark. Nothing serious. I don't even know for sure why I'm telling you, except that the friendship I feel for Lara has another dimension and I don't want to pretend it doesn't."

Mark felt his neck and ears start to turn red. He moved his feet off the table and got up abruptly. "I don't want to hear about this," he said, glaring at his stepfather.

Derek looked a little surprised. "There's not a lot I can do about the way I feel."

"You don't need to tell me."

"I prefer to be honest with you."

"Don't."

"Mark..."

"And don't go telling Mom about your love affairs, either. She might not hear what people say to her, but maybe she does. I don't want her hearing that."

"I'd never say anything to hurt your mother, and you know it."

"Actions speak louder than words."

They stood looking at each other. "I guess it was a mistake to discuss this with you," Derek said. "I'm sorry if I upset you."

Mark could see that Derek was hurt. But it was hard for him to ignore his stepfather's betrayal. And his mother was helpless. If he didn't look out for her, who would? It was pretty obvious Derek was going to be thinking of himself from now on.

"Do you want me to move out?" he asked finally.

Derek shook his head. "Don't be silly. This is your home. You have every right to be here. Besides, it shouldn't sit empty while I'm gone."

Mark contemplated his stepfather for a long time. "If you want me to say it's all right, then I will. Personally, I don't care what you do. But the same as you, I can't help my feelings."

Derek nodded. "I understand."

"Do you?"

"The important thing is that we can talk about it."

Mark didn't respond.

"I think I'll go back up to Mendocino. I was planning on staying here a day or two, but I can see that wouldn't be a very good idea."

"I can go over to the frat house. Don't leave because of me."

"It's not that, Mark. I think we could both use a cooling-off period. And to be honest, I almost feel like an interloper." He went to the window again and looked out through the curtains. "I needed to see your mother. I was up at the crack of dawn and on the road headed down here. But now I've done what I came to do. It's time to go back."

"Sure?"

Derek nodded as he slowly walked toward the door. He gestured toward the staircase. "Have I met your friend?"

"Marcy? No, I just met her myself a couple of weeks ago. In the Bear's Lair. I never go in there, but for some reason I did this time, and...well..."

"Things happen...sometimes when you least expect it."

Mark looked at the back of Derek's head, knowing what he meant.

"Well," Derek said, "I don't want your friend to feel abandoned. I'll get out of your hair." He opened the door and turned around. Reaching out, he took Mark by the shoulder, squeezing him affectionately as he had when he was a boy. "I don't like what's happening any more than you do," he said. "I care about your mother, but I also care about you. I want you to know that."

Mark didn't say anything. Derek went out then, and Mark watched him until he got to his car. Then he closed the door and went slowly up the stairs.

Marcy was lying on the bed, reading. She turned and looked at him when he came into the room. "Everything all right?" she said.

"Yep. Real cool."

She studied him. "You sure?"

"Uh-huh."

"Did your stepfather leave?"

Mark nodded.

"Everything's really all right?"

"We talked about my mother. That's all."

Marcy stared at him. "You're resentful that he took off on his sabbatical and left you to look after her, aren't you?"

"She's taken care of. I don't have to do anything."

"Emotionally, the burden's on you."

"Hey," he said, "I'm the psychologist, you're the profit-and-loss girl, remember?"

"Profit-and-loss *woman*."

"I stand corrected." Mark smiled, but he wasn't feeling very cheerful.

"What's up with your stepfather? Or would you rather not say?" Marcy asked.

Mark shrugged. "Nothing, really," he replied. "But it's becoming more apparent to me every day that there's truth to that old saying about blood being thicker than water."

"Sounds like trouble in paradise."

"No, it's not trouble. And it's not paradise. Maybe that's the point."

"Sorry," Marcy said, showing genuine sympathy.

"Well, I'd say let's get back to work but, to be honest, I'm not sure I'm up to struggling through that last chapter. What do you say we cheat a little and go out for our picnic?"

Marcy shook her finger at him. "Poor study habits lead to poor grades."

"It's either that or chase you around the room."

Marcy got to her feet. "All right, Sigmund, we picnic."

Mark grabbed her by the short hairs on the side of her head and pulled her close to him, kissing her on her petulant mouth. She kissed him back, then pulled away.

"I refuse to be corrupted," she said.

"Then you'd better be a whiz with peanut butter sandwiches."

Marcy made a gagging sound as a commentary on the suggestion, then headed for the door. Mark followed, letting his eyes drift down her body. But it was an automatic thing to do. The truth was, he was sad as hell. He just didn't want to admit it.

STEVE ADAMSON SAT in his truck, swiping at a fly that buzzed through the open window and around his head. It was hot, but at least it was shady where he'd pulled off the road, opposite Lara's drive. He was satisfied she wouldn't be able to see him unless she was looking for him, whereas he would have a full view of her Jeep when she returned.

But where was the bitch? And whose old car was that in front of her cabin? That was the question. That guy, that friend of hers, had been driving a new BMW. Hot and thirsty, Steve was sorry now he hadn't brought along some beer. He hadn't expected to have to wait like this.

Steve still wasn't exactly sure what he would do when he got hold of her. He wanted to believe that after going through the song and dance of acting mad, she'd finally show she was glad to see him. It would be nice if it worked out that way. But he had to be prepared in case she needed some persuading. The key was getting her where she couldn't reach her gun.

After another endless half hour batting the pesky flies, Steve was beginning to wonder if she'd ever come home. Then he heard a vehicle approaching. Instead of passing by like the others that had come along, it slowed. When it finally came into view, he saw that it was Lara's Jeep.

Somebody was inside with her, another woman. Steve saw that it was Tony Bianco's wife. She and Lara had been tight for a long time, so it wasn't surprising, but it still annoyed him. Anything to screw things up.

At least he knew who the other car belonged to. So what would happen now? Probably they'd yak for a while. Broads did that, even if that was what they'd been doing all day long. He'd wait another fifteen minutes, he decided, and if Calle hadn't left by then he'd go nearer the cabin and see what he could see.

Steve thought about the rotten luck he'd had. Somebody always seemed to be getting in the way. He pounded the steering wheel. Everything about Lara frustrated him. The colder she acted, the more he wanted her. For the past week she'd been eating at his gut so hard it almost hurt. Damn, he wanted her.

Even though he'd decided to wait, Steve got out of the truck just to stretch his legs. He paced, careful to stay behind the brush, though he kept his eyes on the drive, hoping he'd see Calle come out at any moment. What the hell was she doing away from her kids for so long anyway? She'd probably stuck her old man with the squawking brats. What a nightmare. Steve was glad he and Mary Beth had never had any, even though for a while that was all she'd ever talked about.

Pretty soon he got tired of waiting and decided to head on down to the cabin, whether Calle was there or not. He could lie low until she was gone. At least it'd be better than watching the road.

CHAPTER SIX

LARA FILLED TWO GLASSES with ice, then poured tea over it. She squeezed some lemon into hers from a wedge she picked up from the counter, then carried both glasses onto the deck, where Calle was waiting. Her friend's eyes lit up at the sight of the cool drinks.

"Manna from heaven!" she exclaimed as Lara handed her the tea. Calle took a long sip, then ran the side of the glass over her forehead. "Every spring I tell myself I've got to lose weight because a hot summer day when you're fat is pure hell. But another summer has come and here I am."

Lara smiled at her friend and sat in the other chair. "You're not that heavy, Calle."

"You should be inside this body." She waved off the remark. "No. On second thought, I wouldn't wish that on anyone."

"We don't get that much hot weather up here, especially where you are, near the water."

"Thank heaven. At least you understand why I don't come to see you so often this time of year."

Lara looked at the sun through the trees. "It'll be cooling off soon. Then you'll be more comfortable." She sipped her drink.

"Yeah, but in fairness to Tony I should be getting home. I don't want to abuse his generosity. The little monsters get to him after a few hours."

Neither of them spoke for a while. They sat listening to the warm stillness around them and drinking their iced tea.

"You know," Calle finally said, "I don't know whether I'm glad about you and Derek, or sorry. One minute I think one way, the next I think the other."

Lara knew that was what her friend had been thinking about. Ever since she'd told her what had happened when Derek followed her home on Friday, Calle had been wrestling with the subject. She wasn't sure whether to take the credit or the blame.

The problem had been that Lara herself was torn, and Calle picked up on her uncertainty. Having feelings for Derek, which she could now no longer deny, was a kind of breakthrough for Lara—a breakthrough in which even she found pleasure. But after all the years she'd spent in purgatory, Derek Gordon was probably the last man on earth she ought to be attracted to. There was really no good reason why they should get involved, and several why they shouldn't.

Lara sensed Derek knew that, too. That was why he had left the way he had after he kissed her. He was in a tough spot. In a way, she felt sorrier for him than she did for herself.

Still, every time she thought about his lips touching hers, and the feel of his body, something inside her came to life. Lara liked Derek Gordon a lot. That was the problem.

"What are you going to do?" Calle asked.

"There's nothing to do. Who knows, I may never even see him again. He loves his wife, and that's no small thing." She sipped her tea. "Actually, I hope I don't see him again. It'd be much easier that way."

Calle had a terribly sad look on her face. "Oh, Lara. It could be so good, the two of you."

"Quit romanticizing, Calle. My happiness doesn't turn on one human being."

"But how many men are there out there who are perfect for you? I mean, who have you met in the past ten years who's even come close?"

"He's not perfect, he's married. And I'm not perfect, either. I've got a rather independent life-style that suits me just fine. A lot of guys wouldn't adjust well to that, even if I were willing to adjust to them."

"I wish you wouldn't talk that way. A negative attitude can be self-fulfilling."

"I'm a realist."

Calle moaned.

"You worry about me too much," Lara said.

"I love you, and I don't think you know what you're missing."

Lara smiled indulgently and got up, going to the railing around the deck. She slipped her fingers into the pockets of her jeans and peered into the heavy stillness of the forest. "And *you* don't know what I have."

Calle put down her glass and stood as well. "Whenever we have this conversation, I get depressed. I think it's time I go home and save my own marriage."

Lara put her hand on Calle's arm. "That's the smartest thing you've said all day."

Laughing, they went through the cabin and then into the bright sunshine out front.

"I've got to get my package out of your car," Calle said.

"I'll get it for you. In fact, I think I'll pull the Jeep around and give it a good washing. With all this dry heat it's gotten really dusty."

"How can you even think of work?"

"There's something about washing a car that gives me pleasure. Besides, it's the coolest chore I can think of."

"You've got a point there," Calle admitted. She watched Lara head for the carport.

In a few minutes Lara parked the Jeep in front of the cabin, next to Calle's car. She got out with her friend's package. Calle took it and patted Lara's hand, then climbed in her car and, after tooting her horn, headed down the drive.

When Calle had gone, Lara got out the hose from the storage locker by the carport and connected it to the bib at the front of the house. She went inside to get a bucket and soap. Deciding it would be cooler to work in shorts and bare feet, she went up to the loft and changed. After filling the bucket in the kitchen sink, she headed back outside.

The sun was sinking, and the long shadows from the trees would soon be covering the cabin. The Jeep was already mostly in the shade, which would make washing it easier.

Lara began wetting down the Jeep, thoroughly rinsing away the light coat of dust. She was spraying the back window when she noticed a flicker of motion in the corner of her eye. Turning, she saw Steve Adamson walking slowly toward her. He was practically between her and the front door, and he had a big grin on his face—probably because he could see she didn't have her gun.

Her first reaction was anger. She glared. "Steve, what are you doing here?" She released the trigger of the nozzle as she spoke, and the stream of water instantly stopped.

He halted near the steps leading to the porch and rested his hands on his hips. The grin on his face turned to a brief laugh. "Thought we might have the talk you never seem to want to have."

"We have nothing to discuss, Steve."

"Oh? Maybe you don't, but I do." He took a couple of

steps in Lara's direction and she raised the nozzle of the hose and pointed it at him.

Steve laughed. "Defendin' yourself with water pistols these days?"

"Don't come a step closer, or I'll spray you!"

Inside, the telephone rang. Steve glanced over his shoulder momentarily, then ignored it. He proceeded and Lara began spraying him, directing the stream of water over his face and chest. "Hey, that feels great!" he said with a laugh, though he held up his hand to ward off the jet of water.

Lara shrieked when he wasn't deterred. He was still a couple of steps away, so she threw the hose at him and began running down the drive. She'd only gone a couple of dozen yards when Steve caught up with her.

"What's the matter, honey?" he said breathlessly as he wiped back his wet hair. "Don't you want to play in the water anymore?"

He had her by the arm, his fingers digging deeper into her flesh than necessary.

"Let go of me!" she screamed, and swung at him with her other hand.

He easily deflected the blow and spun Lara around so that he was behind her. Then he crushed her against him, the wetness from his clothes instantly penetrating her light blouse. She struggled, but he had her arms pinned to her sides. She was helpless. In the distance she heard the phone ringing again, but there was no way she could get to it.

"I swear you'll regret this," she said, turning her head to bite him, though he kept his face at a safe distance. She tried to kick him, but only managed to hurt her bare foot on his heavy boots.

He chuckled at her futile squirming.

"Damn you!"

"Listen," he said into her ear, "if you'd calm down, this fightin' might not be necessary."

Lara stopped struggling then and stood still in his grasp, though his large wet body pressed against her made her want to retch. "What do you want?" she said through clenched teeth.

"A friendly little discussion, same as I wanted the first time I come to see you."

"Is that all?"

Steve shifted his grasp so that he was pinioning both of her arms with one of his. With his free hand, he lightly touched her cheek. Then he slowly and deliberately exhaled onto her neck. "I wouldn't mind some friendly affection," he murmured.

"I don't want you touching me," she said, stiffening.

Steve squeezed her shoulder. "Not even a little?"

"Not even a little. If you want to talk, let go of me first."

"I don't know if I can trust you, honey bunch."

"You can trust me. Just let me go. Please!"

"Mmm," Steve said, "now you're gettin' real polite, aren't you?"

"Please…let go of me!"

He continued massaging her shoulder. Then he leaned over and looked down the front of her blouse. "I see that sweet pair of yours, Lara. They sure look nice."

"Steve…" She tried to get away again, but he held her more firmly than ever, pressing his pelvis against her backside. Lara tried kicking him again, but only hurt her foot worse.

"Hey," he said, his tone growing sharp, "what happened to that politeness?"

"Just…let…go…of…me," she intoned, trying not to get hysterical.

"Tell you what, I'll just feel you up a little bit, then I'll let go of you…if you promise we can talk."

"No!"

But Steve ignored her, moving his hand off her shoulder and across her chest until he'd cupped her breast. Lara trembled with the horror of what was happening. But Steve continued, seeking out her nipple with his fingertips. Hot tears began flowing down her cheeks. As his massaging became more vigorous, she began to sob.

"Lara, baby," he said into her ear. "Don't this feel good? Don't you love it?"

Lara shook her head mutely.

Steve began rubbing his pelvis against her and she could hear his breathing growing heavy.

"No," she sobbed, "please don't."

He drew a deep breath and his body became stiff. She sensed his anger. Letting go of her breast, he straightened. Except for one wrist, which he still clamped tightly, he released her.

Lara moved as far away from him as she could. His expression was leaden.

"What the hell's wrong with me, anyway?" Steve demanded. "I ain't poison! I'm hot for your body, that's all. It's natural, ain't it? Is it you that's screwed up? Are you frigid, Lara? Is that what's wrong?"

She wiped her nose and cheeks with her free hand. "Maybe so," she said. "That's why you're wasting your time with me. Go find somebody who wants you."

"Damn it to hell, I want *you*!"

"I'm not the only woman with breasts," she sobbed.

Steve looked around. Seeing a log not far away, he dragged Lara over to it and sat, forcing her down beside him.

"Look," he said, pointing at her threateningly with his free hand, "it ain't just your body. I want *you*, Lara."

His tone had grown plaintive. Although she hated him with every fiber of her being, she could see that in some way he was suffering. "You can't force something, just because you want it," she said.

"What are you sayin'? I should sit at home and wait until you call me?"

"No, I'd never call."

"See! That's what I mean."

"Don't you understand? A woman's got to care for you first. Forcing yourself on her only makes her hate you."

"You hate me?"

"I hate you for what you're trying to do." Lara looked down at her wrist, which he still held in a viselike grip.

He was staring at her in a way that made her feel naked. "No woman's goin' to say no to me," he murmured, as if he were talking to himself. Then he reached over and gripped Lara's jaw, bringing her face close to his.

When he tried to kiss her, Lara spun away, though the hand on her wrist held her like an manacle. Jerking her hard, Steve threw her to the ground and knelt over her. He put his knee squarely in the middle of her abdomen, trying to force her to stay in one place. Then he began unbuttoning his shirt.

"What are you going to do?" she asked, terrorized.

"I'm going to take what you won't give me."

Lara screamed and began thrashing with all her might. In her white-hot panic she didn't see the blow coming. Everything went black, and when her eyes came into focus Lara saw Steve standing over her, naked from the waist up. Her blouse had been ripped open, and the side of her head felt as if it had been slammed into a brick wall.

She wanted to do something—to scream, to cry, to run—

but her strength and her will had been shattered. She knew it was hopeless. Then, just as Steve began to unbuckle his belt, Lara heard the plaintive whine of a siren in the distance. She wasn't sure if the sound was in her head, or if it was real. But when Steve turned and looked down the drive, she knew it was not her imagination.

"What the hell?" she heard him say. He stood frozen above her then, like a colossus.

Was it a sheriff coming to save her, or an ambulance on the way to an emergency? The vehicle was heading up Flat Pine Road, Lara could tell. In a moment, the siren was close to where her driveway intersected the road. Was it coming up to the cabin? Steve seemed to be wondering the same thing because he picked up his shirt and went to peer through the trees toward the road. Lara raised herself on her elbows and wondered whether this was her opportunity to get away. Despite her grogginess, she managed to get to her feet.

Steve cursed then, whooping with anger. As Lara looked up, he shook his fist at her. "You lucked out this time!" he shouted. "But so help me, I'll be back." With that he took off into the brush, the shirt in his hand flying.

Lara was in a daze, but she staggered toward the approaching siren, holding together the torn flaps of her blouse. As she got to the edge of the driveway, she heard a vehicle coming up the grade at a rapid clip. It was a sheriff's cruiser and its emergency lights were flashing. She almost cried out with joy.

The car skidded to a stop when it got to her, a cloud of dust billowing up around it and drifting slowly into the trees. The driver's door flew open and Wally Stiles climbed out. He hurried over to her.

"What happened, Miss Serenov?" He reached out to steady her, taking her by the shoulders.

Lara was trembling and her face crumpled. She fell heavily against the man. "Steve Adamson," she mumbled into the deputy's shirt. "He tried to rape me. He ran off just as you came up."

Stiles helped Lara to the cruiser, and settled her in the back seat. Then he called the dispatcher on the radio. Lara didn't hear exactly what he said, only bits and pieces.

Though it was hot and her skin was sweaty and caked with dust, she continued to tremble, hugging herself. Her head was throbbing from Steve's punch.

When the deputy had finished, he knelt at the open door beside her. "Which way did he go?"

Lara pointed. The deputy asked her how Steve was dressed, and she described his clothing. Stiles looked at her head and asked if she wanted an ambulance, but Lara insisted she was all right. He had her describe what had happened in detail, and when she had finished, he got back on the radio for a moment to relay some additional information.

With the passage of time, she was beginning to calm down. Her head had cleared some. Except for the throbbing, she was feeling better. Stiles came back and knelt where he had before. "We'll have a bunch of officers up here shortly, ma'am. We'll get him."

Lara sighed with immense gratitude. "How did you know he was here?"

"We had a call from your friend, Mr. Gordon."

"Derek? How did he know?"

"Beats me. I was down on the Coast Highway when the dispatcher sent out the alert. I had a good idea what was up, that's why I came with sirens and lights."

"I don't understand," Lara said.

They heard the sound of a vehicle coming up the driveway. The deputy looked over the door. "Here comes Mr. Gordon now. Maybe he can explain."

Derek's BMW pulled to a stop behind the cruiser, sending up another cloud of dust. He jumped out and came running to where Stiles was standing by the rear door.

"Lara," he said, bending over and looking in, "are you all right?"

She extended her hand to him, emotion welling again. Derek helped her out and she hugged him instantly, squeezing him with all her might. "Oh, Derek," she cried, "I'm so happy to see you."

He kissed her cheek and held her, rocking her in his arms. Lara dug her nails into his back, not wanting to let go of him.

"Maybe I can leave Miss Serenov in your hands," Wally Stiles said. "There's a fellow in the woods I've got to track down."

"I think his truck's across the road, opposite Lara's driveway," Derek said.

"Oh?"

Just then they heard the distant screech of tires spinning on pavement.

"That sounds like him now," the deputy said. "If you'll excuse me, I'll have a look." He jumped in the car and, spinning it around the BMW, took off at high speed down the driveway.

Derek examined the welt on the side of Lara's face. "Steve do this?"

She nodded.

"The bastard."

Lara hugged him again.

"Come on," he said, leading her toward the cabin, "let's put a cold compress on that cheek."

They walked with their arms around each other, Lara holding her ripped blouse together.

"How did you know about Steve being here?" she asked as they went. "I thought for a while there I was dead."

"Calle called me. She said she'd been up here with you, and as she was leaving she saw a reflection of the sun on the windshield of a vehicle across the road from your drive. She couldn't see what kind of car it was because it was in the brush, but she got to thinking about it on the way home, wondering if it might be Steve.

"When she got to her place, she decided to warn you to stay inside, just in case. When you didn't answer the phone, she got worried and called me. Tony and the kids were gone, and I guess she figured I was close enough to check on you. I called the sheriff's office and headed up."

"I owe you and Calle so much. Maybe my life. Steve was about to rape me when the deputy arrived."

They had come to the porch, and Derek stopped. He put his arms around Lara and kissed her forehead. Then he lifted her chin with his finger. "I couldn't have taken that. I couldn't stand you being hurt."

There was a tremendous amount of emotion in his eyes. He leaned down and lightly kissed her lips. "I won't let anything happen to you, Lara. Until they catch Steve, you're coming home with me."

It wasn't the sort of statement a woman could easily argue with. And Lara didn't even try.

DEREK AGREED it would be easier for Lara to get cleaned up in her own bath, so he waited for her to shower and change. Before going upstairs she called Calle to let her know that everything was all right, and that she was with Derek. Then she found an ice bag and Derek filled it while she got cleaned up. It was ready for her when she came down twenty minutes later.

Derek embraced her and was holding the ice bag to her face when they heard a vehicle outside the cabin. It was Wally Stiles.

"Adamson got away," the deputy said, coming up onto the porch. "He's probably off on some back road, but we'll corner him eventually."

Lara leaned against Derek wearily.

"How are you feeling, Miss Serenov?" Stiles asked.

"Tired, but much better, thanks. I can't tell you how much I appreciate what you've done."

"Well, be thankful Mr. Gordon called us."

Lara slipped her arm around Derek's waist. "I am. Believe me."

"I don't know how long it will take us to track down Adamson, but the man's obviously gone over the edge. There's no telling what he might do. I don't advise you to stay here alone."

"I'm taking her home with me," Derek said.

"Fine. We'd be grateful if you'd swear out a complaint for us, Miss Serenov."

"What do I have to do?"

"Just go into the substation in Fort Bragg. I would take you in, but we want to keep as many units on the roads now as possible. We don't want Adamson to slip away for good."

"No, I understand," Lara said.

"I'll drive her to Fort Bragg," Derek volunteered.

"We'd be much obliged. And we'll call you when we've got Adamson, so you can relax. Be sure and leave your number with the dispatcher, Mr. Gordon." Saluting them, the deputy returned to his car and took off.

They watched him leave. "It's terrible that someone can

disrupt lives this way,'' Lara said. ''It's all so unnecessary.''

''Steve's obviously got problems.''

''I tried to reason with him. For a minute—just a minute—I thought I might be getting through to him. Then something seemed to snap and he went crazy.''

''I'm sorry you've had to go through this.'' Derek looked at her, not having thought for a moment about what had happened the last time they were together. The instant that call came from Calle, he had flown to Lara's aid.

Of course, he would have helped any woman in need, but the thought that some harm might come to Lara had consumed him. The instant he saw her in the back seat of the sheriff's car, torn and battered, his only thought was to hold her and comfort her. Now just one thing mattered. He wanted her with him. He wouldn't let her out of his sight until it was safe.

The dust cloud from the deputy's car had disappeared, but they continued to stare down the driveway. Lara put her head against Derek's shoulder, and he pushed her tawny hair back with his fingers.

He wanted to tell her what he was feeling, how much he cared for her. But that wasn't what she needed at the moment. His compassion and protection were all that mattered now. What was in his heart would have to wait.

CHAPTER SEVEN

DEREK OPENED THE DOOR of his cottage and Lara stepped inside, glancing around with curiosity. The air wasn't as warm on the coast, so the house had stayed cool. She rubbed her bare arms and casually looked for the little things that might tell her about him before she gravitated toward the windows overlooking the cove.

After what Steve had done to her, Derek's home was a welcome refuge. With her head still throbbing mildly, the ordeal she'd been through was not easily forgotten. Yet in spite of the terror of what had happened, she was aware of her attraction to Derek and the fact that they were now alone together.

"It's a lovely setting," she murmured as he joined her at the windows, where the sun, now low in the sky, was shining in. She glanced at him and tried to evaluate his mood. Would he simply play the role of the compassionate Good Samaritan? Or would he let his feelings for her impel him along some dangerous course?

"Instead of writing about political theory here, I ought to be painting seascapes, shouldn't I?"

He let his hand rest casually on her shoulder, and Lara felt herself tense imperceptibly. "Do you paint, Derek?"

He turned to her, his eyes drawn to the wounded side of her face, which she could feel was badly swollen. "I fooled around with watercolors years ago, when I was a student."

"Do you have any of your work?" she asked, now genuinely interested.

"No. I don't think I saved anything. If I did, it's buried in a trunk at home."

His look was tender, but Lara sensed more than mere compassion. Self-consciously, she stroked her cheek. She could tell by the touch that her eye was beginning to swell a little, too. His gaze passed over it, taking in her mouth, her hair.

"With the sunlight on your hair, it has the most incredible golden hue," he said.

"You see, you have an eye for color. You *should* be painting. There's an artistic side to you, I can tell."

He smiled slightly at the comment. Then he took her chin and turned her head so he could see her cheek. "We'd better get some ice on this."

Lara stayed at the window while Derek went to fetch the ice pack. She heard him in the kitchen, opening the refrigerator. "You could paint while you work on your book," she called in to him. "For relaxation. You might get more done in the long run."

"If I start losing my creative juices," he replied, "maybe I will get some paints and dabble a bit. I used to enjoy it a lot."

Lara gazed out the window, hugging herself against an imagined chill. Derek returned with the ice pack and she put it against her face. At first the coldness was painful, but after a moment or two it started to feel good. He put his arm around her shoulders again, and together they stared out at the view.

Lara liked his warmth and his tenderness, but they scared her too. It would be easy to become accustomed to them. "I think I'll write a poem about that tree out there," she said, hoping to break the mood. "It's trying to talk to me. Have you felt that since you've been here?"

"I don't know if I would quite put it that way," he said thoughtfully. "But I'm frequently drawn to it. That's one reason my book's behind schedule."

"What is it that appeals to you?" she asked.

"The beauty, of course. But it evokes a mood. Something intangible..."

"It's magical. And with the sky behind it taking on that color..."

He squeezed her shoulder, perhaps unconsciously, and Lara realized that even sharing the beauty of God's nature could be dangerous.

"Would you like to walk out there?" he asked. "It's such a perfect evening."

She nodded eagerly, hoping that...that the tension that was building would somehow dissipate in the ocean air.

Derek opened the doors and they went out onto the patio. There was only the lightest breeze, and it was quite balmy, warmer actually than inside. Usually the wind was brisk and cool, but the heat of the day was lingering into the evening.

They walked along the narrow path that led to the outcrop of rock. Lara went ahead of him, still holding the ice bag to her face. When she came to the low windswept tree trunk she ducked under it, and leaned against the far side. Derek joined her, looking out to sea.

"How's the cheek feeling?"

"Better. I think the swelling's going down already." She propped her elbow against the tree.

"Let me see."

She removed the bag and looked up into his hazel-green eyes. Derek traced his finger lightly around the wound, and Lara felt her chest tighten. She knew there was trepidation on her face, but he didn't seem to notice, or if so it didn't deter him.

Leaning close, his arm on the tree trunk behind her, he lightly kissed her injured cheek. She stood very still, not sure how to respond. She could hardly act offended, because there was as much simple compassion in the gesture as anything more suggestive. Self-consciously she touched the buttons on his shirt, avoiding his eyes. Then he lifted her chin to kiss her lips.

Lara didn't move for an instant. But when his lips grazed hers, she turned her face away. Ducking under his arm, she moved a few steps nearer the cliff overlooking the cove.

"If I could paint a picture," he said behind her, "it would be of you, not a tree."

Lara bowed her head, realizing she had to deflect him from the course he'd chosen. She turned around, having to brush back strands of hair the breeze had swept across her face. "What about your wife?"

"I went to visit Margaret. Yesterday morning I drove down to Berkeley."

Lara stood motionless.

"After Friday night, I had to see her."

More wisps of her golden hair blew across her face. She pulled them back. "Why?"

"I had to put what I was feeling for you into perspective."

Lara lowered her eyes.

"I don't mean to upset you by telling you," he said, "but I did make a decision. Denying my feelings would be as big a mistake as ignoring the fact that Margaret and I are still legally married."

Lara couldn't look at him. She stood motionless, the ice bag dangling from her hand. Derek walked over to her, pulling her several steps away from the precipice behind

her. She felt a desperate agony as he raised her chin with
his finger. There was a sheen of moisture in her eyes and,
noticing, he seemed troubled.

"I've never met your wife," she whispered, "but I feel
compassion for her. I feel almost as much for her as I do
for you."

It was an unusual thing to say, but Derek understood. In
a curious sort of way, he admired her.

Although he sensed her reluctance, he couldn't resist
pulling her into his arms. He held her and put his cheek
against the top of her head, breathing in her scent along
with the pungent sea air. Her body felt so warm. It was
years since he'd really held anyone.

He was sure she was fighting her feelings, but that she
felt something special for him, too. The circumstances
probably troubled her, as much as, or more than, him.

"You know," he said, "I'm an awful cook. But if you're
willing to overlook that, I'd be willing to try and make you
dinner."

Lara looked up at him, smiling, her eyes glossy. "I'd
like that," she said, seeming as glad as he to change the
subject.

"Come on, then." He took her hand. "You can help."

They walked back toward the cottage, which bore a pink-
ish hue from the sky. Derek knew it always looked hospi-
table, but never so inviting as now—approaching it hand-
in-hand with Lara Serenov.

WHILE DEREK WAS CLEANING the kitchen, Lara curled up
in his reading chair, the ice bag pressed to her cheek. He
had insisted she take it easy. They had talked briefly about
his book during dinner, and he had given her one of his
articles to look at.

Lara read through his work with interest—not so much

because of the content but rather because Derek had written it, and it provided insight into the way his mind worked. Despite the philosophical subject matter, which she didn't have the background to appreciate, she enjoyed his prose, which had a nice rhythm and even some sparkle. Usually the authors of scholarly works wrote ponderously. Reading Derek's words, she wondered what he might be able to do with lighter subjects.

But then she stopped herself, asking if it was really wise to become so interested in him. She could rationalize, saying it was just friendship—friends cared about each other. But so did lovers, and with a different intensity.

"Are you reading that, or only pretending to read it?" Derek asked. He was standing at the kitchen door, a suspicious expression on his face.

Lara allowed herself to smile. "I'm reading it for the writing. I don't have the vaguest idea what you're saying, of course."

"It's all part of the mystique," he said. He pulled the desk chair around so that he could sit near her. "How's the cheek?"

Lara turned the side of her head toward him.

"Looking better," he said with a touch of satisfaction.

They stared at each other for a moment. "Why did you become a professor?" she asked, grasping for a safe subject.

"Like a lot of people in academia, I saw the ivory tower as more real than the real world. For some folks, playing with a football can be serious business. In my opinion, so can playing with ideas. Anyway, things intellectual have a way of filtering down into everyday lives. I think we have an obligation to keep inquiring about means of improving the world."

"That's very idealistic."

Derek shrugged.

"I understand the ivory tower part, though," Lara said. "Being a writer is the same thing. It's building with ideas and perceptions rather than with bricks and mortar, as most people do."

He nodded. "It sounds like we have a lot in common."

Lara looked away.

"How did you get into the poetry business?"

"I *had* to. That's what every writer says, of course. But I was also lucky. I couldn't support a pet on what my poetry brings in. But my grandmother was pretty comfortable, and when she died she left me some money—enough to build my cabin and live for several years. The money'll be running out soon, and I've got to start worrying about the real world—things like figuring out how I'm going to pay the bills."

"Any ideas?"

"I suppose I'll go back to school. Maybe teach. After my divorce I got in two years of junior college." She placed the ice bag against her face again. "As a matter of fact, I was seriously considering transferring to Berkeley when I built my cabin and decided to write full-time instead."

"Wouldn't it have been strange if we'd met there?"

"That was several years ago, Derek. Before your wife was sick. I don't think you'd have noticed me."

He rubbed his chin. "Our conversations are taking on a predictable pattern, aren't they?"

"I'm not very good at pretending things don't exist when they do."

He leaned back in the chair and put his hands behind his head. "I suppose what I'm doing amounts to that, doesn't it?"

She nodded, then sighed deeply.

"But Lara, the happiness...no, the joy I feel when I'm with you can't be denied, either," he said.

The words saddened her. They weren't meant to, but they did. "I enjoy being with you, too," she admitted. "And today you were a lifesaver. You've been so very kind. But I've been thinking about being with you. I've decided I shouldn't stay here tonight."

"Why not?"

"I just shouldn't."

"I won't do anything to make it difficult for you."

"It's not that."

"Then why?"

"I'd rather not."

"I won't take you home under any circumstances."

"No, I know I can't go back there. I could probably stay at Calle's, but I've been a burden to her lately, and anyway, Steve has been lurking around there. I don't want to give him a reason to harass them."

"What do you plan to do?"

"Go to a motel."

"It seems so unnecessary."

She shook her head. "It's quite necessary."

He contemplated her, but seemed to understand she was adamant. "You don't have to go just yet. We can talk for a while, or maybe walk down on the beach. The moon is probably up by now. I'm sure it's pretty down there."

"It sounds lovely, but no, I think I'd better not. Besides, I'm tired."

"Yes, I forgot what you've been through."

Lara got up, knowing if she didn't force the issue, she might not be able to resist the comfortable companionship that staying with Derek offered. "Nobody's called from the sheriff's office, so I guess that means Steve's still out there somewhere." She picked up her purse from the couch.

"I wish you wouldn't leave."

"I have to. I'll be fine in a motel. Anyway, my car's at the cabin. If Steve does drive around looking for me, he'll never know I'm at the motel."

Derek relented, carrying her case to the car. They drove half a mile down the highway to a small motel that they decided would be convenient. Derek insisted he'd pick her up for breakfast, and Lara reluctantly agreed.

After she'd checked in, he carried her suitcase to her room. He looked around. "Keep the chain on the door," he said. "I'll call in the morning before I come over."

Lara couldn't help being amused by his earnestness. She struggled to resist the affection she so badly wanted to show. But her hand went to his face anyway. "Thank you, Derek, for all you've done."

He stroked her head, and Lara had a terrible, irrational desire for him to kiss her. She was thankful when he brushed her lip with his fingertip and said good-night instead.

When he had gone, she put the security chain on the door, as he'd suggested. Then, as the engine of his car started, she sat on the bed. The room had a vaguely antiseptic smell. It was clean if simple. But she had to admit she didn't like being there alone.

She was uncomfortable with Derek too close and miserable with him too far away. What a mess. She resented him for making her want to be with him, but craved his companionship at the same time.

At least she'd had the sense to leave his place. She'd have to continue to avoid temptation. Lara smiled sardonically. The notion had a hollow ring to it. Already she was looking forward to morning, and seeing Derek once again.

LARA WAS ALREADY AWAKE when the phone rang the next morning. It was Derek.

"How are you feeling?"

Either she'd forgotten about her face, or she had started taking the soreness for granted. "Just fine, though I haven't looked in the mirror yet. I might be black and blue, but the swelling's down."

"Good. Hungry?"

Lara didn't usually eat much breakfast, but the question made her think of a nice cup of coffee and maybe some eggs and toast. "I guess so."

"How long do you need?"

"Oh, give me half an hour at least. Forty-five minutes would be better."

"Okay, see you in forty-five minutes."

Lara hurried to get ready, ignoring an eagerness to see him that she knew was risky. The night had been difficult for her, and it was hard to pretend she didn't crave refuge from the demons Steve Adamson had set loose. Derek made her feel happy inside, and for the moment she didn't want to think beyond that.

She was just finishing dressing when she heard a car pull up in the gravel parking area outside her room. Suddenly a sinking feeling came over her.

When Derek knocked, she went to the door and asked who it was. He identified himself and she let him in.

"Glad to see you didn't just throw it open," he said, looking her over.

Lara grinned. "I knew that would please you."

"Happy Labor Day."

"Oh, that's right. It's a holiday. I forgot."

He took her chin and turned her head to examine her cheek, much as a father might. "You do look better," he said approvingly. He paused then, gazing into her eyes. He repressed the desire she read on his face. "Ready?"

"I haven't packed, on the assumption I might have to stay another night. I don't suppose the sheriff's office called."

"They did, and the word's not good, I'm afraid. They haven't picked up Steve yet. But he's around. Tony Bianco spotted him prowling around their place late last night. They think he's looking for you, so the sheriff said we'd better stay alert."

Lara closed her eyes, feeling despair.

"The nice thing is Steve doesn't know me," Derek said, "and he wouldn't have the vaguest idea where to come looking even if he thought you were with me. But the sheriff is confident they'll get him today. So don't worry."

"Every time I think things are about to return to normal, something new crops up." She glanced around. "Well, I guess I'll leave my stuff here. If we hear that Steve's been arrested, I can get my things on the way home."

"Okay," Derek said, taking her hand. "Now it's time for breakfast."

They drove back to his place. Going in the door, Lara was greeted by the smell of brewed coffee. She felt better already.

"I've got a few eggs if you want them," he said, leading the way back to the kitchen. "I avoid the cholesterol myself. There's also oatmeal and whole wheat toast."

Lara insisted on fixing her own eggs, since he'd cooked dinner. She made him sit down while she prepared the meal. She'd worn jeans and a long-sleeved cotton pullover—nothing sexy or provocative—but she felt his eyes on her while she worked anyway.

Derek was sitting casually at the table. His jeans-clad legs were crossed and he was lightly drumming the table with his fingers as he watched her, probably unaware of the gesture. Glancing at him, Lara decided he didn't look professorial dressed in a plaid shirt, nor did he seem the artist that she kept imagining him to be.

She stood at the stove, a frying pan in one hand, a spatula in the other. "I thought I would work on a poem today."

"About my tree?"

"Possibly."

"You may have to throw in a few lines about rain. The weather's supposed to turn. According to the radio we'll have showers this evening."

"There's as much poetry in rain as sun. Maybe more." Lara dumped her scrambled eggs onto a plate. She scooped some oatmeal from the pot into a bowl and took it to Derek.

"You're going to spoil me," he said, running his hand affectionately along her arm.

Lara's flesh tingled but she didn't pull away, choosing to ignore the remark instead. "More coffee?"

"I'm fine."

The toast was on the table so she sat down. They began to eat.

"How often in the past five years have you had breakfast with someone?" Derek asked.

Lara looked at him inquisitively.

"I don't mean that as a personal question. I was just wondering if in terms of meals, day-to-day living, you've been as alone as I."

Lara shrugged. "I don't know. Not often. Whenever I stayed over somewhere. I don't have many overnight guests. No men, if that's what you're wondering."

"I wasn't thinking about that specifically."

"How about you?"

"The same."

"How long were you married before your wife became ill?"

"About seven years."

"Then you had a period of normal married life. I didn't, really."

"How long were you and Steve together?"

"Several months. And there was nothing normal about it."

"Then being with me isn't evocative of anything," Derek said. "I mean—having meals, spending a day with a man—has not been part of your experience."

The question seemed to be leading somewhere but she wasn't sure where. "Not really."

He drank his coffee, apparently willing to let the conversation drop.

"Why did you ask?"

"About your experiences? I don't know. Maybe I'm having trouble getting a handle on you. You almost seem like two different women, depending upon the topic of conversation, the mood."

"It might be that I don't know what to think about what's happening."

He looked into her eyes. "What do you mean?"

"To put it bluntly," Lara said, "I'm sort of like a thirty-one-year old virgin who's had a couple of brief relationships."

"There hasn't been anyone you've cared for?"

"Not to amount to anything. In the first five years or so I went out a little—hungering for a normal relationship, I suppose. But I found after a while I didn't need anyone else to be happy. So I stopped trying to connect with men." Lara moved the food on her plate around with her fork. "Some people would say I'm weird, I suppose."

"I don't think so at all."

"You're too kindhearted to say otherwise, Professor Gordon."

"Are you happy with things the way they are?"

"I've always done what I want. But Calle insists that I'm in a shell. She's determined to get me out."

"Does that bother you?"

"She's my friend. I can't help but be affected some by what she thinks."

"Hmm."

"How about you? What's your advice?"

"Do and be what you want—whatever makes you happy. That's the first rule."

The comment struck her as generous. She wasn't used to hearing that sort of thing from a man. Each one who had entered her life seemed to have definite opinions about the way she ought to live. "I've always believed it was my right," she said. "And I intend to continue living that way. As soon as this business with Steve is over, I'm returning to my cabin to write poetry."

Derek leaned back. "Am I wrong, or is there a message for me in that statement?"

"I guess, to be honest, there is. These are unusual circumstances. I shouldn't even be here."

"We're back to Margaret again, aren't we?"

"I suppose."

"Let me ask you this. How would you feel about our friendship—spending time together and so forth—if I were single?"

She ran her fingers back through her hair. "You're putting me on the spot."

"That's not my intention. Maybe I keep coming back to my own feelings. I enjoy being with you, Lara. I like you, but I don't like struggling with the chasm that's between us."

"That's hardly my fault."

"I know."

"Derek, our conversations will keep coming back to the same point. There's no escaping it."

"True. But we're together today, and I want to enjoy the time we have. That's reasonable, isn't it?"

Lara felt a little bewildered.

"Look," he said, "I've got a proposal for you. I promise not to seduce you, and you promise not to think about my wife. Is that fair?"

"I can't promise you what I'll think about, but I can promise you what I will or won't talk about."

"If that's the best you can do, I'll accept it." He extended his hand. "Deal?"

Lara took it with a smile, feeling relieved. "Okay. It's a deal."

"I knew if we tried hard enough we'd come to terms." Derek winked at her, then got up from the table to clear the dishes.

Lara sat mutely watching him. They seemed to be going in circles, but the track was a spiral and it was getting tighter with each turn.

THE WEATHER DID CHANGE radically as the day wore on. The fog grew thicker, and by late morning Lara could barely see the cypress tree out on the point. Derek had been working at his desk for several hours, and she had passed the time moving back and forth between his reading chair and the table, where she worked on her poem.

She wasn't as on edge as she had been earlier, but she couldn't relax completely. Derek couldn't be a lover, nor—it seemed—just a friend.

She tried to write, but her inspiration came only a few words at a time, never complete lines as was usual for her.

She was aware of Derek working quietly nearby, and her mind kept turning to him.

After a while Lara gave up on the poem altogether. What she had written was more about Derek than the tree—descriptive phrases, words that evoked the mood he created, the feelings inside her.

They broke from their work for lunch. Derek asked how the poem was going, and she admitted that it was slow in taking shape.

"Maybe what you need is a field trip," he said amiably. "I like to walk after lunch myself. Want to stretch your legs?"

It was still quite foggy, so they decided to go down to the cove instead of out to the point, where the view would have looked more like the inside of a cloud than a seascape. Derek took her hand while they negotiated the narrow path that wound down the steep slope to the beach. For a long time they couldn't see the water below, though they could hear the waves.

"What an eerie sensation," she said.

"The ocean's out there. I promise you."

Near the bottom the path leveled off and they could see the whitecaps in the gray mist. Spontaneously, Lara let go of Derek's hand and began to run. She went along the sandy beach for a long way before throwing herself down. She was on her back, breathing the salt air deeply, when he came up to her.

She looked up into his handsome, smiling face, thinking how terribly attractive he was.

"You look like a fallen angel," he said. "With your hair fanned out on the sand, you could have dropped right out of a cloud."

"A landing without instruments," she said, trying to keep the mood light.

Derek sat down beside her, holding his knees as he gazed out at the gray-green water. They could hear a gull calling from somewhere, but couldn't see it.

Lara studied his profile, trying to picture what his wife might be like. It seemed strange, thinking of him as married. In her mind she pictured him alone. Yet it was obvious that he loved his wife very much. He had to in order to have stayed with her so faithfully through their adversity.

He seemed so pensive. Lara wondered if his mind was on his wife. "What are you thinking about?" she asked.

He turned to her, his eyes moving over her feature by feature. Then he touched her lower lip. "You wouldn't want to know. It might not please you."

He could have meant several things, but Lara was certain he had been thinking about her. His words had a strangely contradictory effect—evoking both joy and sadness.

"Come on, Professor," she said, pulling him up by his hands, "let's walk on the beach."

The mood broken, they walked side by side, looking at the mist-shrouded water and listening to the sea sounds. The cove was not large and they soon came to the end of the beach. They turned then, and went back the way they had come.

On the way up the path they took turns leading, pulling the other by the hand up the grade. When they got to the top Derek didn't let go, gathering her close to him. She looked up into his eyes, knowing a kiss was possible if she let it happen. But she didn't, and true to his word, Derek didn't force it.

Back inside Lara rubbed her hands together to warm them after the damp chill of the foggy air. Derek put their jackets in the closet. When he returned Lara was holding out his desk chair for him.

"You're going to make sure I finish this book, aren't you?"

"I'm certainly not going to be the reason you don't. How about a cup of coffee to warm your insides?"

"Sounds wonderful."

Lara went into the kitchen to brew a fresh pot. Several minutes later she returned to the front room, a cup of coffee in each hand. Derek had been going through notes and articles all morning and had papers spread over the desk. He cleared a corner for the cup and saucer.

She sat in a chair nearby, sipping her coffee and staring out at the fog as he contemplated her. She knew he was looking at her with admiration, and she thought about how easy it would be to become Derek's lover. Her resolve was all that was standing between them, and she knew that was more fragile than it appeared.

"Going to tackle your poem again?" he asked, breaking into her thoughts.

She sighed. "I don't know. I'm not very inspired."

"Maybe it's the weather."

"Maybe." Actually the fog did make her want to curl up and get as cozy as she could. All she needed was a fire to make the effect complete.

"You know, I hadn't thought about it until now, considering it's September," Derek said, "but I could build a fire."

Lara had to laugh.

"What's the matter?"

"I was just thinking about that myself. The very second you said it."

"Well. I guess we're on the same wavelength." He got up and went to the fireplace. "I'll have to get some wood from outside, though."

Derek went out the front door, leaving it ajar. Lara

peered out at the fog drifting by the cottage. Though it wasn't exactly cold, she wanted him back inside and the door closed. She wanted the snug intimacy they'd shared all morning. And maybe part of the feeling was knowing Steve Adamson was out there somewhere, searching for her, though she hadn't thought about him all that much.

Considering what had happened the day before, that was remarkable. In bed at the motel she had hugged her pillow, trying to fight off the terrifying recollections of the attack. But somehow, with Derek, she felt safe.

A moment later he came back inside, his arms filled with firewood. Lara closed the door behind him, locking it securely. He was kneeling at the hearth, selecting pieces of kindling to start the fire, and she squatted beside him.

"Were you a Girl Scout?" he asked cheerfully.

"No. I'm completely self-taught in the ways of the wilderness."

"I have to confess to being an Eagle Scout," he said.

Lara couldn't help chuckling.

"What's the matter?"

"You aren't your typical all-American scout type," she said, "but somehow the Eagle Scout image fits."

"I seem like someone who's always helping little old ladies across the street, is that it?"

"Exactly!"

He glanced at her, smiling wryly. "I've been accused of that before."

"By your wife?"

He hesitated. "Among others."

"I'm sorry," Lara said. "I wasn't supposed to mention her, was I?"

Derek turned to face her, resting his weight on one knee. "Maybe it was selfish to ask that of you."

Lara picked up a piece of newspaper, twisted it and put

it on the grate amid the kindling. "Are we going to rub two sticks together, or be sissies and use matches?" Lara asked, wanting to get away from the subject of Derek's wife.

He tweaked her nose. "If you want this fire going before winter comes, Miss Smartypants, I recommend we resort to matches."

Lara tweaked him back and got to her feet. "You're the Eagle Scout." She went to the couch and flopped down insouciantly to watch the final preparations.

In a couple of minutes the flames were lapping up the chimney and Derek started adding some small logs on top of the kindling. When he had them going, he stepped back to admire his efforts. "First fire of the season," he said with satisfaction.

"If you don't already have a merit badge for fire building, I'll see that you get one," she teased.

Derek went over to where she lay on the couch and playfully tickled her ribs in retaliation. "That was definitely sarcasm!" Lara shrieked and clamped her elbows against her sides. "Well, well," he said, continuing to torment her, "I think I've found your Achilles heel."

"My Achilles rib, you mean!" Then, laughing, she squealed, "Stop that!"

He sat on the edge of the couch, gazing down into her flushed face, his hip against hers, his face inches from hers. He could easily kiss her if he wished. With that realization, the mirth instantly faded from their expressions. He looked steadily into her eyes. Then very solemnly he said, "Every once in a while a man makes a promise he really regrets. I made one today." Brushing her cheek with the backs of his fingers, he got up and returned to his desk.

Lara lay very still, staring at the flames blazing brightly in the fireplace, pondering his words. What he had just said was very telling. She understood completely, because she felt exactly the same way.

her. In some way still, buried in the subconscious, maybe in a place beyond the meaning of his words. When he met her eyes once—

she couldn't tell—she understood something, because she couldn't be sure why ...

CHAPTER EIGHT

DEREK WAS PEELING potatoes for dinner and Lara was just starting to make a salad when the phone rang. It was Calle Bianco.

"You all right over there?" Calle asked without ceremony.

"Yeah, why?"

"Steve Adamson has gone berserk, honey. I just wanted to make sure you've got the shutters down."

"What happened?"

"He was here this afternoon. An hour or so ago. I was coming home from the store with the kids and he jumped out of the bushes. About scared me to death."

"Oh, Calle!"

"He didn't hurt anybody, but he demanded to know where you were. I told him it wasn't any of his business, and even if I knew where you were, I wouldn't tell him."

Lara felt heartsick. "Why is he doing this?"

"He's nuts, I guess. When he grabbed me by the shoulders, Jodie started screaming. I guess it scared him off, because he took out of here like a bat out of hell. I called the sheriff, but by the time a deputy got here Steve was long gone."

"Calle, I'm so sorry."

"I'm fine. Everybody is. Tony was over at Art McNew's, helping him fix his motorcycle, when it happened. He's home now and he's got his Italian blood up. Says he's going to shoot Steve on sight. But I doubt he'll be back. The deputies say they don't know how he's managing to avoid them, but he is. Knows the roads as well or better than they do, I suppose."

"I wish they'd catch him. This is turning into a nightmare."

"Tony said it's just a matter of time. But I had to call you. Don't take any chances, Lara. I don't know if Steve'll be able to find Derek's place or not, but you should be prepared."

"I doubt if he'll find us. But who knows?"

"How are things going otherwise?" Calle asked.

Lara knew what her friend meant, but she wasn't sure how to answer—not with Derek in the next room. "Derek's been very kind," she said. "He's taken personal responsibility for my safety, and I can't tell you how good it makes me feel."

"Well, I can tell you how good it makes *me* feel," Calle said.

Lara could almost see the smile on her friend's face. "Hopefully this won't go on much longer," she said evenly. "I'm in the middle of a salad, so I'd better get going. But thanks for calling. And I'm awfully sorry about what you're going through on account of me."

"We *all* love you," Calle said, making the word sound like an informed judgment rather than simple politeness.

"Thanks."

Back in the kitchen Lara found Derek still up to his elbows in potatoes. She started to tell him what had happened when the phone rang again. With a groan she returned to the living room and picked up the receiver. "Hello?"

There was silence on the line.

A stab of fear went through her. Somehow, she was sure

it was Steve. But she summoned her courage and tried again. "Hello?"

"Uh...is Derek Gordon there?"

It was a man's voice, but not Steve Adamson's. The caller sounded young, and definitely tentative. "Just a moment please," she said.

Lara called Derek, who walked in with a towel, wiping his hands. With a smile for her, he took the receiver and watched as she retreated into the kitchen.

"Hello?"

"Dad?"

"Mark! What a nice surprise. How are you doing?"

"Okay."

"What's up?"

There was silence on the line. "Was that her?"

"You mean Lara? Yes, it was." Derek could tell by the boy's tone that the surprise of hearing her voice had set him back. "She's had some problems, Mark—threats from a former husband—so she's spent the day with me."

"I see."

Derek knew he didn't. Not really. But there was nothing he could do about it now. "How's everything at home?"

"Okay, I guess."

Something was wrong, but it was apparent the boy wasn't going to come right out with it. "Your mother all right?"

"Yeah, sure."

Derek waited.

"Look," Mark said, "I wanted to talk to you about her."

"About Margaret?" He drew a deep breath. "Okay. What do you want to say?"

"No, I don't really want to get into it over the phone, but I've been thinking. I've decided we ought to sit down face-to-face and hash everything out. Is it all right if I come up next weekend? I don't have any classes Friday."

"Sure. Make it a three-day weekend. I've got the guest room."

"Okay," Mark said. "It'll probably be afternoon when I get there—early."

"I'm looking forward to it. Have you been over to see your mother, by the way?"

"Yeah. Today. Just got back a little while ago, as a matter of fact."

Derek had to fight the hypocrisy he was feeling. But he did care about Margaret, no matter what else was happening in his life. "How is she?"

"Same as always."

"Was she awake? Did she seem to recognize you?"

"She was awake, and she looked at me. But it was hard to tell how aware she was."

Derek felt the same old stab in his gut whenever he pictured Margaret in her hospital bed. It was so hard to know what to say to Mark. Most of what could be said had been, many times over.

Mark was silent for a moment. "Happy Labor Day, by the way."

Derek suddenly felt guilty. He should have called Mark. The family had always been big on Labor Day outings. The past several years he and Mark had usually gone to a ball game, followed by dinner out. "You know, the holiday slipped right up on me, Mark. I've been working all day and just now stopped to fix dinner. When you're up here, we'll go out. How about that?"

"I wasn't hinting at anything," Mark said.

"I know, but I feel badly because I didn't call."

"Hey, no guilt trips, huh?"

"Okay, no guilt trips."

"Will I get to meet your new lady?" Mark asked, his voice adopting a tone of false innocence.

Derek didn't answer for a moment. He wasn't sure if Mark's comment revealed unintentional callousness or thinly disguised sarcasm. He decided to give the boy the benefit of the doubt. "It's nothing like that," he said, glancing into the kitchen. Lara was out of sight.

"Whatever you say..."

But Derek didn't want to get into it. "How's your new girlfriend, by the way?" he asked. "What was her name?"

"Marcy."

"Yeah, Marcy."

"She's fine."

"Want to bring her when you come?"

"You mean to double-date?"

"Mark..." Derek could see they did need to have a long talk. The visit was probably a good idea. "We can discuss it when you get here."

"Yeah, okay. And if you don't mind, I might bring Marcy. We're getting pretty tight."

"What sort of arrangement should I make? There's just the one bed in the guest room."

Mark chuckled. "Not quite the libertine you pretend to be, eh, Dad?"

"Underneath it all, I guess I am of a different generation."

"Don't worry. I can sleep on the couch."

Derek smiled. "We'll work it out."

"Well, I won't keep you from whatever you're doing," Mark said. "See you on Friday, I guess."

"Yeah, see you then."

Derek hung up and went back into the kitchen. Lara was at the counter, tearing lettuce leaves into the salad bowl. Her back was to him. She was completely silent. He shuffled his feet and waited for her to turn around, but she didn't.

"I didn't know you had a son," she said, continuing her work.

"Mark is my stepson, though for all intents and purposes he's mine. We're very close."

Her back was still to him. "I'm a problem between you, aren't I? I couldn't help overhearing."

"No, of course you aren't."

She turned around abruptly. There was a somber expression on her face. "I'm starting to realize how much my predicament with Steve is disrupting other people's lives. And it's not a very pleasant thing to discover."

Derek walked over to her. He put his hands on his hips and looked down into her blue-green eyes. Just looking at her delicate, lovely face stirred him. "I'm going to break my promise, but only for a second," he said softly. Then he leaned over and lightly kissed her. Putting his arms around her, he held her close.

After a moment in his embrace, Lara hugged him back. Soon he felt dampness on the shoulder of his shirt. When Lara gave a little sob, he knew she was crying. The discovery sent a stab of anguish through him. His predicament had very clearly become her predicament, too. Mark was just another complication.

He stroked her head and held her tightly against him. Kissing her on the heels of Mark's call probably hadn't been very considerate, but at the moment his emotion and his desire were a lot stronger than his common sense.

WHEN MARK GOT BACK downstairs Marcy was sitting at the kitchen table, a half-empty glass of milk in front of her. The dishes had been cleared away, and her bare feet were propped up on his chair. He glanced at her legs protruding from the knee-length T-shirt she wore as a nightgown. Marcy pulled her feet out of the way and he sat down.

"How'd it go?"

"All right. He said we could come up this weekend."

"Was he surprised?" she asked.

"No, I don't think so. We were both thinking about something else. *She* was there."

"His new girlfriend?"

Mark nodded.

"Who are we to talk?" Marcy said with a shrug.

"*I'm* not married to somebody else."

The girl fingered the milk glass. "Him finding somebody else really bugs you, doesn't it?"

Mark leaned on the table, rubbing his temples with his palms. "I suppose it shouldn't. He hasn't had much of a life, I know. But she's my mom. It's tough knowing how helpless she is."

"Your stepfather's hung in there pretty long. I wish my dad had. My mother already divorced him because of another woman, and Mom isn't even sick."

"Yeah, I know. Derek's not so bad. It's all in my head, I guess. But I've got to talk to him anyway. If he wants to fool around, fine. He just ought to get a divorce first."

Marcy leaned forward and stroked Mark's arm. He looked up and smiled. She grinned her crooked grin that was so elflike and sexy. Mark took her hand.

"Hey, Gordon, want that ice cream now?"

He put his hand on her knee. She took his wrist and put his hand back on top of the table.

"I said ice cream."

"What's wrong with both?"

"Nothing," she said, getting up. "But first things first. I'm hungry for dessert." She went to the refrigerator.

"I'm hungry, too," he said suggestively.

Marcy glanced at him over her shoulder and rolled her eyes. "Men."

Mark smiled as he scanned her slight but curvaceous body. He liked Marcy a lot. He liked it that she had practically moved in with him. He hadn't lived with a girl before. There was a lot about the arrangement that was appealing.

That made him think about Derek and how lonely he must have been the past few years. One day he had a wife, the next day he didn't—no one to sleep with, or share a carton of ice cream with. Despite himself, Mark understood his stepfather's need. And he wondered if maybe up in Mendocino things between Derek and his lady weren't a lot like they were between him and Marcy. Still, loving his mother as he did, it was a hard thing to take.

LARA AND DEREK HAD a candlelight dinner with the fire still burning in the fireplace. It could have been romantic, but her concerns hung over them like a cloud. Derek made it as easy for her as he could, returning to the friendly manner he had affected all day.

They talked about everything except what was happening between them, though her problem with Steve came up in the context of the incident with Calle. Mostly they spoke of the past. Derek was very interested in her life as a child. He was sympathetic when she told the story of losing her mother and her affectionless relationship with her father. Derek asked why Lara never saw her dad, and she replied it was probably because he made no effort to see her.

Lara admitted that her resentment toward her stepmother was probably as much a cause of her problems with her family as anything. The two women simply didn't get along.

"It must be nice to have a good relationship with a stepchild,'' she said wistfully. "Have you and Mark always been close?"

"Yes," Derek said. "The fact that he didn't know his father probably helped. There was never an issue of me being an interloper."

"Is leaving on this sabbatical a problem between you?"

"More than I thought it would be. But maybe I over-estimated his understanding of my situation."

"He can't help but be protective of his mother. She *is* helpless." Lara felt a strong compassion for Margaret Gordon, though she had never laid eyes on the woman. Ever since Derek had talked about her at the Guild meeting, she'd felt for her. And it made the pain of her own inner conflict worse.

Derek nodded in response.

"And I must be salt in the wound," she added.

"Don't say that, Lara. If Mark was fully informed, he'd understand."

"My problems aren't the issue."

"Sure they are."

She shook her head.

"What are you saying?" Derek asked. "That if it weren't for Steve, we wouldn't be together?"

"I don't believe we would." In spite of the way she felt about Derek, Lara was sure she wouldn't have put herself in the present situation if it hadn't been for Steve.

Derek didn't look pleased.

"I'm not trying to belittle either your feelings or mine," she explained. "But if Steve had been arrested, I wouldn't be here tonight." She lowered her eyes. "The truth is, I'm beginning to care for you more than I should. And that makes me uncomfortable."

Derek was silent. When Lara looked up, he was staring

glumly at his wineglass, turning it slowly by the stem. "I can't say those feelings should be ignored," he said.

She put her hand on his in a friendly way. "Don't deceive yourself, Derek."

"I don't like this pretense."

She removed her hand. "I shouldn't be here. It's a needless temptation for us both. I should return to the motel."

"I'd prefer you stay here."

She shook her head. "I can't. In fact, if you don't mind, I'd like to go back now. I'd really like to be alone."

Derek sat silently for a minute, but he didn't argue. He got up from the table, and she helped him carry the last of the dishes into the kitchen. He wouldn't let her wash them, insisting he'd do them later, but she rinsed and stacked them anyway.

When they went out to the car a light drizzle was falling, the first rain of any consequence that season. Several minutes later, after a silent drive, they arrived at the motel. Derek went into the office with her to pick up her room key.

"You've had a call," the clerk said as he handed her the key, "but no messages. He didn't leave a name, either."

"He?"

"Yeah. Phoned just a few minutes ago. I told him I didn't think you were in, but I rang your room anyway."

Lara and Derek looked at each other.

"Did he say anything else?" Derek asked.

The man rubbed his chin. "He asked how long she was registered for, but I told him we don't give out that kind of information."

Derek turned to Lara, whose eyes had rounded with concern. "He must have checked all the motels in the area, asking for you. A long shot, but it paid off. The guy's persistent. I'll give him that."

"Is there something wrong?" the clerk asked.

"Yes. Miss Serenov is checking out. If the guy calls back or drops by, tell him she hasn't returned yet, would you? Don't say she's checked out." Derek took out enough money to cover the bill and put it on the counter. "Come on, Lara," he said, taking her by the arm, "we've got to get your things."

They left the office.

"Steve's probably on his way over to watch the place. Throw your clothes in your suitcase and let's get out of here," Derek said as they entered her room.

"Shouldn't we call the sheriff?"

"Yes, but from my place. I don't want to take the time now."

Lara was packed in thirty seconds. Derek took her bag and they were out the door and hurrying to his car. A few moments later they were speeding out the drive, the wheels of the BMW spinning in the gravel. Derek turned up the highway, in the opposite direction from his cottage.

"Where are we going?"

"I don't want to head straight for my place in case Steve called from nearby and is watching the motel. If I drive around for a few minutes, I can tell if we're being followed."

Lara moaned. "This can't be happening."

"Let's be glad we've managed to stay a step ahead of him. This could turn out to be a lucky development, though. If the sheriff stakes out the motel, they might be able to catch Steve when he comes looking for you."

Derek kept watching his rearview mirror. The windshield wipers slowly wagged back and forth in the drizzle. He pulled off the road and waited a minute, then made a U-turn and headed back toward his cottage. "So far, so good."

Derek scanned the road as they passed the motel, but there was no sign of Steve's truck, or any other suspicious vehicle. Just to be safe, he went a quarter of a mile past his drive before returning and entering it. Once off the highway he stopped, extinguished the lights and waited, looking back to see if anyone approached the drive.

The rain fell in light droplets on the windshield. Lara watched the accumulation slowly snake down the glass in tiny rivulets. After a minute Derek was satisfied they hadn't been followed, and proceeded down to the house.

Lara was silent the entire time. When he shut off the engine she turned to him, studying his face in the dark. "If they don't catch Steve tonight, I'm going to my father's place in Willits in the morning."

"If it's important to you, I'll take you there tonight."

"No, it would take forever to get there. I couldn't ask that of you."

"You'll be safe with me."

Lara wasn't sure if he meant safe from Steve, or safe from the risk of further involvement. At the moment she could only deal with one danger, though. As before, she put herself in Derek's hands.

They went inside and he immediately phoned the sheriff's office, explaining what had happened. Lara sat on the couch while he talked, staring at the fire, which was reduced now to hot coals. When he finished the call, Derek stoked the fire and added some wood. When the blaze was going again, he sat beside her, putting a protective arm around her shoulder.

"I hate this," Lara said. "It's so unfair what he's doing."

"It can't go on much longer."

"It makes you think how much in life you take for granted."

"That's true. What you do have can be snatched away at any moment."

Lara considered the words. Derek could have been referring to the loss of his wife, or to their friendship. She thought about what they'd discussed earlier, when she insisted they wouldn't be together were it not for Steve. Could the whole business be fated? she wondered.

Derek massaged her shoulder with his strong fingers. "You're really tense. Your muscles are tight as a knot."

"I know. I feel like a spring ready to be sprung."

"Can I fix you a drink? How about a hot toddy? I've got some brandy."

"All right. Maybe I'd feel better."

Derek was only gone a few minutes, but Lara was acutely aware of every sound outside during his absence. She heard the rain blowing against the windows. In the distance she heard the surf, and a truck passing by on the highway.

When Derek returned, she felt much better. He handed her a mug and she took it eagerly. They watched the fire and sipped their drinks. Derek tried to put her at ease by talking about other things.

When he was younger he used to do a lot of backpacking and mountain climbing, and he recounted stories of his adventures in the mountains. Loving the woods herself, Lara was soon caught up in his tales. They were sitting close, and between his body heat, the fire and the hot toddy, she was getting a cozy, warm feeling.

At one point Derek took her hand and unconsciously rubbed the back of it with his thumb. Her mood amplified the sensuality of the gesture, and she leaned against him.

"You know," he said, "we both love the wilderness so much, we ought to go on a serious hike sometime, maybe along the John Muir Trail."

"When, Derek? When Steve's out on bail, or after he's paroled?"

He looked at her with surprise.

"I'm sorry," she said. "That wasn't a nice thing to say. I'm afraid my frustration is showing."

"No need to apologize. My tendency to romanticize things has gotten out of hand. I shouldn't have said what I did." He twisted an end of her hair around his finger.

Lara could tell he wanted to kiss her. And she was afraid if she stayed there any longer he would. What she ought to do, she knew, was to get up and go over to the easy chair. But she couldn't pull herself away from him. It was as though she were suspended between two poles of a magnet. She wanted him, but couldn't have him. And it was pure agony to resist.

When Derek ran his finger lightly over her cheek—the sore one—she trembled. But her reaction had nothing to do with the injury. She looked pleadingly into his eyes.

"I made you a promise," he whispered, "and I've never regretted anything more." He hesitated. "I want to kiss you, but if you don't want me to, I won't."

Derek was putting the burden on her, but at least he was giving her a choice. The truth was she wanted him, wanted his love, and he knew it. She touched his face in a silent response. He lowered his mouth to hers.

They fell back on the couch, his lips pressed against hers. Lara dug her fingers into his hair. All day long she had fought the temptation, holding it at bay. Now there was no stopping. Her teeth bit hungrily into his lips. She arched against him.

Moments later, when their mouths parted, Derek eased his body down beside her. He held her close, kissing the corner of her mouth and combing her pale hair back with his fingers. Then he ran his hand up under her sweater and cupped her breast, making her nipple swell.

Except for Steve's unwanted advances, it was ages since a man had touched her that way, and practically as long since she had dreamed or fantasized about it. But she managed to relax and enjoy the pleasure of Derek's touch. Her body came alive.

When he took her hand and pressed his lips to her fingertips, tremors went through her. The raspy sweep of his tongue across her palms made the place between her legs pulse.

Lara accepted his eager kiss, opening her mouth to take in his tongue. And she felt him, even as he felt her. She tore at his shirt to get her hand inside. She caressed his chest and shoulders, wanting badly to explore the rest of his body.

In the course of their growing excitement he'd removed her sweater and bra. After lightly running his thumb over her nipples until they stood erect, Derek kissed her breasts, his tongue spreading a trail of moisture over her creamy flesh.

When he started to pull away, Lara held his face against her, wanting the feeling to never end. She was powerfully aroused now, moaning at each rasp of his tongue. But when he stood and began unbuttoning his shirt the realization that they were moving toward the ultimate intimacy hit her. Though her body was still throbbing, she began seeing Derek as a man—a man she didn't belong with, a man who was married to someone else. And she realized that even if his feelings were genuine, they were misguided. He was blind to a reality he was pretending didn't exist. And until this moment, so was she.

Rising, Lara put her arms around him, covering herself by embracing him. She pressed her face against his shoulder and breathed in the scent of his flesh. Desire coursed through her once more, but she fought it.

"Oh, Derek," she said on the verge of tears, "why do these things have to happen to me?"

He gently pulled back her head so that he could see her eyes. "What, Lara? What's wrong?"

"We can't do this. I want to, but we can't." She let go of him and bent over to pick up her sweater, which she slipped on to cover herself.

He studied her with consternation. "I thought it was what you wanted."

"It was. I do want you, in a way. But not for the right reasons. It's not your fault, though."

"What are the right reasons?"

"Please, Derek, let's not go into it. Isn't it enough that I don't want to be with you?"

"It's because of Margaret, isn't it?"

"It's because of her, your son, the situation, Steve, my life, your life, our friendship, my fear. There are a million reasons."

"The last one, fear, is the only one that really matters. And it can be handled."

Lara got up and went to the fire, wanting a substitute for Derek's strong allure. "Maybe I should go to another motel. Or to Calle's."

"No."

"It was my fault it went too far. But I wanted you to kiss me."

"I'm glad you did," he said.

"It was weakness. A lapse. It won't happen again."

Derek tucked in his shirttail. Then he went to where Lara stood by the hearth. "I can accept everything you said except that last point. We have to find a way to make it all right with you."

She shook her head. "Don't you see? It's not a matter of rationalizing."

He had moved very close. And the way he was looking at her told Lara he didn't much care what she was saying. Taking her face in his hands, he leaned over and kissed her lips tenderly, as if to prove the point.

It was a brief kiss, but arousing. Steeling herself, Lara backed a half step away. "If you don't mind, I think I'll go to bed now." She turned without waiting for an answer and headed for the guest room.

CHAPTER NINE

DEREK SAT for a long time staring into the fire. Lara had been in the guest room for half an hour, and her light had been off nearly as long. The crackle of the burning logs was the only sound in the house. Outside, the wind had picked up and was gusting and whistling about the eaves.

The urgency of his desire had dissipated, but that longing for her was still lying heavily within him. He had never craved a woman as he did Lara—not even Margaret at the height of their love.

Wanting her—loving her, if that was what it was—was easy enough. Knowing what to do about it was the hard part. Margaret and Mark—his family, the people he had always loved most in the world—couldn't be swept under the carpet. They would have to be taken into account.

Besides, it wasn't only his feelings that were at issue. Lara was struggling, too. And Margaret had to be at the heart of her concern. He was, after all, a married man.

Restless, Derek went to the French windows and peered out into the darkness. He couldn't see much. The light from the fire was bright enough that the panes of glass were like mirrors. The reflection of the flames dancing in the window drew his eyes.

The wind continued to whistle, blowing scattered raindrops against the panes of glass. Occasionally he could hear the crash of a large wave against the rocks.

Suddenly he sensed a presence. Then he saw her reflection in the windowpane. Lara was standing in the doorway. A half-buttoned shirt coming to the top of her thighs was all she wore. Her blond hair cascaded in a tangle to her shoulders.

Derek turned slowly. In the firelight she looked sensuously beautiful, her mouth slightly petulant in the shadows. In her eyes there was doubt…and fear. In them was the question…and an answer.

She didn't say anything. After a moment of staring at him, she turned and went into the darkness of her room. But she left the door open in silent invitation.

Slowly Derek walked over to the doorway. In the dim light he could see she had gotten back into bed, and the shirt she'd worn moments earlier was draped over a chair. He realized she was naked under the covers, so he undressed.

As he climbed in beside her, she scooted over to give him room. Her flesh felt warm as he took her into his arms. Then Derek kissed her gently. It was his answer to her question.

She was holding him very tightly, her mouth against his shoulder. As though in frustration she nipped at him with her teeth, gingerly sinking them into his skin. "I'm not strong enough to resist you," she whispered plaintively.

"Don't think about it. Just let me love you."

She turned her face to him. The tip of her tongue grazed his lips and the sweet scent of her filled his lungs. He grew hard, aroused by her softness.

She was an exquisite creature, heart-stoppingly beautiful. He ran his hand over her body, following its curved lines under the covers. But he had to pause to get control of himself. He didn't want to rush her. Lara had said she wanted to be held first. She wanted things long and slow and gentle. And he wanted their lovemaking to be perfect for her.

Then, while he was still waiting for his desire to subside, Lara touched his chest, entangling her fingers in his mat of hair before letting her hand roam down over his hip and thigh. Derek stiffened at the pleasure of her touch. What she did was more loving than erotic. He kissed her deeply, wanting her. And he could tell that she wanted him, too.

Lara hardly breathed. Her heart was pounding desperately. When Derek drew his tongue across her breasts, all the fire that had been within her flared again. She closed her eyes, and her legs opened slightly to accept his touch. She clenched the sheets and trembled as Derek found her center.

Lara's hips began to rock. She moaned with each caress, the desire quickly building to a breaking point.

Derek must have sensed her release was near because his hand stilled. But Lara wouldn't let him stop. She dragged his fingers back and at the same time she reached down to find his sex. Her own pleasure overwhelmed her.

"Please, Derek," she whispered, "don't wait any longer. Take me now, please."

Her pleading nearly ended in a cry. Kissing her deeply, he moved over her. He felt her stiffen, this time in fear rather than excitement.

He badly wanted to penetrate her, yet he made himself hold back. His mind screamed at him to be gentle, so he tried to focus again on her pleasure, her need.

Gradually the tension seemed to drain from her. She slid her hand to the small of his back and lightly pressed, signaling for him to enter her. As he did, she gasped again. But he could tell it was more with uncertainty than discomfort. Slowly, ever so slowly, he thrust deeper until their bodies were locked.

For a long moment they clung together, her fingers digging into his back. She began to undulate, her movements gradually more frantic, building to a heightened pace. She began crying out.

Her cries undid him. He climaxed then, as their bodies surged against each other. They clung together panting, then he collapsed on top of her.

Under him he could feel the rapid beating of her heart. He kissed her lips, her cheeks. She lay motionless, almost lifeless, though the purr in her throat told him she was still in her pleasure. After a while he rolled off her, but she still didn't move. Her eyes remained closed. She hadn't said a word.

Derek would have told her he loved her if the words had been permissible. But he sensed somehow they wouldn't be welcome. He found her hand under the covers and interlaced his fingers with hers. Lara's eyes opened, but she didn't look at him.

He considered asking her if she was upset, but decided if she wanted to say something, she would. If she was thinking about Margaret, the question was better left unasked. He himself hadn't thought about his wife. Not until now. Then it occurred to him that Lara was the first woman he'd made love to in years, and the only one besides Margaret since his marriage.

A wave of guilt washed over him, but he felt as badly for Lara as anyone. He raised himself onto his elbow to see her face. Her eyes were glistening. When he bent to kiss her mouth she turned away, slipping her hand from his. A lump of emotion formed in his throat, and after a few seconds Lara quietly began to cry.

STEVE ADAMSON GEARED DOWN as he approached the motel, seeing the red neon No Vacancy sign lit up. The battered pickup belched and coughed as it backfired. Tim Easterly's truck wasn't half of what his was, but the advantage was the police weren't looking for Tim's old junker. They *were* looking for his.

Steve peered at the motel through the rain-streaked windshield. The wiper on the driver's side barely worked, and the other one didn't work at all. He cursed the weather, hating the rain more than anything about the north coast.

But Steve knew he was lucky to have any transportation at all. If it weren't for Tim, the cops would have probably picked him up by now. There were only so many roads. He couldn't dodge them forever, but at least trading trucks with Tim had given him a little more time. "If you're in trouble, I don't want to hear about it," his friend had said. "The less I know, the better."

Steve continued on past the motel, not exactly comfortable with what he saw. He was jumpy—it might not be any more than that, but he wanted to make damn sure. Lara's Jeep wouldn't be there, but he half expected to see that guy's BMW. But it didn't seem to be around, either. In fact there was only one vehicle at the entire place. Steve didn't know whether that was a good sign or not.

A quarter of a mile past the motel he swung into a driveway and turned around, intending to pass the motel for a third time before going in. One shot at Lara was all he wanted. Then he'd hightail it out of the county, and probably out of the state. If he could just get her alone...

Approaching the motel again, Steve studied it, satisfied nothing was wrong. His fear was probably groundless. Knowing he was vulnerable out on the highway, he decided to pull into the drive and get it over with. He parked a ways from the office. The light was on inside, but he couldn't see anybody. It was late, and the night clerk might be lying down on a cot or something.

Steve got out of the truck, slamming the squeaky old door with its half-rusted hinges. He started toward the office in the drizzling rain, the gravel crunching under his boots as he went. The door to the office was locked and he started to ring the night bell, when he suddenly realized what was bothering him. If the No Vacancy sign was lit, why the hell weren't there cars all over the place?

Steve spun on his heel and took a step back toward the truck when he saw two sheriff's cars coming down the highway—one from each direction. He turned toward the corner of the building as a deputy stepped into view, his service revolver pointed directly at Steve's midsection.

"Freeze!" the man shouted.

Steve looked over his shoulder and saw two more deputies appear from the other side, guns drawn. Before he could flinch a couple more cops appeared. "Damn it to hell!" he said through his teeth, seeing his situation was hopeless.

"Put your hands up!" one of them hollered at him.

Numbly Steve obeyed, cursing under his breath. They were on him then like a pack of dogs. His arms were pulled behind him, the cuffs clamped onto his wrists. He had an urge to start swinging, but he knew they'd just beat the hell out of him.

He looked into the eyes of the big guy in front of him. There was a grin on his face. It was Wally Stiles.

"Evenin', Mr. Adamson," he said, the cocky grin spreading wider.

"Screw you."

"You should have listened to me," Stiles said as they frisked him, "it would have saved the taxpayers some overtime money."

"The hell with the taxpayers and the hell with you."

Even though they were standing in the rain, Stiles pulled

a card from his shirt pocket and started reading Steve his rights. But he was so numb, and the adrenaline was pumping so hard, that he didn't hear a word. All he could think of was wanting to pound the cop into the ground. But it was too late.

"You know," the deputy said, "in a way I wish you'd been stupid enough to try something. I'd have enjoyed returning the favor you did that woman."

"She asked for it," Steve said, squinting into the rain. "She ain't nothin' but a tease. She was eggin' me on, makin' me think she was interested. I didn't hit her until after she kicked me a couple of times. It was self-defense."

The deputies laughed at the remark.

"It's true!" Steve shouted. "I was married to the bitch once. This whole thing was to get revenge on me. I didn't do nothin' she didn't ask for. You ain't heard my side of the story."

"There'll be time for that," Stiles said, gesturing for the two officers holding Steve to take him to the cruiser. "The judge and jury will be glad to hear all about it."

"This ain't fair!" he called out as they led him away. "Ask Lara. She'll tell you. She wanted me. I know she did. If she said she didn't, she's lyin'!"

They had him at the car. One of the deputies pushed his head down so they could get him in the back seat. It was uncomfortable with his hands manacled and his face dripping wet. A helpless feeling came over him, knowing he was headed for jail. "Damn her!" he screamed to no one in particular.

"Knock that off!" one of the deputies snapped.

"Jeez, this ain't fair," he moaned. It wasn't as if he hadn't been arrested before. A time or two he'd been in bar brawls. But he was always out the next day, and drunk enough when they hauled him in that he didn't remember much about what happened. He knew this was different. He wouldn't be getting out any time soon. They might even send him up.

He kicked the seat in front of him. The deputy getting in next to him gave him a sharp poke in the ribs with his nightstick.

"I said cool it, Adamson!"

Steve doubled over with pain. "I hate her guts," he moaned. "This is all Lara's fault."

SHE STARED AT THE CEILING in the darkness, listening to the rain. Beside her, Derek was asleep. Lara didn't know exactly when he dropped off, but it must have been an hour ago. She'd cried for quite a while, despite the pleasure he'd given her.

She remembered the miracle of their lovemaking. Lara had never known such sensation. How would she be able to resist sharing herself with him in the future?

Stopping what she started was every bit as necessary now as it had been to invite him to her bed in the first place. Her only hope was to get away from him. If she could escape, disappear into the night... Facing him in the morning seemed impossible. She didn't want to have to look at him over breakfast. If she were to remember him, better the recollection be of his kindness and the mutual pleasure of this solitary night.

But even if she couldn't leave, Lara yearned to be alone. Pulling back the covers and getting out of bed woke him.

"Lara?"

"Sorry," she whispered.

"Where are you going?"

"It's too cramped to sleep. I'm going to the couch."

He took her arm. "I'll leave, if you like."

"I didn't mean to disturb you." The conversation struck

her as bizarre, an unnatural politeness considering they had been lovers, intimate only hours ago. Now they were suddenly strangers.

Derek sat up on the edge of the bed. She watched him in the darkness. He was searching the floor for his clothes. She felt wretched, chasing him away.

When he had found his things, he stood and looked down at her. She could barely see his features, but judging by the way he stared at her, he was trying to find the right thing to say. He sat on the edge of the bed again, and reached out to caress her face.

"I didn't hurt you, did I?"

"No," she whispered.

He took a breath to say something more, but instead rose from the bed and left her, silently closing the door behind him.

For a moment she held her breath, wishing the compassion, the affection she felt for him, would go away. But it didn't.

LARA AWOKE the next morning to the sound of a telephone ringing. For a second she thought she was at home, but then she remembered...everything. She sat upright and the sheet fell from her naked body. The ringing stopped. She heard the muffled sound of Derek's voice, though she couldn't hear what he was saying.

Several things hit her at once: she had made love with Derek Gordon; Steve Adamson was looking for her; the smell of brewing coffee was in the air. Her next thought was to get cleaned up and dressed. She looked around, trying to orient herself. Derek's voice stopped in the next room. A moment later there was a soft knock on her door.

Lara pulled up the sheet to cover her nakedness. "Yes?"

"Can I come in?"

She hesitated. "Okay."

The door opened and Derek stood there. Dressed in cords and a sweater, he looked handsome and bright-eyed. His expression was friendly. She could smell his cologne from across the room.

"Good morning," he said, smiling. "I've got good news. The sheriff's office called. They picked up Steve last night at the motel. He walked right into their trap."

Lara sighed with relief. "Thank God."

"You won't have to live in fear now."

She sensed caution in him. He was being cheerful, perhaps intuiting that what she craved was normalcy.

"How about some coffee?"

"I'd love it. But first I want a bath."

"Right. I'll have a cup ready when you're finished. Hungry?"

Lara shook her head. Derek seemed aware she was embarrassed, so he gave her a wink and withdrew. When she headed for the bathroom, she heard him in the kitchen. The sun was shining and he was whistling.

Lara soaked for a long time, trying to figure out what tune Derek was whistling. She smiled at the innocence of it. Derek was so...endearing.

As she listened, the whistling drew nearer, then stopped. He knocked on the door. "You still afloat in there?"

"I haven't sunk yet. I'll be out in a minute."

"Just wanted to make sure you're okay." He went off again, humming now.

Lara got out of the tub and quickly washed her hair in the basin. She toweled it thoroughly, then got it about half dry with her blower before dressing and going to the kitchen.

Derek was sitting at the table with a cup of coffee, reading over some notes. "There she is." He got up and examined her injured cheek, noting with a nod that it was much improved. Then he got the coffeepot, pouring some of the steaming liquid into the cup at her place.

"Sorry I took so long," Lara said. "It felt so good to soak."

Derek returned to his chair. "Did you sleep well?"

"Fine." She glanced at the papers in front of him. "Hard at work already?"

"I was checking over my notes. I'm going to tackle part one of the book today." His eyes settled on her.

Lara could hardly meet his gaze. Pretending nothing had happened last night wouldn't work. She knew that. "Now that they've got Steve, I'd like to get on home," she said evasively. "I hate to ask you to drive me, but there's no other way. My trials and tribulations have interfered in your life enough."

"Don't be ridiculous."

A vague sadness in his voice moved her. Still she was determined. "If you want to drive me back as a break from your work, I can go for a walk to kill some time. Whatever is most convenient."

"It's up to you."

She avoided his eyes, staring out the window at the wind-swept point. "Well, it certainly cleared up, didn't it? Wait until you have to endure your first full-blown winter storm. You'll think the ocean is about to come through your living room."

"I've heard the weather can get pretty rough."

Lara felt uncomfortable. They were both silent. She picked up her coffee cup, glancing at him uncertainly. His expression was unaccusing, deferential, but she knew he had to be feeling the same torment. "Oh, Derek, why do we have to suffer this way?"

He didn't reply for a moment. "What would be easiest

for you," he finally said, "if I take you home, pretending our lovemaking didn't happen, or if I ask you to tell me how you feel?"

She stared down at the cup, running her finger self-consciously around the rim. "I suppose I owe you some sort of explanation."

"No, you don't."

Lara looked up to see what he meant.

"Your motivations don't matter. All I care about is the future—what you want."

She thought for a moment. "I won't insult you with banalities. I want to return to my life…as it was."

He considered her words. Then nodding, he said, "I understand."

"Do you really?"

"Sure. And there's no point in me spouting banalities, either. You're a mature woman who knows her mind. You're aware of my feelings. There's no need to go any further than that if you don't wish to."

Lara reached over to stroke his hand. "You're a decent, considerate human being, Derek. I'll always love you for that."

Derek gave a little laugh. "Thank you."

"It's not what you want to hear perhaps, but—"

"That's all right. You don't have to explain. Compliment accepted."

"I've offended you."

He reached over and took her chin in a sort of paternal gesture. "No, you haven't."

She was grateful for the manner in which he was handling the situation, though in a way his stoicism almost hurt worse than a more emotional reaction would have. Recollections of the night before passed through her mind before she forced herself to concentrate on what was happening now. This—the morning after—was the reality that mattered.

She got up from the table. "I'll get my things."

When she returned to the living room, Derek was standing at his desk shuffling some papers. Seeing she was ready, he took her case from her and they went outside to the BMW. The air was clean and brisk. Derek put her bag in the back seat and they took off.

As they drove past the motel, Lara saw that the vacancy sign was lit. A maid was outside the rooms with her service cart. Lara shuddered at the thought of what might have occurred if it hadn't been for Derek. In spite of herself, she glanced at him longingly.

His expression was peaceful, accepting. Her eye traced his profile. When she looked at his mouth she thought of the incredible things he'd done to her. The memory sent a sharp twinge through her. Would she really be able to forget?

When they entered her drive and began the climb to her cabin, the familiarity of place gave her a sense of well-being. She was glad to be home. But the illusion of security was soon shattered.

As they drove up, she saw that the rear window of the Jeep was smashed. The front door of the cabin was standing wide open.

"Oh, hell," Derek said, noticing what had happened.

Lara seethed as she got out of the car.

The inside of the house was a mess. The slider had been broken, her new drapes pulled down. Chairs were overturned, lamps knocked over. Her underclothing was scattered all over the place, apparently thrown down from the loft. Even her books had been stripped from the shelves. And in the kitchen the contents of the refrigerator had been dumped on the floor, and a sack of flour had been spread over everything.

"I hate him!" Lara screamed, staring at the mess.

"Better this than you," Derek said. "Why don't you call the sheriff, so that they're aware of this when they question Steve. I suppose it's possible it was someone else—kids, vandals—but I doubt it."

"Yes, maybe I shouldn't jump to conclusions."

While Lara was on the phone, Derek set the living room furniture upright. He stacked the books on a table and collected her clothing and put it on a chair. When Lara came back in, he was picking up pieces of broken glass. The place looked somewhat better.

"It's not as bad as it seems," he said. "The drapes aren't torn, they just need to be rehung. Only one lamp is smashed beyond repair. The main damage seems to be to the sliding glass door and your car window. You should probably get a glass man out right away." He pressed his foot on the carpet. It made a squishy sound. "The rain soaked this a little, but it'll dry out."

Lara sighed. Derek put an arm around her shoulder. "You've had a couple of rough weeks."

"You're a master of understatement, Professor Gordon." She looked at him and saw not only compassion but wistfulness in his eyes. He seemed sad. Lara suddenly regretted her hard-line stance.

"I'll help you clean up the kitchen," he said.

"No, you've got work to do. This'll keep me busy till the glass man gets here." She tried to smile. "Maybe I'll turn this into a plus and do my spring cleaning."

He pinched her chin again. "You're early by about six months."

"Or late. I'm not sure which."

Judging by his expression, Derek read into her comment

a double entendre that she only half intended. "It's never too late," he said simply.

When her eyes dropped, Derek turned and walked slowly toward the door. She followed him onto the porch.

He stood for a long moment, staring out at the trees bathed in warm sunshine. There was a light breeze. The air was pleasant. It was the sort of day she loved to go down by the creek and lie in the tall meadow grass.

Derek had a smile on his face when he finally turned to her. He was telling her it was all right, not to worry.

He touched her cheek with the backs of his fingers. "I'll probably come to the Literary Guild meetings," he said. "And I'll look forward to seeing you at them."

Lara felt a huge lump in her throat.

"I do have a request, though, if you don't mind," he said.

Lara nodded, biting her lip.

"I'd like you to write me a poem. It doesn't matter what it's about. I'd just like something you wrote for me."

She nodded, unable to speak. Her eyes filled.

Derek grinned as she wiped away a tear.

"You know what?" he said, his voice dropping to a hoarse whisper. "You're terrific, Lara Serenov." Then he leaned over to kiss her.

Lara's arms hung limply. She wanted to put them around his neck, but held back. Then, finally, she couldn't resist any longer. She hugged him and kissed him goodbye.

When the embrace ended, Derek smiled a last time, tweaked her nose and went to his car. As she watched him go, the only thing Lara could think of was how much she hated what had happened between them.

CHAPTER TEN

THE MAN FROM the glass company had just finished installing the new door when Calle's car pulled up in front of the cabin. She had Theresa with her, and they sat together on the couch while Lara wrote a check for the workman. Once she had seen him out the door Lara came back into the living room and plopped in a chair.

"If I have to face one more disaster, Calle, I may not make it."

"At least Steve's in jail."

"How'd you hear about it, by the way? I would have called you but I've been cleaning up this mess. You should have seen the way it looked when we got here."

"I phoned Derek and he told me he'd brought you home and everything that's happened."

Lara gave her an inquiring look. "What do you mean by 'everything'?"

Calle smiled. "I have a feeling I don't quite mean *everything*."

"What did he say?"

"That you spent the night in his guest room because Steve had found out you were at the motel."

Lara nodded. "That's true."

Theresa started squirming, so Calle put the toddler on the floor. The girl promptly went over to Lara, who brushed back her pretty, dark hair.

"Do I get the rest of the story?" Calle asked.

"You can guess, can't you?"

"You didn't!"

Lara nodded. "I did." Theresa tried to climb onto her lap, so Lara lifted her up.

"And?"

"And so I'm miserable."

"It wasn't good?"

"To the contrary, it was too good. And a big mistake."

Calle beamed, despite the disclaimer.

"It was the worst possible thing that could have happened, so don't go getting smug," Lara said.

"You mean because he's married? Well, I can certainly understand that. Lord knows, I'd hate the thought of Tony with anyone else. But there is a difference, Lara. He doesn't have a real marriage. He can't have a normal relationship with his wife so ill. It's not as though he's—"

"Cheating? Let's face it, that's exactly what it is. And somehow I have trouble picturing myself as the other woman."

"You feel guilty."

"Of course, wouldn't you?"

"It isn't as though you set out to seduce him. And he wasn't an innocent bystander, was he?"

"No, but he didn't exactly initiate things, either."

"*You* started it?"

Lara bounced Theresa on her knee. "I made the definitive overture. Let me put it that way."

"Good for you!"

"Calle!"

"I don't mean to sound like the devil's handmaiden, but even if you never see him again, you weren't exactly breaking up a marriage. Believe me, if anyone wanted to defend the institution, it'd be me. But I'm a realist. The poor man's been deprived. And so have you, for that matter."

"I'm glad you're taking such a charitable interest in our sex lives," Lara said a bit sarcastically, "but this is my life we're talking about. And his. And his wife's. And his son's."

"His *son*?"

"His stepson," she replied, nodding. "I found out over the weekend. He's college age. A young man." Lara gave Theresa a big hug and a kiss on the cheek, which made the child giggle with glee. "We're talking about a family, Calle."

"All right, so you don't want to be a home wrecker. I can sympathize with that. But how does Derek feel? I mean, what did *he* say?"

"What could he say? I made it pretty clear how I feel."

"That you don't want to see him again?"

"More or less. He mentioned the Literary Guild, but I'm not even sure I could handle seeing him there."

Calle raised her eyebrows. "This guy really got to you, eh?"

Theresa became impatient and Lara put her down. The little girl went to the window and began chattering at the jay that had landed on the railing of the deck.

Lara crossed her legs and looked at her friend thoughtfully. "I think I could care for him a lot."

"I see."

"And so, rather than hurt a bunch of people needlessly, including myself, I decided to put a stop to it immediately."

"And he said…"

"He was really most understanding. Not pleased, but he understood. I have to hand Derek that. He's a very, very mature and selfless individual."

Calle hesitated a moment before asking her next question. "How is he in the sack?"

"Calle, sometimes you can be downright…heartless."

"The term is *ribald*, honey."

Lara laughed.

"So how was he?"

"Fabulous. Just fabulous."

Calle's grin was genuinely salacious.

"So you see why it was the worst possible thing that could have happened."

"I see why you can't blithely continue hiding out in this convent of yours."

Lara gave her a look. "You're incorrigible."

Theresa went running to Calle. She plopped her head down on her mother's lap. Calle stroked the child's hair. "What's next?"

"I get the window of my Jeep fixed. Then I start writing poetry with a vengeance."

"Do poets write with a vengeance?"

"This one will. At least until I'm back in the groove."

"How about coming over for some lasagna?" Calle said.

"Thanks, but I really need to be alone for a couple of days. I want to get centered."

Calle had a sincerely triste expression on her face. "For a woman of letters, you're a painfully rational creature, Lara Serenov."

Lara grimaced. "It's a matter of survival, Calle. Survival."

DEREK TYPED THE LAST WORDS on the page, then rolled up the paper to reread the final paragraph. He deleted a phrase, added a word, then decided the writing was good enough for the chapter to be moved to the ready-for-revision pile. He leaned back in his chair and glanced out the window.

It was Friday, the fourth sunny day in a row. He was glad. If Mark was going to make the long drive north, it would be nice to have fine weather for his visit. Derek looked at his watch. His stepson could be arriving at any time.

He went into the kitchen and felt the teakettle. The water was still hot enough to make another cup. He dropped a tea bag in his mug and filled it from the kettle. After tasting the steaming brew he returned to the living room, sat in his reading chair and thought about Lara. Only a few days had passed since he'd seen her. It seemed like a year.

From Lara there had been only silence. He had decided not to contact her. But he had called Calle the night before and she had immediately guessed his motive.

"She's doing okay," she had said. "She's doing fine."

He couldn't tell whether Calle knew what had happened, but he suspected that she did, judging by her solemn tone.

"How's your book coming?" she asked. "Have you managed to get church and state together?"

"Only until it's time to separate them."

Calle laughed. "It's good that you can have a sense of humor about it."

"It's one of the requirements of teaching political philosophy."

But Calle had no news of Lara. He suspected that what she could have said, he wouldn't have wanted to hear. But maybe it was just as well. Making love with Lara had been among the more wonderful experiences of his life. Still, he couldn't escape the fact that he had broken his vows to Margaret.

He had been faithful for so many years, yet he had been unable to resist Lara. Did he love Margaret any less, or was it simply because, until now, he had never been truly tested? He didn't know the answer.

The worst part was knowing that ultimately he would have to choose between them. Lara hadn't left much doubt she was unwilling to have a relationship with him as things stood. And there was Mark to think of, as well. Derek's family, duty—everything he believed in—stood on one hand, and Lara on the other.

Outside the cottage Derek heard a vehicle. It was Mark and his girlfriend. He watched as they got out of the truck. The sight of Mark, with his mother's auburn hair and distinctive nose, was heartening to Derek. He glanced at the leggy young woman with the faddish haircut, then at Mark, who was getting a couple of bags from the back of the pickup. "Well, you made it," Derek said, greeting them on the porch.

Mark introduced Marcy and they shook hands. Derek took one of the bags. "Have you kids eaten?"

"We brought some snacks along for the trip," Marcy said as she walked through the door. She went over and looked out the French windows. "What a neat place! Did you see this view, Mark?"

He dropped the bag and ambled over to where she stood. "Yeah, not bad."

Derek took their things into the guest room. When he came out they were still at the window. Mark's arm was resting on Marcy's shoulder. "So, how about some lunch? I've got the fixings for sandwiches. And some soup is on the stove."

"Sure. Why not?" Mark said. He turned to Marcy. "You hungry?"

She shrugged.

"Tuna okay?"

They both nodded.

"Give me ten minutes," Derek said. "If you want to walk out onto the point and get a feel for the place, go ahead."

They went outside, and when they came back ten

minutes later Derek was putting things on the table. Mark wandered into the kitchen while Marcy went to the bathroom to freshen up.

"So, how's what's her name—Lara?" he said, straddling a chair.

"I haven't seen her for several days."

"Mom's fine, in case you're wondering. She's the same, anyway."

"Yes, I was going to ask if you've been over to see her."

"Sure. I try to go two or three times a week at least."

"I'm glad."

Mark's expression turned sober. "I do it for her, not for you."

Before Derek could reply Marcy came into the kitchen. She had a scrubbed, wholesome look about her, despite the faddish hairstyle and the exotic-looking earrings that hung nearly to her shoulders. "You've got a great place here, Professor Gordon," she said cheerfully.

"Thanks, but I'm on sabbatical, so for a year at least it's just Derek."

She smiled and sat next to Mark. "That won't be easy. My roommate last year was in your Poly Sci 100 class. All she talked about for three months was Professor Gordon."

"I hope it was the quality of the instruction that impressed her."

Marcy giggled, lowering her eyes. "Not exactly."

Derek put the last bowl of soup on the table and sat down.

"Well, it looks like you haven't lost your knack for lunches," Mark said, taking a bite of the tuna sandwich on his plate.

"It wasn't always that way, was it?"

Mark laughed. "Heck no. I'll never forget you making

my school lunches when Mom first got sick. Remember that time you made a mayonnaise sandwich?"

"I was in a hurry and forgot the baloney," Derek said defensively. For some reason he had always been sensitive about his parenting mistakes. He'd regarded his role of surrogate father as terribly important, perhaps taking it more seriously than if Mark had been his own child. "It was a mistake even a mother could make."

"Mrs. Arigoni didn't think it was so cool," Mark replied. "She sent a note home suggesting you put something more nutritious between the bread!"

"Yes, and I was offended. It's not like it had happened every day for a week."

"At least you tried," Marcy said. "My father can't boil an egg. Of course, that may have changed now that he's on his own again. I really don't know because every time I see him, he takes me out to dinner someplace expensive."

"Guilt," Mark said, munching.

"No, I don't think so. It's like generosity is a way of expressing love. Not being with my mom anymore, he's got to find his own way of saying it."

"What do you think, Dad? Your situation is practically like being divorced," Mark said.

"I wouldn't describe it that way. Your mother and I are still very much married."

Mark didn't reply, and there was an awkward silence.

"Speaking of cuisine, how are you doing on your own?" Derek asked. "Still having bowls of cereal half an hour before dinner like you did when you were in high school?"

"Naw. I don't cook that much, to be honest. And neither does Marcy. We usually eat at the cafeteria and study at the library before going home."

"Mark…" Marcy said, poking him with her elbow.

"He knows. Anyway, he's got a girlfriend himself."

Derek's look hardened. "I wish you wouldn't say that. When you called, Lara was here because of a problem she was having with her ex-husband. He'd tried to attack her and the police were hunting him. He'd been checking out her friends' places, the motels in the area and so forth. She was with me because her husband wouldn't have looked for her here."

"What are you saying, that she's really only a friend, that she doesn't mean anything to you?"

Derek glanced at Marcy, who had lowered her eyes. "Maybe we ought to discuss this later," he said.

Mark looked at each of them. "Yeah, sorry. I didn't mean to bring up a sore subject."

"I can go down and have a look at the beach, if you want to talk," Marcy volunteered.

"That's not necessary," Derek said. "We've got plenty of time to discuss things this weekend."

The girl picked up the uneaten half of the sandwich. "No, really. I'd kind of like to get some air. I can have this down by the water." She got up and went out of the cottage.

"She's a nice girl," Derek said after a bit. "Things getting serious between you two?"

Mark shrugged. "We're pretty close."

"Didn't you just meet?"

"I've known her longer than you've known Lara."

"Is that what you want to talk about?"

"She may not be any of my business, but Mom is."

"Meaning?"

"I don't think you should take advantage of the fact that Mom's incapacitated."

"What do you mean, 'take advantage'?"

Mark rocked his chair back on its rear legs and clasped his hands behind his head. "You aren't having an affair?"

"Not an affair, no." He looked into Mark's eyes and discovered he was more uncomfortable than he had expected. "Not exactly, anyway."

The boy stared at him. "What are you saying, you got laid a time or two?"

"I wish it wasn't necessary to be so crude."

Mark seemed annoyed. "Okay, sorry. but what do you want me to say? What Mom doesn't know won't hurt her?"

"What I do is my business."

"True, you can do anything you want, and you don't have to account to me. But the least you can do is have the decency to divorce her."

Derek felt his blood pounding in his veins. "That's what you came up here to say, isn't it?"

"I'm sure a lot of people think you're crazy not to leave her, or at least to get a little on the side...."

"Mark!"

"Maybe even I would in your shoes. But who's looking out for Mom's interests? If I don't, who will?"

"I understand how you feel, but you're assuming an unnecessary burden."

"Do you have a better solution?"

"I wouldn't do anything to hurt Margaret."

"You're saying you're going to look out for her?"

"I'm saying if the time comes that I can't be a husband to her, I won't."

Mark sat silently, studying him for a while. "I'm not sure that's good enough."

"I'm not going to divorce her just because I've discovered someone else I'm attracted to. These things happen. It's probably a miracle it didn't happen sooner. The question is where it will lead."

"So, where do you think it will lead?"

Derek pushed back his plate. "That's the problem. I'm

not sure. At the moment I'm *not* having a relationship with
Lara. She doesn't want one. It may be over between us, or
it may not. I don't know at this point. But I'll be honest
with you. I care for her very much.''

"Then maybe it's time you let go of Mom. I know you
don't care what I think and that you don't need my permission to have a fling. But you might as well know I've
already started taking responsibility for my mother—emotionally, anyway. Like I said before, I can't divorce her.
You can."

"Your mother is my responsibility, Mark."

"Bull."

"What do you mean by that? Just because someone else
has come into my life I've lost my rights?"

"I'm not talking about you. I'm talking about myself.
I'm not a kid anymore. True, Mom's married to you. But
she's *my* mother. I know you think I adjusted well to her
getting sick. I can't even remember how many times I heard
you saying how proud you were of me. But I'll tell you
something, it was a lot harder than I let on."

Derek kept his silence, letting the boy get out what he
had to say.

"When Mom first got real bad…when she had to go to
the nursing home, I used to lie awake at night worrying. I
was afraid she was going to die. I knew everybody does
eventually. But she was so young, and I didn't want her to
leave me.

"Once they'd taken her away, and there was just the two
of us, I knew I had a lot more responsibility. I worried
about what was going to happen to me. Even at fifteen, I
figured you'd leave eventually, and it would be just me and
her."

"Oh, Mark."

"That's no slam at you. To be honest, I'm surprised it

took you this long to realize how little you've got out of being married to her. And if I think about it, I don't blame you. Like I said, in your shoes I'd probably do the same.''

Mark's words cut deeply. Derek had had no idea how hard it had been for him. The loss of his mother was an obvious enough tragedy, but the extent of the inner turmoil came as a surprise. "So, all that time you seemed to be handling things well, you were really suffering."

He nodded. "I wasn't just worried. I guess I was resentful, too. Most moms were pushing their kids out of the nest and mine was lying there in bed, helpless, needing me. It made me feel guilty just wanting to be my own person, wanting to get away. But it wasn't her fault. And the more guilty I felt, the more resentful I became."

"I had no idea." Derek felt awful, knowing he'd been oblivious to Mark's needs. It wasn't much of a defense, he knew, but the fact was he'd been pretty absorbed in what Margaret's illness would mean to his own life. It hadn't been easy coping with the fact that he would be a widower in all but fact, and have sole responsibility for his stepson.

"I wasn't exactly aware what was going on at the time," Mark explained. "A lot of this has only become clear recently. I tell myself you've got to be feeling something similar. That's why I think you ought to divorce her."

Derek felt so selfish just then. He reached out and took hold of Mark's arm. "I hope you weren't afraid I'd abandon you."

"I don't know if I consciously felt that way. But...nothing's forever."

"That's not true, Mark. You're my son, the same as if you'd been born to me. You didn't think that once Margaret was gone I'd forget you?"

"Not like that. But hey, that's all in the past. I'm not a kid anymore."

"No, it's not in the past. I'm dealing with some of the same things you've struggled with. And they don't involve only your mother and me. Or Lara. They involve you, as well."

"Please don't lay that on me. I don't want your sympathy."

Derek got up and walked to the other side of the room. He leaned against a counter. His frustration was as strong as it had ever been since Lara Serenov had come into his life. "We seem to be going in circles," he said.

"What are you going to do? That's what I want to know. It's why I came up here."

"I'm not divorcing your mother. One doesn't resort to divorce simply because a spouse becomes inconvenient. Besides, I still love her."

They looked at each other for several moments. Then Mark got up and wandered into the front room. When Derek joined him, he was looking out the window at the cove. "I guess I'll go find Marcy." He glanced at Derek.

"We may not have decided anything, Mark, but we both had something to get off our chests, and we did. That's good."

The boy nodded.

"You and Marcy enjoy the beach. I'll try to get some work done. Then tonight I'll take you both out to dinner."

Mark smiled. It was the most relaxed and friendly he'd seemed. "Okay. That's not a bad offer."

Derek went to the window after Mark had gone out. He watched until the boy disappeared over the edge of the bluff. Then he turned and looked around the room. His eyes came to rest on Lara's book of poems. With a sigh he went in to clean up the lunch dishes.

LARA PARKED down the street from the Mendocino Hotel and hurried along the wooden sidewalk toward the entrance. She was supposed to meet Shirley Wilsey at seven and she was twenty minutes late. Inside, she found her friend sitting in the bar. A guy was with her. He looked vaguely familiar, but Lara couldn't place him.

When she came up to the table, the man got to his feet and Shirley introduced him. His name was Jim Cole, and he had come to a couple of Literary Guild meetings with Shirley a year or so earlier. They had been dating and, when the relationship ended, Jim stopped coming to the meetings.

"I haven't seen you for a while," Lara said.

"No," Jim replied, "I've been down in the Bay Area the past six months. I just got back recently."

It took Lara only a minute to figure out that Shirley was really pleased to see Jim again. When he left them to get a pack of cigarettes at the bar, Shirley let it slip that he'd invited her to a party that evening but that she'd refused because of her dinner date with Lara.

"If you want to go with him, don't stay because of me, for heaven's sake."

"Lara, I couldn't go off and leave you," she protested without much conviction. "Besides, if he's really interested, he can call me."

"Why play games? And why waste a perfectly good evening?"

When Jim came back, Lara instantly complained of a headache, saying if Shirley didn't mind she might skip dinner and go on home. Shirley protested it wasn't true, and told Jim not to believe a word Lara said.

"Hey, why don't you both come?" Jim said, lighting a cigarette. "There'll be food. It'd save you the cost of dinner."

But Lara didn't want to tag along. "Seriously," she said,

"you two go on. I'll finish my wine, browse in the bookstore for a while and head on home. I mean it."

Shirley and Jim exchanged looks. It took a few more minutes of insisting, but Lara finally got them out the door together. Watching them go, she was shocked to see Derek Gordon in the hotel lobby. He was with a young couple, a nice-looking boy and a tall blond girl with spiky hair. They seemed to be going into the restaurant and hadn't yet seen her.

Lara stared at them as the maître d' approached Derek. It was the first time she'd seen him since the night they'd made love.

Lara was staring so intently she didn't notice at first the boy was watching her. Flustered, she glanced away. When she looked back, he was saying something to Derek, who turned her way. Their eyes met.

She didn't know what to do. When he started walking toward the bar, her heart began pounding. He came up to the table and stopped, resting his hand on the chair Jim Cole had vacated.

"May I intrude?"

"Hello, Derek."

"You looked lonely sitting here. I couldn't help coming over." There was a wistful, vaguely sad look in his eyes.

"I just had a drink with Shirley Wilsey and a friend of hers."

"Are they coming back?"

"No."

"My son, his girlfriend and I were about to have dinner. Why don't you join us?"

"Thanks, but no. I was about to head home."

"Have you eaten?"

"No, but…"

Mark and the girl were at the entrance to the bar and

Derek signaled for them to come over. "At least let me introduce you," he said to Lara.

Mark Gordon seemed a bit dour as Derek made the introductions. The girl was more friendly.

"I suggested Lara join us for dinner," Derek said to them, "but she's afraid of intruding."

"No, why don't you join us?" Marcy said. She turned to Mark then, realizing she'd spoken out of turn.

"I'm sort of a third wheel in this group," Derek offered. "Four makes a better dinner party than three."

Lara looked at Mark, who nodded. "Yeah, Derek's in danger of getting bored."

Lara got up, accepting the invitation as much to end their importuning as for any other reason. Derek had been kind to her, and it seemed a safe way to satisfy his obvious desire to see her. He took her arm as they followed Mark and Marcy to the entrance to the restaurant. She was aware of his touch, realizing his effect on her hadn't diminished in the days they'd been apart.

They were shown to a table and, as they took their seats, Lara observed her dinner companions, sensing a strained atmosphere she hadn't fully picked up on at first. She wondered if she'd made a mistake. But Derek didn't let the tension linger for long. He was effusive, directing the conversation through the get-acquainted stage, seeming to care that things go smoothly.

After initial hesitation, Marcy became chatty. Only Mark was taciturn.

Lara tried to engage him in conversation. "I was the one you spoke with on the phone that night you called," she said.

"Yes, I know. Derek already explained why you were there."

"It was kind of him to take me in. I didn't have any other place to go."

"He's like that," Mark said with a glance at his stepfather, "always taking in strays."

"Lara was hardly a stray," Derek rejoined sharply. "You'd have done the same thing in my shoes."

Mark shrugged.

"I was a stray," Lara offered, trying to smooth things. "And Derek is kindhearted."

There was a brief lull in the conversation that neither Derek nor Marcy filled. "You haven't met my mother, have you?" Mark asked.

Lara felt the sting of the question and lowered her eyes. "No."

"Of course she hasn't," Derek said pointedly.

"She's not much to look at now," Mark went on, ignoring his stepfather, "but before she was sick, she was really a very nice person...attractive, intelligent. She had a pretty good marriage."

"Mark," Derek said under his breath, "this is completely unnecessary."

"Look," Lara cut in, "you came here to have a nice family dinner together, and I'm spoiling it." She scooted her chair back. "I think it would be best if I left. I was planning on going home anyway."

"Don't leave," Marcy said.

But Lara was standing. She glanced at Derek, who looked sick at heart. "I'm sorry," she said softly to them all, and headed for the door.

She was already out the front door of the hotel when she heard Derek behind her. He took her arm, stopping her.

"Listen, Lara, I'm awfully sorry about that. I thought Mark was more mature. I thought if he actually met you, he might see you as a person and it might soften his hostility."

"I can't blame him," Lara said, taking a ragged breath. "I shouldn't have agreed to join you." Her eyes had filled with tears and she wiped the corner of one. "I guess he knows about us."

"Yes," Derek said.

"Then it's not his fault. It's mine."

"Of course it's not. And I feel terrible for letting it happen."

"Don't be silly."

She turned to go, but Derek took her arm again. "Maybe I was being selfish in wanting you with us. But seeing you alone there, I couldn't resist."

"You know what your problem is?" she said, smiling despite her tears. "You *do* take in strays."

Derek was looking at her wistfully. He didn't respond. But he took her hand, his face full of emotion. She felt a lump rise in her throat, remembering his expression when he had come into her room to make love with her.

"I've missed you," he whispered. "I've only known you for a little while, but I really miss you."

Lara shook her head. "We've both been through a lot. It's the circumstances. Don't be deceived by things, Derek. Don't." She gave his fingers a squeeze and freed her hand, backing away a bit.

"I want to see you again," he said.

"No."

"Mark's problem has nothing to do with you."

"What I'm feeling has nothing to do with Mark. He's entitled to his feelings, and so am I. I made a mistake sleeping with you. I don't want to repeat it."

"That isn't what I'm asking."

"There's no point in titillating each other."

"I didn't have that in mind, either."

"What we have in mind, and what happens, don't necessarily relate. I'm not blaming you. I take responsibility for what I do. That's why I don't want to see you again."

"You don't mean that."

"Yes I do, Derek."

He looked terribly sad.

Lara stepped forward and kissed him lightly on the cheek. "Despite everything," she said, her eyes gleaming with tears, "I don't regret what happened. But it's over. And now you've got to let go of me. Your son needs you. And so does your wife."

CHAPTER ELEVEN

SUNDAY MORNING DEREK SAT at his typewriter. He'd written a page and not much more. Mark and Marcy had gone to one of the redwood parks for a hike before heading back to Berkeley, leaving him to work on his book. But he was preoccupied with Lara.

It had been a tense two days. Mark had apologized when Derek returned to the restaurant that night, but that didn't do Lara any good. She was the one who'd been hurt, and Derek told him so.

For the balance of the weekend, the kids were mostly off exploring along the coast while he wrote. Saturday night he had made dinner for the three of them, and afterward they sat around the fire until he went to bed, leaving Mark and Marcy to enjoy each other's company alone.

Derek was wondering again whether he'd mishandled the situation with Lara, when he heard Mark's truck pull up outside. A moment later he and Marcy came in the door, their cheeks rosy from the brisk outdoor air.

"We've got to get going," Mark announced.

"Want some lunch first?"

"No," the boy replied, "we'll grab something on the way back."

"I'll pack," Marcy said, going off to the guest room.

Mark wandered over to the desk where Derek sat. "Do you have a minute or two so I can talk to you?"

"Sure."

"Want to go outside?" Mark asked. "Maybe walk down to the beach?"

"Okay."

They went out, making their way down to the small beach ringing the cove. Mark dropped to the sand, and Derek sat beside him. For a moment they watched the waves lapping onto the shore. Half a dozen gulls swooped and soared above them. Mark leaned forward, took a stone and tossed it in the general direction of the birds.

The gesture reminded Derek of Mark as a boy, when he and Margaret would take him to the beach. Now, instead of two of them together watching Mark, it was Derek alone. Instead of a lad of twelve, Mark was a young man of twenty. So much time had passed, so much had changed.

Mark still hadn't said anything, and Derek knew he was searching for the right way to express whatever was on his mind. Finally, his stepson turned to him.

"I've been thinking about what I did the other night at the restaurant," he said, "and it's been bothering me."

"Forget it. You've apologized. There's no point in brooding over it."

"I apologized to you, but Lara's the one I offended."

"She understands. She as much as said so."

"Still, it's been bugging me. It was a pretty childish thing to do. If you don't mind, I'll call her before I go."

"That's considerate of you, but it's really not necessary."

"Don't try to spare me, Dad. I've got to right my own wrongs. The only reason I'm discussing it with you is to make sure I don't compound the problem. I really don't know how things stand between the two of you, but I sense they aren't going too well."

"You're right about that."

"Because of what I did?"

''No. You don't have anything to do with it. But wanting to talk to Lara is very thoughtful. I appreciate it.''

''Mind if I call now? We've got to get going. I'd just as soon do it before heading home.''

''Sure. Suit yourself.''

After a few more minutes together they went back to the cottage. Marcy had packed their things and was reading a magazine. Mark told her he was going to make the phone call and, to give him some privacy, she helped Derek take their bags out to the truck. Mark waited until they were outside, then dialed. The phone rang for quite a while before Lara answered.

''Marcy and I are heading for home in a few minutes,'' he explained. ''But before leaving Mendocino, I wanted to apologize to you for what I said the other evening.''

''There's no reason to, Mark. Your feelings are understandable.''

''Still, I was acting like a kid. You didn't deserve that, and I want you to know I'm sorry.''

''You're very thoughtful. I hope Derek didn't put any pressure on you to call.''

''No, not at all. I asked if he minded, that's all. I didn't want to cause any more problems between you than I already have.''

''You haven't caused any problems, honestly.''

''I know things aren't going well between you,'' Mark said, choosing his words carefully, ''but don't blame Derek. My mother's dying, and she won't keep him tied down much longer. It's just a question of how long it will take.'' It hurt him to utter the words, but they were the truth. And even if Lara had been told the same thing by Derek, she ought to hear from someone else, too. ''I don't know if it makes a difference,'' he added.

"You may not believe this," Lara said, her voice husky, "but I feel a great deal of compassion for your mother."

The words made him suddenly emotional. And, though it was difficult, Mark knew Lara was sincere and that she meant to be constructive. "I'm sorry about what you've been going through, your problem with your ex-husband," he said, wanting to find something positive to say.

"Thanks."

"And I hope you'll forgive me for what I said."

"No need. There's no forgiveness required." Lara was silent for a moment. Then she asked, "How old are you, Mark?"

"Twenty."

"I want you to know how refreshing it is to talk to someone who can come to terms with his feelings in a constructive way. My former husband is thirty-one, and he's still incapable of that."

"Apologizing is the obvious thing to do."

"You have every reason to feel hostility toward me, and I very much appreciate what you've said."

"What's happened to my mother has been rough for our entire family," Mark said. "It's hard not to let it spill over."

"I can understand that. But I want you to know I'm determined not be part of the problem."

He would have liked to reassure her that she wasn't before they said goodbye, but they both knew that she was. Derek was married and Lara was the other woman. There was no denying that.

Sighing, Mark went outside. Marcy was sitting in the truck. Derek was talking to her. They both looked at him apprehensively.

"I apologized and she was gracious," he announced.

Derek looked relieved, but Mark didn't know whether to

express his suspicion that the call had only served to complicate things with Lara, or not.

"If nothing else, I cleared the air," he said lamely.

Derek clasped his shoulder, smiling, and Mark got into the pickup. They said goodbye, and Mark swung the vehicle around and drove up to the highway. He waited for the traffic to clear, but even when it did, he didn't go. Instead he sat, staring across the road, thinking about what had happened.

"You all right?" Marcy asked.

"Yeah," he said unconvincingly.

"What's wrong?"

"I have a sneaking suspicion I screwed things up."

"What do you mean?"

"I think coming up here, seeing Lara and talking to her just now, hardened her feelings against my stepfather. I think because of me she sees him as a family man, whereas before it was only an idea."

"Why? What did she say?"

"That she was determined not to be part of the problem."

"That doesn't mean anything. She could have felt that way before."

"Maybe," he said. With that he turned the truck onto the highway. A car was coming pretty fast and so he punched the accelerator, making the tires screech as the pickup sped away.

Marcy reached over and stroked his arm. "You can't take responsibility for everything, Mark. Whatever happens between them won't be because of you."

"Maybe you're right." He tried to smile. "I may be blowing things out of proportion."

"Anyway, why this sudden compassion for your stepfather? I thought his relationship with Lara upset you."

"It did. And I was mad at Derek for leaving Mom. But I'm beginning to see it's inevitable. So now I want to spare us all the pain of dragging things out. I want him to divorce her and get it over with."

"Does Derek know that?"

"Yeah, I told him. But he's into denial. He's not ready to face things."

"Maybe he's not sure. He did love your mother, didn't he?"

"Yes, and he claims he still does."

"The poor guy's in a tough spot," Marcy said sympathetically. "If I were you, I'd cool it. Let him work things out his own way."

Mark thought about her comment as he stared up the highway. "I don't know if I can do that. Whenever I think of Mom, it tears me up. Whether she's conscious or not, she doesn't deserve this."

Marcy leaned over and put her head on his shoulder. Though she didn't say anything, he knew she understood what he was going through, and it touched him. Then she kissed him on the neck and said, "Thanks for the nice weekend, Gordon. Even though there were problems, I had a good time."

Mark glanced over at her and tweaked her nose. He could tell she was doing what she could to lighten his burden. He appreciated her a lot just then. He needed a friend. The fact was, his family was in a hell of a mess and he might have to take the lead in solving the problem.

DEREK LET A FEW DAYS pass without trying to contact Lara. He didn't want to cause any more unhappiness. It was pretty obvious she didn't want to expose herself to temptation, but it was equally obvious to him that he needed to see her. The only question was under what circumstances and when.

He had pretty well decided to let their meeting come about as naturally as possible, perhaps at the Literary Guild, when a letter from the district attorney's office in Ukiah arrived. The case against Steve Adamson was being prepared, and the DA wanted to interview Derek to determine if his testimony might be used in the trial.

He had forgotten that Lara still had that ordeal to face. It wouldn't be easy for her, and it was something they would have to go through together. He wondered if, under the circumstances, she might permit his help and support.

Derek went to the phone and called the district attorney's office. The DA, Carolyn Buchanan, asked him to come in at his earliest convenience for an interview.

"Will you be talking with Lara Serenov soon?" he asked.

"She'll be meeting with me Wednesday. Why?"

"It occurred to me I might come in at the same time. We could share the ride that way."

"That would be fine, but I would prefer to speak with you separately."

"I understand. Can we schedule my interview either before or after Lara's appointment?"

"Certainly."

They set a time, and Derek decided to call Lara right away so that she could plan on going with him, if she was willing. He dialed her number, but there was no answer.

He tried several times before finally reaching her late that afternoon. "I was afraid you'd been eaten by the bears," he said.

"No," she replied, ignoring his halfhearted attempt at humor. "I was down by the creek with my tape recorder and notepad. The weather's been so nice."

"It has been, hasn't it?"

There was silence on the line.

"How have you been, Lara?" he asked.

"Okay. I've gotten back into a routine."

"I've thought about you."

"You shouldn't have."

He didn't like talking around the issue. "I can't let you go that easily," he said.

"You really haven't any choice, Derek."

There was a distance, a coldness in her voice that he didn't like, even though he understood it. "That isn't why I called. I spoke with the district attorney this morning. I have an appointment on Wednesday, about the same time you do. I thought we could ride over to Ukiah together."

"I don't think that's a very good idea."

"Listen, we went through the business with Steve together, and we'll be going through the trial together, too. You can't pretend I don't exist."

She didn't reply immediately. "That's not it."

"What are you afraid of?"

"Nothing."

"Then let me help you. Let me be with you. I'm not Steve, Lara. I'm on your side. Remember?" He listened, waiting for her to reply.

"I don't mean to seem ungrateful. I just don't want to make another mistake."

She was quiet for a long time, and he knew she was struggling with his proposal. He let the silence hang, hoping she would relent.

"Okay," she said in the end. "If it's that important, I'll ride over with you. But please don't make it hard for me."

"I respect your feelings. And I'll make it as easy for you as I can."

LARA SPENT an uneasy few days until Wednesday morning finally came. Then she became truly nervous. She looked into her eyes in the bathroom mirror as she applied pale peach lip pencil to her mouth. Her hair was up in a simple, elegant twist. She wore a white silk blouse and the skirt to her navy suit—the only suit she owned.

She was sorry now that she had agreed to go with Derek. It would have been so much easier if she hadn't. But as always, the man tore her in two directions.

She blotted her lips lightly, then secured a loose tendril of hair. She heard a car outside, so she put on her suit jacket and went downstairs.

When she opened the front door Derek was standing there, a smile on his face. He was wearing a sport coat and tie, and appeared more formal than she had ever seen him. Much as she hated to admit it, he was a welcome sight.

"Hi," he said.

Lara struggled to suppress the pleasure that must have been evident on her face. "I'm ready. I just have to get my purse."

She went back inside. On the table next to her purse was an envelope. Inside was the poem he had asked her to write.

When she returned to the porch, Derek was gazing out at the woods. It surprised her how serene he seemed. It was an alluring quality.

She handed him the envelope. "It's the poem you asked for."

Derek fingered it almost affectionately. "When can I read it?"

"Later. When you're alone, if you don't mind."

"You feel shy about it?" he asked.

"It's the first thing I've done specifically for someone. So, yes, I guess I do feel shy."

Derek placed the envelope in his inside pocket. "All right. I won't embarrass you."

They got into his car, Derek holding the door for her before going around to the driver's side. She glanced at him as he slid into the seat. Their eyes met and she looked away. She felt his gaze a moment longer before the car started.

They went down the drive toward the road. Derek let the silence continue. There was a vague tension in the air, but at the moment Lara preferred no conversation.

"Is this going to be hard for you?" he asked after a while. "Having to go over everything that happened with Steve, I mean."

"I've tried not to think about it. Maybe I've been repressing things, but I want it all to fade into the past as quickly as possible."

"That won't be easy. You have the trial to get through."

"I know that. And I'll do what I have to. But I try not to dwell on what happened. I'm so grateful Deputy Stiles got there before Steve really hurt me. I don't even want to think what he'd have done if...he'd had the chance."

"To the extent that you'll let me, I'd like to be there for you," Derek said.

His comment made her feel good. Derek was the kindly professor again—the man who had originally come to her rescue, the one she let herself fall for. Still, apprehension went through her at the thought of his compassion. It was so easy to be lulled by his presence. But it was dangerous, too. She kept telling herself that. Over and over.

"Would that upset you?" he asked, bringing her back into the conversation.

She shifted uncomfortably. "Maybe it's something I should deal with on my own."

"Whatever you want."

They followed the highway through the mountains. It was a secondary road, twisting slowly through the wooded ravines and around steep mountain slopes.

Derek said very little. He was giving her space. And she was grateful. But still, she had been wondering what was going on in his life—particularly between him and his stepson.

"It was very sweet of Mark to call," she said. "It was a mature thing to do."

"He's taken my leaving Berkeley harder than I thought. And I found out some things I hadn't known before. He's suffered over his mother more than I realized."

"And our relationship has compounded the problem," she said.

"That's something Mark has to work out for himself. And I'm confident he will. We talked quite a bit."

"I hope he knows what happened between us was just a slip, a transitory thing."

"He's aware of your feelings," Derek said succinctly.

They drove for a while in silence.

"I don't want to hurt you, either," she whispered.

Derek reached over and took her hand. His touch made her feel weak and good at the same time. Already her resolve was beginning to crumble.

They arrived in Ukiah and headed for the courthouse. After a short wait in the outer office, the district attorney, an attractive brunette with a pleasant but businesslike manner, came out to greet them. Carolyn Buchanan was perhaps a couple of years older than Lara, tall and rosy-cheeked. She wore a gray suit and black pumps. She shook each of their hands and took Lara into her office first.

They had barely disappeared down the hall when Derek reached into his pocket and took out the envelope Lara had given him. He tore it open.

Her poem was handwritten, a couple of pages long, in large flowing script. The verse was simple and straightforward. It was about his tree on the point, but he also decided it was about him, the way she saw him. There were allusions to adversity—storms and gales—but also to beauty and tranquillity. The tree was resplendent with nobility, a nobility built on its long life and continuity.

The poem contained no feminine force, no suggestion of Lara, except as observer. The distance implicit in that saddened him, but he knew it was reflective of her state of mind.

Still, he liked the poem, reading it over several times. It was a personal observation, intended only for his eyes. He would treasure it, just as he treasured the brief hours he'd been with Lara herself.

CAROLYN BUCHANAN WAS SEATED behind her desk, a yellow legal pad in front of her. A tape recorder was running as she and Lara spoke. She had explained that it would help in preparing her lines of questioning at the trial.

The attorney indicated she had gone over the police reports. Because the accused was a former spouse of the victim, she wanted some background information, asking Lara to tell her about when she and Steve first met.

Lara had known there'd be questions like that. Still, actually having to address the past aroused her emotions more than she had anticipated.

She began at the beginning, when she and Steve were in high school. She described their brief marriage and the traumatic way in which it had ended. When she got to the events of the past month, Carolyn Buchanan stopped her occasionally for clarification on certain points.

The attorney took notes from time to time, but mostly she listened, carefully watching Lara, probably measuring the credibility of her words and manner. When Lara had finished answering questions, the attorney leaned back in her chair, steepling her fingers like a judge.

"How are you holding up, personally?" Carolyn asked.

"What do you mean?"

"Rape and assault cases are very difficult to try. They're hard on victims. Obviously there's a lot of stress, facing your attacker in the courtroom. It can be extremely difficult for a woman."

"I've thought about that. I think I'll be all right."

"Going through a trial can be a healing process, too," Carolyn observed. "When a victim has been degraded and defiled, she feels helpless. Bringing her assailant to justice can have a therapeutic effect. It can work for you, if you let it."

"I've heard about that. Fortunately, the deputy arrived before Steve raped me. I didn't have to suffer that."

"You're lucky. But control over your body has been taken from you in an attempted rape, too. I want to get a feel for your mental and emotional state on this point. It isn't critical to our case in a legal sense, but I see my job as not only representing the people against the accused, but also as an advocate for the victim. It's a personal aspect of my work."

"I appreciate that. I really do. I have to admit I was pretty upset at the time, but I don't believe I was seriously affected. I've had a few bad dreams, but no terrible nightmares. My life is otherwise fairly normal."

"Good." Carolyn Buchanan brushed back her hair and contemplated her. "There's another reason I brought all this up, though."

"What's that?"

"Steve Adamson sent word to us that he'd like to talk to you."

"Why?"

"I'm not certain, but it's probably to ask you to drop the charges, or at least not to cooperate with us in the prosecution."

"Does he think he can charm me out of it?" Lara asked bitterly.

"I'm not sure how this cuts," Carolyn said, "but there's another wrinkle that's been added in the last week. Adamson's wife has come back into the picture. She's visited him in jail, but I don't know much more than that."

"Mary Beth has seen him?"

The attorney nodded. "Adamson's lawyer said there's been talk of reconciliation, but I don't know how much stock to put in it. Defense counsel likes to have the loyal wife standing behind her man in this kind of case. I guess eventually we'll find how much is behind it. For now it amounts to Adamson wanting to talk to you."

"Do I have to see him?"

"No. Only in the courtroom. The choice is yours."

"Then I won't," Lara said without hesitating. "If I could, I'd never see him again as long as I live."

"I'll pass that on to Adamson's lawyer." The attorney leaned forward. "I don't have anything else, unless you have some questions."

Lara shook her head.

"Well, then, I'd like to speak to Mr. Gordon."

Lara got up and went back into the waiting room. Derek rose as she approached. His eyes searched hers. She tried to smile, to let him know she was all right. Derek took her arm, squeezing it reassuringly. Then he followed Carolyn Buchanan into her office.

Lara dropped onto the couch. The news that Mary Beth had seen Steve came as a surprise, and Lara wondered if somehow he had conned her into feeling sorry for him.

From what she knew, Mary Beth's relationship with him wasn't a whole lot better than her own had been. Lara hoped, for Mary Beth's sake, that she hadn't been taken in by him a second time.

WHEN DEREK FINISHED his interview, he and Lara left the county building together and walked to the car. The day was warm, and the shade of the elms and maples lining the quiet street was welcome. The leaves had begun to change color and the air had that rich, autumn smell to it.

Derek glanced over at her as they walked. "Everything go okay?" he asked.

"Yes. Did Ms Buchanan tell you about Mary Beth?"

"Yeah. I don't know the woman but it kind of surprised me."

"It surprised me, too. I don't really know her, either, so I can't say what would have motivated her."

"People do strange things in a time of crisis," he said.

"I hope she doesn't do anything to make it harder on herself."

"You can't worry about it, Lara. There are some things you can affect, and others you can't. There's no point in worrying about what you can't change."

They came to the car and Lara took Derek's arm. "Are you anxious to get home?" she asked.

"Not especially. Why?"

"Could we walk for a while before we head back?"

"Sure," he said. "If you want."

"I'd just like to get a little exercise, clear my mind."

They started walking slowly up the street past the small houses, all looking as though the occupants were napping, or waiting at the kitchen table for a pie to finish baking. Ukiah was a place where time was measured by the ticks of a living room clock.

"You seem a little anxious," Derek said after they'd walked a block.

"Maybe I am. I'm wondering why Steve wanted to talk to me. Do you think I did the right thing by refusing to see him?"

"Sure. You don't owe him anything. If I saw him, I'd want to shoot him."

"That's the way I felt, but I'm not so sure now."

They rounded the corner, passing a little girl on a tricycle. Derek tousled the child's curls as they went by. "Don't worry about it. It's time to think about yourself."

"I don't believe you mean that—not completely. You think about your son and wife. You consider their needs and your responsibilities to them. Why should I forget about others?"

"That's different. You don't owe Steve a thing."

"Maybe not now, but I'm starting to wonder if there haven't been too many people in my life that I've cut off. Steve was understandable, granted, but there's my father. We have no relationship to speak of. And you. Look what's happened to our friendship."

Derek put his arm around her shoulders in a friendly way. "You put me in the awkward position of defending you against myself. It's hard to say you're entitled to do what you did, but to be honest, I have to admit you are." He massaged her shoulder before letting his arm drop.

"I appreciate you saying that," Lara said.

"But that takes nothing away from my feelings for you. The fact is I care for you very much, and I don't want to fight that anymore."

Derek glanced at her, to gauge her reaction. Surprisingly, her expression remained thoughtful. She was looking ahead, down the sidewalk, though he could tell she was rolling his words through her mind. She was so desirable, so lovely, that he wanted to touch her again. He wanted to kiss her. But he didn't. They continued strolling.

Finally she turned to him. "I guess I don't want to fight it anymore, either. I'm reluctant to admit it, but I'm tired of being alone. Still, it's hard letting go of defenses you've built up over the years."

"Sometimes it's not easy knowing when to fight and when to surrender to your feelings."

She gave him a smile of appreciation for his understanding. Derek took her hand then, interlocking his fingers with hers. They came to the next corner and turned again. She held his hand tightly.

"I don't know why," she said, "but I feel better."

"So do I."

They strolled a bit farther before she said, "I've decided there's something I'd like to do before we start back. My father's ranch is only half an hour or so from here, and I'd like to see him. Would you mind if we drove up to Willits? If it's not convenient, or you'd rather not, it's okay."

"No, I don't mind at all. I'd be happy to drive you up."

Lara beamed. "I should probably let him know we're coming."

"We can stop at a pay phone."

Derek noticed a bounce in her step. It was as though something very important had just happened, and he couldn't help but share her joy.

CHAPTER TWELVE

IN A FEW MINUTES they were on the Redwood Highway, headed north. They stopped at a service station on the edge of Ukiah. While Derek waited, Lara went to the phone booth. He watched her, noticing that the impression she gave in a suit, with her hair up, was unlike the one he was used to. But she didn't look unnatural. To the contrary, she was showing a different side of herself—a measured, thoughtful woman spiced with equal amounts of maturity and fresh innocence.

After a few minutes she returned to the car. "He said fine, come on up," Lara said.

Derek didn't know why she would have questioned her welcome, even if the relationship with her father had been difficult.

Lara was silent on the drive up the broad agricultural valley. She seemed a bit tense, but eager. When they neared Willits she directed him on a series of side roads. Finally they pulled into a long driveway that divided an orchard, coming eventually to a comfortable-looking farmhouse, shaded by tall trees.

As Derek and Lara climbed out of the car, a tall slender white-haired man of about sixty came out on the porch. Despite the heat, he wore a long-sleeved work shirt and long pants, both clean and pressed. He was sober faced, but nodded in greeting.

Lara approached him self-consciously. They exchanged

a few words and she introduced Derek. "This is my father, Nikolai Serenov," she said.

Derek saw blue-green eyes like Lara's under the man's heavy brow. They shook hands, but Nick Serenov's severe expression hardly changed. "Why don't we sit under the oak?" he suggested. "Ellen's mixing up some lemonade."

They walked across the grass to where some lawn chairs were set up in the shade of a mighty tree. Lara walked beside her father and Derek followed, noticing how tentative she appeared. It saddened him to think that parent and child should feel that uncomfortable in each other's presence. In the few minutes he had known Nikolai Serenov he could tell that he was not an easy man.

When they were seated, Nick asked Derek about his business and he explained what he did.

"I know it's prestigious what you do, Mr. Gordon, but as far as I'm concerned, colleges are mostly places where they spend tax dollars. I'd sooner see the money spent on roads and water projects."

"We all have our priorities," Derek said in reply.

"I take it this is just a social call," Serenov said to his daughter. "You aren't here to announce anything, are you?"

"We're good friends," Derek answered for her. He suspected it was easier for him to deflect the question than it would have been for Lara.

"Derek and I were in Ukiah on business," she said, "and I thought I'd take the opportunity to see you, since it's been a while."

The man nodded. "Been a year or two, anyway, hasn't it?"

Ellen Serenov, a woman in her fifties, came out the front door of the house, carrying a tray. She walked carefully across the grass. Though her general appearance was pleasant, her expression was as severe as her husband's.

"Hello, Lara," she said as she approached. "We were certainly surprised to get your call."

Lara introduced Derek to her stepmother. After small talk, the woman pleaded work to do in the house. She left the pitcher of lemonade and some glasses on a table, then went back inside. Lara poured them each some juice.

"I read in the papers you had trouble a while back," Nick said, as his daughter handed him a glass. "I figured everything must have worked out all right, because we never heard from you."

"Yes, it did. I saw no point in bothering you since there wasn't anything you could do."

"Don't want to say I told you so, but living alone in the woods is no place for a woman."

She glanced at Derek. "I know how you feel, Dad. But it's the life I've chosen."

Their alienation was apparent, and Derek couldn't help feeling sorry for them both. Lara was obviously struggling with it, though Derek still hadn't been able to figure out what she was up to.

While they drank their lemonade, Nick Serenov made conversation about the farm. Derek offered an occasional comment, but mostly he watched and listened, curious about the family dynamics. Lara, it seemed to him, was building toward something. Finally, she asked her father to walk out into the orchard with her so they could talk alone.

"I can go for a stroll," Derek offered.

"No, that's all right," Lara said, "I like to be on my feet while I'm talking. Do you mind, Dad?"

"Whatever you want is fine with me."

As Derek sipped his lemonade, the two went off. They walked slowly. He couldn't tell what was going on, but he surmised it was stressful for them both. They headed directly out between two rows of fruit trees, stopping occasionally to look at each other. Lara seemed to be doing most of the talking, at times in a very animated fashion.

They had gone at least a hundred yards into the orchard when they turned and headed back. Derek watched them closely, sensing that something important was happening. When they got to the edge of the trees they stopped. The conversation continued. Lara's voice carried, and he could hear the emotion in it, though he couldn't make out her words.

Derek couldn't be sure, but he thought much of the problem must concern the strain between Lara and her stepmother. He well knew the potential dangers in the stepparent role. He was thankful that his own relationship with Mark had been, in the past at least, a largely positive one.

Of course, even before the recent tension there had been ups and downs. They had the same problems other fathers and sons might have. But there had always been love, respect and acceptance between them.

Derek had been lucky, he knew. His success could be explained in part by the fact that he had not supplanted Mark's natural father. The opposite seemed to be the case with Lara. She probably never came fully to terms with the loss of her mother, and Ellen Serenov probably didn't help matters by the way she reacted. The pattern was all too familiar.

Fortunately, Margaret had understood both his own and Mark's needs and had helped to make the relationship work. He suspected that Nikolai had compounded the problem between his daughter and wife.

Soon Lara and her father returned to where Derek was sitting. Nikolai was ashen-faced. Lara's eyes were red, her cheeks streaked with tears. With barely a glance at Derek she picked up her purse and took a handkerchief from it, blowing her nose. Her father shuffled uncomfortably, his hands thrust into his pockets.

Lara looked at Derek. "We can go now."

He got up and, with a glance at her father, followed her to the car. Lara climbed in without waiting for either of them to open the door for her. Derek shook hands with Nick, then went around to the driver's side. As he climbed in he saw Lara's father move toward her window. Derek pushed a button to lower it.

"Lara," Nikolai said, "if there's blame in this business, it lies in me."

She sniffled. "Blame's not the issue. Maybe it wasn't fair to say the things I did, but I felt the need."

There was silence, then Nikolai reached his hand through the window, toward hers. Their fingers touched, and he pressed hers tightly. "Please come back," he said.

"I will," she whispered, barely controlling her emotion. Then she looked at Derek, beseeching him to go.

He started the car and they retreated down the drive. After they were off the property and headed along the paved road, Lara began sobbing, lowering her face to her hand. She wiped her nose with her handkerchief.

"You all right?" Derek said, reaching over and rubbing her hand.

She nodded.

"Sure?"

She took his fingers and pressed them against her cheek. "Thank you for being here," she murmured. "It helps knowing you care."

He squeezed her affectionately.

They had gone through Willits and were on the highway to Fort Bragg before she finally began to explain what had happened. He reached over and took her hand.

"I'm sorry to put you through a family thing like that," she said. "It wasn't fair."

"I'm concerned about you. I don't mind at all."

"There were some things I've never said to my father," she explained. "Some bitterness and resentment I've carried in my heart. Today I expressed it. I didn't know it would happen when I asked you to take me. Actually I was expecting something very different. I was going to try to make peace, explain my feelings. But once I started talking, it all came pouring out."

"This is a day for catharsis, isn't it?"

"It seemed to be the right thing to do. There were some things he needed to get off his chest, too. All these years he'd been afraid, and when I spoke my heart, it gave him permission to do the same. I can't say our relationship will be a lot different in the future, but we've opened the door a crack."

Derek slipped his hand behind her neck, caressing and massaging her taut muscles. She moaned contentedly.

"While you were in talking to the district attorney I read your poem," Derek said. "I liked it very much."

"It wasn't an easy one to write."

"Because of me?"

"Yes."

"I felt your detachment. But underlying it were some very strong feelings. I could sense you were fighting them."

"You saw that in my poem?"

"I may have been reading things into it a little," he confessed, "but I could certainly discern your feelings for me."

"That's because they're strong."

He touched the corner of her mouth with his finger.

"We've been through a lot together, haven't we?" she said.

"In a short span of time, more than a lot of married couples."

"You probably know as much about me as any person in the world—with the possible exception of Calle."

"You know," he said, pulling her hand to his lips and kissing it, "there's something about that I like a lot."

"Oh, Derek…"

"What's the matter?"

"I feel myself slipping again."

"Don't worry about it."

"I have to."

"No, you don't. There are some things you can do something about," he said. "Others, you can't. The important part is knowing which is which." He kissed her fingers once more.

"Isn't this something I should do something about?"

"No," he whispered, "not this."

LARA PEERED OUT the kitchen door at Derek, who was on the deck. He was standing at the railing and looking out into the darkness. It was a balmy, Indian summer evening and very still. The only illumination was from flickering candles on the table. Derek had proposed a candlelight dinner on the deck and Lara hadn't been able to deny that it would be lovely.

She turned from the doorway and put the champagne that he had bought into the silver ice bucket on the table. It was a wedding present from her father and Ellen, something she hadn't seen since the day she'd moved into the cabin. It was tarnished, but somehow that didn't seem to matter.

She packed ice around the bottle and added some water from the faucet. Then she dried off the bucket and examined it, running her finger thoughtfully along its rim. It was strange that today of all days she should be using it, perhaps for the first time ever.

She took the champagne out onto the deck. Derek turned around just then and caught her with his eyes. She stood still. He somehow seemed different to her, though she couldn't say why. The shadowed lines of his face, the way he held his mouth, struck her.

She had been aware of how attractive he was almost from the beginning, but she hadn't been as strongly drawn to him as she was now. Derek was like a fine portrait that had been wrapped in gauze, then revealed. Now she was able to look clearly in his eyes and see the way she was being seen. She liked the feeling.

"What a lovely sight," he said. "Come here." Derek held his hand out and she went to him, pausing only to put the ice bucket on the table.

He slid his hands under her jacket and rested them on her hips, holding her at arm's length so that he could look at her. Color crept into her cheeks, but she didn't turn from his gaze.

His expressive eyes methodically took in her features, one after the other, lingering especially on her blue-green eyes. The twitch at the corner of his mouth signaled his approval. Although Lara was shy and uncertain, there was a comfort in what was happening that she hadn't experienced with him before. Not with any man really. What had happened? What had changed?

"I like what I see," Derek said. "Do you?"

Lara nodded and touched his warm cheek with her fingertips. Their faces moved closer. Their mouths hadn't yet touched. She heard his breathing deepen. Derek was staring at her lips as though considering how he wished to take them.

She smoothly turned away then, easing herself from his arms. She took the champagne bottle from the ice bucket and handed it to him. Derek looked at her for a moment then tore off the foil and unfastened the wire. He aimed the bottle away and the cork popped loudly, sailing over the railing and into the darkness. He turned back in time to direct the surging bubbles into one of the glasses she had picked up.

When the flutes were filled they held them up to the candlelight. "It's been quite a day," she said softly.

"But the best part is just beginning, if we let it." He touched his glass to hers. "To you, Lara."

They drank their champagne at the railing, looking off into the dark coolness of the woods. To the east the moon was rising above the ridge line, highlighting the dark silhouette of the pines. The sky was getting brighter all around them, and they could even see the thin band of ocean on the western horizon.

He put his arm around her as they continued to drink the champagne and take in the majesty of the night. Lara eased close to his warm body.

"It's beautiful up here," he said, kissing her temple.

"I've never really shared it before. Not like this."

"I'm glad you decided to share it with me."

She looked up at him. She studied his face in the moonlight. "Are we wrong to do this? Are we being selfish?"

Derek's expression grew more sober. "I don't know. I'd like to say it's all right." He sighed deeply. "I suppose what matters is that no one's hurt."

"I don't like relying on the fact that your wife is too ill to know."

"I'd never hurt Margaret. And I take consolation in the fact that what I do won't affect her." He set his glass down and took her by the shoulders. "But we have a responsibility to each other, too—a responsibility not to be hurtful. That's what I'm most concerned about.''

"What about Mark?"

"Yes, he matters, too. But I can't live my life for him. He's starting to let go, anyway. If anything, he's pushing me away from his mother in an attempt to get a grip on the situation.''

Lara shook her head. Derek lifted her chin and brushed her lips lightly with his own.

"I won't hurt him, either," he said.

She turned away, put the champagne glass on the railing and gazed out into the moonlit woods. "I've never been a live-for-today person.''

"Neither have I. And I'm not suggesting we throw caution to the winds and damn the consequences.''

She glanced his way. "What are you suggesting?''

"I know I care for you, that we share something special. I guess I want to find out how special, and what it means.''

"You're saying we should follow our hearts, not our heads.''

Derek put his glass down and turned her toward him. "At least for a while, to see where it takes us. I'm willing. Are you?''

Lara drew a deep breath. "I don't know...."

He pulled her closer. Her thighs came up against his. Their lips touched. His breath, warmer than the balmy evening air, caressed her skin, and his scent filled her lungs with his distinctive musk. Their lips met again, but not for long, the feathery kiss made of breath as much as flesh.

Lara was suddenly overcome by excitement, just as she had been that night in his cottage. Physically he overwhelmed her, drew her, provoked her desire.

"You make it so hard to resist," she murmured into his lips. She pressed her breasts softly against his chest, her nipples hard and pulsing through her clothing. Their lips collided and parted—once, twice, a third time.

She started to turn away again but stopped. She wanted to be in his arms, but she was torn.

"How can you say no to this?" he whispered into her hair.

"I can't. That's the problem."

Derek took her face in his hands. "It's not a problem, Lara. Not unless we make it one." He kissed her fully but not forcefully. He was holding back a bit, letting her eagerness play out, though she could hardly help herself. He kissed her; she kissed him. It went on and on until their mouths parted breathlessly.

She pulled back to look into his eyes. They exchanged smiles and she straightened herself, moving back a few inches, though remaining within his reach. "You knew this would happen, didn't you?"

"I didn't know. But I was hoping."

"That I'd be too weak to resist?"

"That you'd see we have to be together."

"Maybe in my heart, I do." She reached out and touched his face. Then she stepped closer, running her fingers back through his hair. It was both an affectionate and possessive gesture. His eyes settled on her as they had at first. Only this time there were subtle signs of triumph playing at the corners of his mouth. They kissed.

"Let's finish our champagne," Lara said.

"That sounds like a good idea."

They took their glasses from the railing and went to the table. It was warm enough that she slipped off her suit jacket and hung it over her chair. They finished the champagne. The candles flickered as they stared into each other's eyes. After a while, Derek slid his hand across the table and captured hers.

"In spite of the things that have happened the past few weeks, there have been moments of wonderful, incredible happiness," she said, "happiness I've never known before. It's almost scared me."

"I understand that."

"I'm afraid, Derek."

He stroked her hand. "I know."

Lara felt warm inside. And she was happy. She glanced up at the moon. It was nearing the treetops. She looked down at Derek's hand holding hers.

"Are you hungry?" she asked.

"At the moment I'm feeling too good to be hungry." He drained his flute, then refilled both their glasses with champagne.

Lara took a long sip. "I'm beginning to get tipsy," she said, liking the feeling. "But I can't get drunk. I'll never get dinner on the table."

"I'll help you. Or we can skip it."

"I've already put all the shrimp in the salad. It won't keep."

"Then let's have the salad with the last of the champagne. We can save the steak until tomorrow."

His fingers trailed partway up her forearm, painting it with gooseflesh. Lara shivered.

"I think you were a masseur in a previous life. The things you do to me..."

"I enjoy beautiful things. I like to touch them."

Lara gazed at him over the rim of her wineglass, seeing, sensing, an extraordinarily passionate man beneath the gentleness she had come to associate with him. There was a whole side to Derek Gordon that she was only coming to appreciate.

"How could you have been lying dormant for years and

still be this way?'' she asked. ''Is making love like riding a bicycle? Once you've learned...''

He grinned broadly, his teeth gleaming in the candlelight. ''It's you.''

''I don't believe that for a moment. Tell the truth. You aren't a college professor. You're a notorious rake who preys on widows and divorcées, aren't you?''

Derek chuckled, throwing his head back. Then he looked her squarely in the eye. ''Yes.''

Lara laughed then. ''I thought so. I may not be terribly experienced, but I can spot a professional a mile away.'' She took a big sip of champagne.

When she put her glass down he ran the palm of his hand up the underside of her arm, bringing back the goose bumps. Her back and chest were alive with a tingling sensation. He couldn't rub the feeling away, but she wished he could. Lara took a ragged breath, letting her desire show in her eyes.

''How about if I get the salad?'' he said.

''I'll do it. I'm not too drunk to walk. I'm just feeling good, that's all.

''You were the chef. I'll be the waiter.''

He got up before she could protest, and disappeared inside. Lara leaned back with an audible sigh. Was the champagne making her fall in love, or was it simply numbing her resistance?

Derek came out a few minutes later with two plates piled high with salad. He placed one before her, taking the opportunity to lean down and kiss her behind the ear. It made her spine tingle. She purred and caressed the side of his face.

He took his place and refilled both their glasses. ''The moon's lovely tonight,'' Lara said, staring at it beyond his shoulder.

Derek turned around and peered at it. "It's beautiful."

"Last night I lay in bed watching it," she said wistfully. "It seemed sad. I was wondering what it would be like seeing you today, knowing I was eager, but that I shouldn't be."

"Did you think it would come to this?"

"No," she replied without hesitation. "Not for a moment."

They finished their salad and Derek poured the last drops of wine into their glasses. Observing him across the table, she decided his look mirrored her own deep-seated desire.

When she had drained the last of her drink, Derek blew out one of the candles and picked up the other. Taking her hand, he drew her into the cabin.

He said nothing, leading her up the stairs to the loft. He put the candle on the bedside table, then gathered her gently into his arms, hugging her against his body. Over his shoulder Lara saw their shadows, cast by the candlelight onto the vaulted ceiling. She observed the figures blending together above her: a man and a woman.

It was hard to believe the woman was she. But when Derek kissed her and she tasted his mouth and felt his strength, the reality struck her. She wanted him. With all her heart.

Lara stepped back to better see his face. A feeling of awe came over her—awe at the depth of her emotion, amazement that they were together in her loft, and alone, She backed against the bed and sat down abruptly. A slight smile touched his lips, and he sat next to her. Nuzzling her neck, he began to unbutton her blouse, his hand moving down the front of it.

"You're so lovely," he whispered. "So beautiful."

It was going to happen, she knew. And she felt powerless

to do anything, though because she couldn't risk getting pregnant, she had to stop him.

Still, she didn't resist as his fingers slid inside the opening of her blouse. He touched the flesh swelling over the top of her bra and she tensed. Remembering the feel of his lips and tongue, her nipples hardened.

Derek started to undress her then, but she managed to stop him. "This is not a safe time for me," she murmured. "I took a chance last time, but I can't again. I don't want—"

He touched his finger to her lips. "Don't worry, I have something. I figured you probably weren't on the pill."

"Really?"

He nodded, reassuring her.

She let him remove her blouse and skirt and bra. Then, as she lay back, he dropped beside her, kissing each breast in turn, running his tongue round and round her nipples then over the hardened peaks. The sensation made her womb pulse.

He got up and undressed then, all the while his eyes riveted to her. When he was stripped to the waist he sat on the bed again. By the candlelight, her gaze traced the line of his shoulders. Then she touched his chest, intrigued by the feel of his soft mat of hair.

He leaned over to kiss her neck. He drew his tongue along her taut flesh, sending flames along her spine. She moaned. "Oh, God, how you excite me, Derek."

"I want you," he said. "I want you so very much." He finished undressing, then took something from his pocket and turned away. Lara removed her panties, and when he was finished, he crawled beside her.

Lara watched his eyes, seeing hints of love as well as desire. Derek was not a frivolous person. This was for them both. What they could do with their bodies was evident. Now she wanted the reassurance of his love.

He held her against him for a moment before drawing his hand down her hip, molding her curves with his touch. She felt the swell of him against her. She was ready, but he seemed to be in no hurry.

"I could hold you like this forever," he said. When the moist tip of his tongue flicked her ear, she trembled.

Her entire body was alive, expectant. She wanted Derek to penetrate her. He was eliciting her to invite him; he was making her crave his intimate touch.

Derek drew his hand across her stomach. She tensed. Then he pulled his hand up the inside of her leg until it neared the delta between her legs. Her heart tripped in her chest.

She moaned, her breathing coming now in short, anxious gasps. His fingers tightened and slipped a bit higher, almost as though he were testing the strength of her need. She stiffened instantly, wanting to press his hand between her legs. But she didn't move.

The bedding under her filled her fists as he bent over and drew his tongue up the inside of her leg. She wasn't sure he was really going to kiss her there. And if he did, she wasn't sure that she could stand the pleasure.

He inched higher and higher, kissing the wet patches he had drawn. Lara lifted her head once to look at him. Her heart raced.

When his breath warmed her flesh she convulsed involuntarily and her legs parted wider. His tongue swept across her.

Lara clenched her teeth, moaning. She was balanced on the hard edge of desire and she knew that she couldn't let herself go, for if she did, the wonderful feeling would subside. When Derek licked her again, the same charge coursed her body. He began kissing and stroking her. It was so much, too much—she could hardly stand it.

Although she tried to stay at that miraculous point of pleasure, she felt her excitement begin to consume her. Tiny pulses began rippling in her core, and she couldn't help but convulse her hips. Just as her joy threatened to hurtle out of control, he stopped.

She lifted her head to look at him, but he began moving up over her body. Lara took his shoulders, kneading the muscles. He rested above her on his hands, his knees between hers. They searched each other's eyes.

His gaze penetrated her. Her lips parted in response. He pressed himself against her, and when he slid inside, she drew in a sharp breath, then arched to maximize the penetration.

Slowly he began to thrust. She saw his jaw tense and his lips part. Wanting his mouth, his tongue, his very breath, she pulled him down upon her. His tongue penetrated the deepest recesses of her mouth, and she submitted completely. She cried out, then Derek climaxed. For a long minute their bodies convulsed together, until they were spent and he collapsed on top of her.

After a minute his breathing recovered, and he murmured, "Are you all right?"

She nodded, because she couldn't speak.

"I didn't hurt you, did I?"

She shook her head. "No, I'm okay. But I don't think I'll ever be the same again." She saw him smiling in the candlelight.

"I hope that's good."

She kissed his shoulder. "Mmm. Wonderful."

He lifted his head so that he could see her. His eyes were liquid in the flickering light. "I love you, Lara," he whispered. "I love you so very much."

The words caught her off guard, though they shouldn't have. But she was moved by them. And grateful. She wanted his love. Badly. "Do you?"

"Yes, can't you tell?"

"I can tell you enjoyed yourself."

He kissed the fullness of her lip. "That was only the half of it."

Lara hugged him. She wanted to tell him she loved him. But she couldn't. Not yet.

When she released him, he rolled off her, though he was right beside her, one arm holding her close against him. "I want to spend the night with you," he said. "I know that's inviting myself, but I don't want to leave you."

"I don't sleep with anyone very well. I'm not in practice."

"I'm not either, so that puts us on equal ground."

They lay side by side. Derek took her hand and held it, his large thumb running over the back of it. Lara didn't move, savoring his affection.

"You're sure this wasn't a mistake?" she said.

"Positive."

"How can you be so sure?"

"Could anything that good be wrong?"

"That sounds like a philosopher's trick to me."

He gave a low laugh, then rolled onto his side, facing her. "I love you, Lara. It's that simple. There are no other words to describe the way I feel."

She squeezed his hand. "It's not simple, no matter what you say."

He put his arm around her, cuddling her against him. He inhaled the scent of her hair. "Time will tell, my darling. But I'm not worried."

"I wish I were that brave," she said, turning her head away.

"It has nothing to do with bravery."

"Yes, it does. You don't know how difficult it is to give yourself up to someone, especially when you've trained yourself not to."

"What's the worst that could happen?"

"I don't know."

"Think about it. What's the absolute worst thing?"

"I guess if I fell in love with you and you went away," she replied.

"Then where would you be? Where you are now, right?"

"No, not where I am now. Already I'm a different person. And the change can only become greater." She turned so she could see his face in the dim light of the candle. "The hardest part is knowing we shouldn't even be together, that you really belong to someone else."

Derek touched his finger to her lips. "You don't know the future, Lara. No one does."

CHAPTER THIRTEEN

LARA AWOKE IN A TANGLE of sheets. Her nightgown was twisted around her waist, her hair was across her face. She was lying diagonally across the bed.

The next thing Lara noticed was that Derek wasn't there.

She'd hardly slept during the night. It had been like sleeping with a bear, though she had to admit the companionship appealed to her. But all those elbows and legs would take some getting used to, not to mention the deep breathing that hovered somewhere between a purr and a snore.

But where was Derek now? She'd obviously gotten some sound sleep if he'd been able to slip away without her knowing it. Lara got up on her elbows and sniffed the air. Coffee. He was downstairs, perhaps making breakfast. It had been like that last time, at his place. He must think her terribly lazy, sleeping in every morning.

She looked at the clock. It was just after nine. That wasn't too bad, considering the night she'd had. And her head was throbbing—probably from a combination of champagne and lack of sleep.

She remembered the warmth of Derek's skin as they fell asleep in each other's arms. His body heat had almost been too much, but how nice that would be in the winter when the bed was always cold.

Fleeting recollections of their lovemaking went through

her mind. She colored at the thoughts. And she felt embarrassed when she thought of the things she'd said.

Lara sat up anxiously, clasping her knees. The smell of coffee was strong now. She had to dress and get downstairs. She took her jeans and a T-shirt into the bathroom, showered, dressed, dried her hair and went downstairs. Derek was sitting on the deck with a cup of coffee and a book from her collection.

"Good morning," he said, greeting her. He held out his hand and she went over to him. He pulled her down and kissed her. Then he swung a director's chair around beside him, for her to sit in.

The sun was above the treetops, bathing the deck in warmth. Lara had to squint through the brightness. "How long have you been up?"

"A couple of hours. How'd you sleep?"

"It fell somewhere between mud wrestling and the roller derby," she teased. "But the intermissions were nice."

"It's all rhythm, Lara. When you sleep with someone long enough, you learn to turn over at the same time, share pillows and avoid flying elbows aimed at snakes and alligators."

She was glad he was being lighthearted. It made it easier. "Do you wrestle alligators often?"

"Was I that bad?"

"I don't have a lot to compare you with."

He took her hand and kissed it. "I made some coffee."

"I smelled it first thing."

"Can I get you a cup?"

"No, I'll do it. Have you eaten?"

"I found some oatmeal. Hope you don't mind."

She grinned at him. "Not as long as you washed the pot."

"It's soaking."

They exchanged smiles and Lara went into the kitchen. She poured some coffee into a mug and returned to the deck. Derek was leaning back in his chair, inhaling the fresh morning air. She watched him, reading his contentment. The realization that he was her lover gave her a strange feeling, although at one level it made her so very happy. Did she love him? She decided that she probably did, though the implications concerned her.

How would she ever be able to put the fact that he was married out of her mind? She couldn't spend her life high on champagne. But being with him by the light of day wasn't as distressing as she had expected. Actually, it was rather comfortable. He took her hand again, stroking her fingers with his thumb.

"What are your plans for today?" she asked.

"I wanted to talk to you about that. Would you prefer to spend the night at my place, or shall I stay here again?"

The corners of her mouth twitched with amusement. "Are those the only choices?"

"I suppose we could meet somewhere in between." He poked his tongue into his cheek.

"Are you making some kind of not so subtle announcement, Derek?"

"I've already declared my love. This is the next step."

Lara contemplated him, watching the amusement playing on his mouth. He still had her hand, and didn't seem inclined to let it go. "I can't say what's bothering me, can I?" she said.

"You can say anything you want."

"But you'd prefer that I didn't."

"Do you like being with me?"

"Yes."

"Was last night so bad you wouldn't want to try again?"

"You mean sleeping with you?" she asked.

"Yeah, the mud wrestling."

Lara laughed. She tried to pull her hand away, but he seemed determined to make it his personal possession. "I would be willing to try again."

"Then let's. We'll make it a no-obligation deal for as long as you're happy with the arrangement. Money cheerfully refunded if not completely satisfied." He nibbled at her knuckles playfully, until with an effort she managed to yank her hand free.

"You're a devil in more ways than one!"

Derek laughed with that full-throated laugh of his. She had a strong physical sense of him, liking it when he was being playful. But the reality that she had become his mistress—his woman away from home—was inescapable. It wasn't an image she liked.

He'd said he loved her, but how? In what context? As a surrogate for his wife? In addition to Margaret? Lara was really the only woman in his life at the moment, but even so, his situation haunted her. And it would continue to haunt her, no matter what he said.

"So, decide," he said. "Do you want to suffer my company, or shall I suffer yours?"

"I think I'd rather stay home, if you don't mind."

"Could I go to my place and fetch my typewriter and some of my things? Perhaps a suitcase?"

She considered the question. "A small one."

Derek laughed again. "Agreed. A small one."

Lara took their mugs inside to get more coffee, and when she came out she had a duplicate front door key with her.

"Is this a vote of confidence?" he asked.

"It's for convenience. Returnable on demand."

"I must say, Lara, you don't plunge into things headfirst, do you?"

"I appear more worldly-wise than I am."

They drank their coffee companionably for a while. Then Derek announced he was going to his place to get his things. "Can I pick up some groceries while I'm out?"

"I thought I would do the shopping myself."

"We can make it a joint enterprise."

"How about next time?" Lara was a bit reluctant to give up her independence entirely, yet she didn't want to hurt his feelings. Having a houseguest was strange enough, let alone a sleeping mate and live-in lover.

"Right you are," he replied smoothly. "But would you object if I picked up a case of that champagne?"

"Expecting lightning to strike twice?"

He grinned. "A guy can hope, can't he?"

"Let's wait on the champagne, too."

He leaned over and kissed her on the cheek. "You drive a hard bargain, my love."

The fresh, now familiar scent of him was arousing. And when he lingered a bit, she made her mouth available so that he could kiss her. In seconds their slightly self-conscious banter had been transformed into a friendly intimacy. Sensations from their moonlit night returned.

When her arousal grew serious, Lara pulled away. "If you really need to do some work, maybe we'd better reconsider spending so much time together."

He shook his head. "No, it's character building."

"Whose character? Yours or mine?"

Derek tweaked her nose and got to his feet. He took the door key from the table and slipped it into his pocket. "I'll be gone a couple of hours. Sure there's nothing I can bring back with me?"

"Just your typewriter and a small suitcase."

He winked. "'Small' being the operative word." He kissed her again and headed out the door.

WHILE DEREK WAS AWAY getting his things, Lara ran out to the grocery store. She still had the steaks from the night before, so she didn't buy food for another dinner on the assumption that by tomorrow he would either be leaving or they would be buying groceries together.

On her way back to the Jeep, Lara passed an art gallery and noticed a watercolor seascape in the window. The picture reminded her of her comment that Derek ought to take up painting again. It also gave her an idea.

She was pretty sure that George Krumholtz kept a few art supplies in his store, so she went over to McGaffy's to see what he had. The stock was limited, but George did have two different-sized sets of watercolors, an assortment of brushes and paper. Lara bought the larger set of paints and some other art supplies, and hurried home.

Derek was already there when she returned, so she left the paints, brushes, drawing pad and paper in the Jeep, deciding to give them to him as a surprise after dinner. His things were stacked in a pile, so they discussed what physical arrangements would be most suitable for their work. They finally decided Derek could set up shop in the living room.

That afternoon, as he typed, Lara sat on the deck with her notepad, trying to summon her muse. The clickety-clack of the typewriter didn't do wonders for her powers of concentration, so after a while she gave up trying to write. She couldn't really blame Derek. It was probably her state of mind.

Learning to live with someone wasn't easy. No one had to tell her that. Yet she wondered if her fear was causing her to search for problems that might not be there. In any case, she was determined not to be passive. She had her life to live, even if she would be sharing her time with someone she cared for.

Late in the afternoon she took her tape recorder and note-pad and told Derek she was going down to the meadow to find some inspiration.

"Need any help?" he teased.

"Not that kind of inspiration!" she said, pinching his nose.

And so she took off, Derek tapping away in her living room. When she got to the meadow, she found it bathed in the warm rays of the afternoon sun. She sat on the log and closed her eyes as images of their lovemaking the night before came tumbling through her mind. She pictured their bodies entwined, the deep fulfillment she associated with Derek alone. Just thinking about it made her heart beat swiftly. A few deep breaths did little to calm her. It was Derek. What power he had over her if she let him!

It seemed useless to try to work. Derek was everywhere. He'd thoroughly invaded her world. Picking up her things, Lara headed back up the path to the cabin.

She found him in the kitchen, making a salad.

"I ran out of gas," he said, "so I thought I might as well do something productive."

She looked at him forlornly. "I never got my engine started today."

"What?" he said, taking her in his arms. "No creative juices?"

She shook her head.

"I think I know the solution. You must write love po-ems."

She gave him a telling look. "That's the most self-serving statement I've ever heard."

He laughed and spun her around the kitchen, holding her by the waist. She let her head fall back, giggling gleefully along with him. And then, when they stopped, he gathered her to his chest. Lara listened to the beating of his heart and wondered if such joy was really due her.

She fixed the steaks and they had a quiet meal at the kitchen table. Derek had a glass of red wine with his dinner, but after the champagne the night before Lara wasn't ready for any alcohol.

They did the dishes together and she showed him where she kept everything. They made little jokes about it, funny comments with double entendres.

When they finished cleaning up the kitchen, Lara made Derek sit in the living room while she went out to the Jeep to get the gifts. After presenting them, she knelt beside him and watched his face expectantly. He seemed very pleased, perhaps more with her thoughtfulness than with the paints themselves, though he did have a gleam of past joys in his eye as he examined them.

Derek leaned over and took her face in his hands. "That was really very sweet of you," he whispered.

"It wasn't to pressure you. I thought it would be nice to have them around in case the urge struck."

"I wish I had the talent to justify your confidence."

"It's for happiness, not achievement," she said. "Isn't that what life's about?"

Derek ran his hand along the side of her neck and kissed her lower lip. "Yes. It's certainly the most important part."

It was too warm for a fire that evening, though it was somewhat cooler than the night before, so they read in the living room, both of them on the couch, Lara with her feet on Derek's lap.

After an hour or so she put down her book and watched him until he became aware of her. He looked over and smiled.

"Is it supposed to be this comfortable?" she asked.

"If you want it good, it is."

She wondered again what would happen if she became accustomed to this togetherness and then all of a sudden he went away. She didn't express her misgivings, though. He'd dismissed the notion the night before. Anyway, he'd only brought a small suitcase, and their arrangement had included a money-back guarantee.

They read a while longer, then Derek began rubbing her feet. Lara realized he wasn't concentrating on his book any more than she was on hers. About the third time their eyes met he took her hand and they went upstairs to bed.

Derek undressed her, slowly removing each garment, even her underclothing. He hadn't taken off his own clothes, but he held her, tenderly caressing her skin, kissing her shoulders lovingly.

She climbed into her bed then and watched him undress in the lamplight. He joined her and they embraced, the feel of his warm flesh familiar now. They lay together, kissing and reveling in each other's bodies.

Lara hadn't realized how much she had been looking forward to this, though she hadn't consciously thought about it much until just before they came upstairs. Then, when he'd gotten her very excited, they began to make love. The pace was slower than before. Every time she was about to come he would stop, until the pulsing subsided. Then he'd begin again.

The dance continued for what seemed like hours. Each time the deprivation became more acute and her level of excitement higher. She begged him to take her.

"Why are you doing this to me?" she said into his lips as she kissed him deeply. "Please don't torture me."

The next time he didn't stop. He took her to completion, having expertly sharpened her desire and deepened her fulfillment. Afterward, as she lay panting in his arms, struggling to calm her heart, he told her again that he loved her.

Lara again wanted to confess that she loved him, but she still couldn't. She did love him, it was true. She knew it with absolute certainty now. But deep in her heart there was doubt about what they were doing. She kept it to herself this time. It was pretty clear he would refuse to share her misgivings.

THE NEXT EVENING Lara was in the kitchen doing the dishes. The window over the sink was open and the breeze wafted in, gently fluttering the curtains. She could hear Derek outside, chopping wood. He had complained that he needed some exercise, and after another day at his typewriter, he'd wanted a chore that would tax him physically.

Not one to look a gift horse in the mouth, Lara had taken him out to the wood pile and told him he could split the larger logs and stack a supply of firewood for the winter. Derek had happily set to work. She'd watched him for several minutes, noting it hadn't taken him long to get the hang of it.

Then she had come inside to clean up the kitchen and do the dinner dishes. She liked the sound of the ax echoing in the woods. And it appealed to her particularly that there was someone to share the burden, someone she cared for making the everyday life a joint enterprise. The image of Derek working up a sweat in the balmy twilight, readying them for the coming winter, was very appealing. She contemplated baking a cake for him or preparing some other treat as a reward.

Lara went to the pantry to see what she could find when she heard a vehicle coming up the drive. At about the same time Derek's chopping stopped. She went to the front window and, peering out into the fading twilight, saw a car with its headlights on, pulling to a stop in front of the cabin.

The car was not familiar, and Lara couldn't imagine who

the visitor would be. She went to the front door as Derek came around the side of the house.

There were two women in the automobile. The driver was older. Lara had never seen her before. The younger one got out and Lara recognized her. It was Mary Beth Adamson.

Steve's wife was a slender brunette, slightly taller than Lara. She was pretty in an old-fashioned way, having the earnest innocent look of a country girl. Lara didn't really know Mary Beth, having met her only once, not long after Steve had remarried. The woman had sought out Lara at a fair at the Mendocino Art Center. She had introduced herself, saying she thought they ought to be acquainted, so there wouldn't be any mystery between them.

At the time it struck Lara as strange, but later she recognized the wisdom of the idea. They had only spoken a minute, and never again after that, but the contact did give Lara an impression she hadn't forgotten.

"I don't know if you remember me, but I'm Mary Beth Adamson," the brunette said, approaching the porch. "Would it be all right if we talk?"

Lara nodded. "Yes." She felt uncomfortable. Over the past few days her ex-husband had hardly entered her mind, but seeing Mary Beth brought back all the bad memories. "Come in, if you like."

Mary Beth looked at Derek. He took her glance as a cue to leave and headed back to the woodpile. Lara saw there was no point in introducing him. And she had no desire to explain his presence.

Mary Beth looked nervous and uncertain as she came up on the porch. She saw Lara looking at the older woman.

"That's my mother," Mary Beth explained. "She wants to wait in the car."

As they entered the cabin, Lara noticed that Mary Beth's

dress looked a little tight on her, and maybe a bit too short. But she was neat and well groomed. She hesitated inside the door, rubbing her hands together.

"Go on back into the living room," Lara said. She turned on a lamp and they sat down, Mary Beth on the sofa, Lara across from her.

"I know it's not very polite to drop in like this," Mary Beth said apologetically, "but I couldn't say what I have to on the phone. I needed to see you."

"That's all right."

Outside Derek resumed chopping wood. Mary Beth turned at the sound. "Is that the man who's going to testify against Steve?"

"Yes."

Their eyes met and Mary Beth bit her lip, lowering her head. She fidgeted with her hands. "I'm sorry about what happened to you, Lara. Steve gets crazy sometimes, but I guess you know that."

"Yes, unfortunately." She wanted to ask Mary Beth why she was there, but she could see the woman was struggling. Whatever her errand was, it was obviously painful for her.

"I guess you know that Steve and I split up," Mary Beth began. "We were separated. I was planning on divorcing him. I think that's why he got crazy—because he was upset and mad. So in a way, it's my fault what happened to you."

"It's not your fault. Steve acted on his own. No one else can be responsible for what another person does." Lara had suddenly become emotional. "I hope you didn't come here to apologize for him, because it's not necessary."

Mary Beth shook her head. "No, it's something else."

"What?"

The woman looked down again, her lip trembling. "I've come at Steve's request. He's wondering if you could find it in your heart to talk to him."

"The district attorney already gave me that message, and I said no."

"I know you did. But I'm asking now." She looked up, her eyes flooding with tears. "I thought you might do it for me."

"Why? If you're divorcing him, what do you care?"

"I'm probably not going to divorce him now. I mean, maybe I won't. I don't know." The woman wiped a tear from the corner of her eye. "I haven't decided what I'll do."

"I don't understand. What's happened? Did Steve put pressure on you to come here?"

"He asked me."

"You don't have to do what that man says. Don't let him intimidate you."

"It's not that."

"Then what is it?" She looked at Mary Beth, who sat mute, her gaze averted.

The steady thump of Derek's ax came from outside. There was a reassurance in the sound. Lara was glad he was there. Even though he wasn't in the room, knowing she wasn't alone was a wonderful feeling.

Mary Beth remained silent. Then she sniffled, wiping away another tear. "I wasn't going to tell you this, but maybe I have to." She hesitated.

"What?"

Mary Beth glanced up at her through shimmering eyes. "I'm pregnant, Lara. I'm going to have Steve's baby."

"You're pregnant?"

Mary Beth lowered her face to her hands and began to sob softly. "Yes, I didn't find out until a few weeks ago. It must have happened the last time—when he forced me."

"Oh, God."

"I was so upset when I found out," she sobbed. "I

wanted a baby for years, and it didn't happen. Then just when…'' She began weeping hysterically.

Lara got up and went around the coffee table to sit beside her. She put her arm around the sobbing woman. After a minute Mary Beth got control of herself. She took a tissue from her purse and wiped her eyes and nose.

"I'm sorry," she said. "I didn't want to do this."

"It's got to be a terribly emotional thing. Does Steve know?"

"Yes, I went to see him in the jail. I told him then."

"What happened?"

"He cried. Like a baby. I've never seen him cry before."

The situation hit Lara hard. She almost felt as though she would be sick. She couldn't ever imagine feeling compassion for Steve Adamson, but in a funny sort of way she did. "Now you want me to drop the charges so that the father of your baby won't be in jail."

"I'm asking you, yes," Mary Beth replied. "But I told Steve that wouldn't be enough, that he would have to make his peace with you. He agreed. That's why he wants to see you."

Lara got up and paced across the room. "I can't believe this."

"I know you're bitter toward him. I would be in your shoes."

"What about you?" Lara snapped. "Do you really think anything's different just because Steve happened to get you pregnant? Do you think fatherhood will change him? Just because he forced you and a child came out of it, doesn't mean he's somehow worthy."

"I know that," Mary Beth said, the tears starting to flow again. "At first I was horrified to think I'd have his baby. But it *is* his. And we *are* married. I knew I couldn't keep it a secret. So I decided to go to the jail and tell him the truth. I didn't know what would happen, what to expect.''

"Because he cried doesn't mean he's reformed, Mary Beth.''

"It's not just that. When I saw him that way I knew I didn't want that for my baby's father. No matter what happened between me and Steve, I didn't want that for my baby.''

Lara paced some more. "Now I'm supposed to forgive and forget for the sake of your baby. Is that it?''

"No. I wish you could, but I know I've got no right to ask that. This is between you and Steve. So I'm begging you to talk to him. To give him a chance.''

Lara shook her head. "I can see you're in a tough spot. But that doesn't change what Steve did, nor does it change who he is. How you feel about him is your business, but I don't think he should benefit from the accident of his crime against you or me, either one.''

"I know you hate him. I did, too. But I think the baby has changed him, Lara.''

"Because he broke down and cried?''

"No. I really think it's made him wake up and see what he's done to his life.''

"What about our lives—yours and mine? And now his baby, too.''

"He sees that now.''

Lara still wasn't convinced. She sat back down in the chair. "I think it's wishful thinking on your part, Mary Beth.''

"It's not only what happened over the baby. Believe it or not, Steve actually got better the past year or two. I thought he was growing up. But then he got laid off and it got to him. He started drinking heavy, fighting with me.

After he beat me that night, I couldn't take it anymore, so I left. But I think he'd started changing, I really do.''

"So that's what you want for yourself and your baby— a husband and father who's all right until he's got a problem? Every time he gets laid off you want to face that?''

"You were only married to Steve a few months,'' Mary Beth said, "and it was a long time ago. You didn't love him. But I do. In spite of his faults, I love him. I gave up hope, that's why I was going to divorce him. But now that I'm going to have a baby, I want to try again.''

Lara sadly shook her head. "Steve doesn't deserve you, Mary Beth.''

She sniffled. "I've got to try. I've got to give him one more chance. Please, Lara. I'm begging you. Just talk to him.''

Lara closed her eyes and put her face in her hands. "I don't think I could do it. Even for you and your baby.''

"Will you at least think about it?''

She sighed deeply, drawing an uneven breath. "Yes, I'll do that much. I'll think about it.''

Mary Beth got up. Lara rose, too. They stared at each other for a moment, then Mary Beth stepped around the table and they embraced. Neither said anything.

Mary Beth started for the door, but stopped short. Derek, his brow and shirt soaked with perspiration, was standing there. Mary Beth looked back at Lara, who immediately introduced them.

"If it hadn't been for Derek,'' Lara said, "Steve might be in a lot more trouble than he is. And I might be in the hospital or dead.''

Mary Beth bowed her head. "Thank you,'' she mumbled. "I'm so sorry about everything. I wish I'd been here. None of it ever would have happened.''

Lara went over to Derek and put her arm around his waist, craving his protective embrace.

"I don't know what this is all about," he said, "but there's some good in almost every situation. If it weren't for Steve, I probably wouldn't be here now."

Mary Beth looked at Lara hopefully, though she didn't say anything.

"I promised I'd consider it," Lara said, knowing what she was thinking. "But beyond that I can't say."

Mary Beth nodded, then headed for the door. Lara followed her, watching her descend the steps and get in her mother's car. When they pulled away, she closed the front door. Derek was wiping his brow with his handkerchief when she went back into the living room.

"What was that all about?"

She put her arms around him again. "Mary Beth is pregnant by Steve. They want me to drop the charges so he can play Daddy and become a good citizen."

"Good heavens!"

"My thoughts exactly."

"What are you going to do?"

"She asked me to talk to Steve, I guess to give him a chance to beg for forgiveness. I said I'd think it over."

Derek kissed the top of her head. "Poor Lara. It's getting awfully tough to put that business to rest."

"That's true. But you want to know something?"

"What?"

"Even when Mary Beth was here, telling me her sad story, I was thinking how lucky I was to have you, how nice it is not to have to face this alone."

Derek lifted her chin and kissed her lips. "Believe it or not, I'm the one who's lucky."

THE NEXT DAY Lara wrestled with Mary Beth Adamson's request. She was torn. She and Derek talked about it some, and he told her he didn't think she would be doing Mary Beth a favor by helping Steve. Still, if she felt that talking to him might somehow benefit her, she ought to do it.

Lara decided there were different kinds of benefit, one of which was the satisfaction of helping others. But the problem was she didn't know what was truly in everyone's best interest, including Steve's. Some time in jail might do him more good than anything.

Derek suggested that if she wanted to talk over the problem with anyone else, she might give Carolyn Buchanan a call. Lara agreed that was a good idea, and after lunch she phoned the attorney and explained what had happened.

"The first thing you should know," Carolyn said, "is that it isn't up to you alone whether we drop charges or not. But you can torpedo the prosecution's case if you refuse to cooperate."

"Then there's not much I could do for Steve, even if I wanted to."

"Basically, that's correct."

"Well, I'm not going to lie for him, and I'm not going to pretend that it didn't happen."

"Then forget about it, Lara, until the trial."

"But Mary Beth wanted me to talk to Steve. Whatever else I do, I can still do that, can't I?"

"If you want to. I won't advise against it," Carolyn said. "It might do you good to confront him. We've talked about that."

"If I decided to, when would I see him?"

"Anytime before the trial. There's no rush. Take your time. Personally, I think you ought to let him cool his heels for a while. I've tried to keep him locked up. The judge set a high bail at our request. There's no way Adamson is going to get out, unless bail's lowered substantially."

"Will it be lowered?"

"Adamson's attorney is trying to get it reduced. The mother-in-law apparently has some money and is willing to help, so if they can get the judge to agree to reduce bail, he could be released."

Lara felt her heart stop. "Oh, no!"

"I'm not saying it will happen, though. My position has been to oppose any reduction because of the danger to you. Adamson's violent tendency and his threats will be enough to defeat the motion as long as our office opposes it. That's my position on it, unless you want me to do otherwise."

"No, I wouldn't want to take a chance just because Mary Beth's convinced he's a changed man."

"I agree," Carolyn said. "Why don't we do this? I'll get word to Mrs. Adamson through the defense attorney that you're considering the accused's request for a meeting, and that you'll make your decision within two weeks. That'll give you some time and keep them off your back."

"That sounds good."

"In the meantime, try to relax and forget about Adamson. If I were you, I'd be thinking about Mr. Gordon. He seemed like an awfully nice guy, and my impression is that he's very fond of you."

Lara couldn't help smiling. "Yeah, that's my impression, too."

The attorney laughed. "Something tells me I just stepped in something, so I'll let it drop there."

"No comment."

"Lucky lady," Carolyn said after a pregnant pause. "My secretary asked me about him after you two were in the other day, if that's any indication how he's viewed in the marketplace."

"I believe it," Lara said. And she knew Carolyn Buchanan was right. She was very lucky indeed.

CHAPTER FOURTEEN

IN THE DAYS FOLLOWING Lara tried to forget about Steve Adamson. Because of Derek she largely succeeded. She had actually begun a new life with him. They worked together, cooked together, shopped together, and they became more than lovers. It was as though they had both found the one person who would make their life complete.

Living with someone was a new experience for Lara and a happy one for the most part. They discovered each other's foibles and sensitivities. They learned how the habits from years spent living alone could become a problem, but they always seemed to find a way to work things out.

And she never ceased marveling at how fufilling their intimacy could be. She never tired of Derek, finding her desire flaring at the most unexpected times. Their relationship became a wonderful game, in which they acted on their mutual desire whenever the whim struck.

Lara seduced him while he was sitting at his typewriter, and again when he was sketching her as they sat out on the deck. Once, when she had gone down to the stream to work, he appeared out of nowhere with an old blanket under his arm and they made love in the meadow.

But the feelings she had for him went far beyond the physical joy they shared. There were tender moments, funny moments, even angry moments that managed somehow to end up in the same place—in love and harmony.

Though he'd done a lot of sketching, Derek hadn't tack-

led the watercolors Lara had bought him. At first he didn't
let her see his drawings. But when he told her he wanted
to sketch her nude, Lara playfully insisted his bona fides
as an artist had to be proved first. She wasn't, she said,
going to be the object of a lecherous ruse. So Derek had
handed her the sketch pad and, for the first time, she was
able to see his work.

The fact that he had talent didn't surprise her. Still the
quality of his work came as somewhat of a shock. He was
an accomplished draftsman, though he didn't draw with the
freedom his subjects demanded. She did notice improve-
ment though, a gradual loosening of his style. She was eager to see what he could accomplish with watercolors, but
didn't press him.

Sometimes in the evening Lara would work on a poem
while Derek sat opposite her, sketching. Sharing that creative time together, in quiet companionability, was joyful.
It was something she'd always assumed she wouldn't be
able to experience with anyone.

But for all her joy, Lara was vaguely troubled by the
future—the distant, dark cloud on the horizon. Steve Adamson, Mary Beth and the trial were an immediate concern,
but there was also Derek's marriage and the impending
storm surrounding his family.

Derek never gave any indication that it was troubling
him. She decided he was still assessing the love they
shared. Besides, what were his choices? His options with
Margaret weren't happy ones. And their own lives, as they
were living them now, weren't unhappy. Still, Lara couldn't
forget all that was out there waiting for them.

One afternoon during the second week Derek had been
with her, Lara went to visit Calle Bianco. Her friend was
aware that she and Derek were living together, but they
hadn't really had a chance to talk about it.

"If you love each other," Calle said as they sat in the kitchen, "that's an awful lot. The unknowns will work themselves out eventually."

"I keep telling myself that, but I'm beginning to wonder if Derek has decided to ignore the future. You know, the if-this-is-paradise-why-rock-the-boat syndrome."

"His marriage has to be on his mind. He's probably just trying to figure it out."

"I wish he'd say something. It's wonderful being with him, Calle, but sometimes I feel like we're trying to live a dream."

"Have you told him that?"

"I haven't forced the issue. I sense he's not ready to confront things head-on yet."

Calle put her plump arm around Lara's shoulder. "If it bothers you enough, then you ought to let him know."

"I've thought about that. I'm aware that I've got rights. But every time I get ready to say something, I ask myself if I'm worse off than I was before. I have to say I'm not. The truth is, I was probably more lonely than I realized. And now I'm scared."

"Derek is a sensitive man," Calle said. "He's got to be aware of what's going on, to know you're concerned."

Lara went to Calle's stove and got more hot water for her tea. "He isn't selfish. He makes it plain that our staying together has to be a mutual thing. And he doesn't put any pressure on me—actually gives me opportunities to tell him if I'm unhappy."

"He's showing he cares about your feelings," Calle said. "He wants to make sure you're not being hurt while he works everything out in his own mind."

"I suppose. I guess I've been telling myself that, too. I just wish he'd decide what he wants to do. If it goes on much longer, I'm going to have to talk to him about it."

Calle took a cookie off the plate in the middle of the table. "Maybe the problem is you're living too artificially, like a couple of hermits. Maybe you ought to try for a more normal life—socialize together. Face the outside world."

"That's not a bad idea." Lara reflected for a moment. "Maybe I'll suggest we do something. We could have you and Tony over for dinner. That would be a change of pace."

"Yes, or we could go out someplace. Maybe dancing. I haven't gotten Tony on a dance floor in a hundred years. There's that disco, the Jukebox, in Fort Bragg. We've never been, but I hear it's nice and some of the music is more our generation."

"What generation is that, Calle?" Lara said, poking her tongue in her cheek.

"All right, *my* generation. But you'll be seeing the dark side of thirty-five before too very long yourself."

Lara laughed. Calle started to reach for another cookie, but thrust her hands into her lap and frowned.

"I'd give five years for more willpower," she groused.

"At least the married man you're living with is your husband," Lara replied. "You don't have such a bad deal."

Calle patted Lara's hand. "Everything will work out for you, too, honey. I know it will."

Lara smiled faintly at her friend.

"Any word about the trial?" Calle asked.

"No, but I forgot to tell you the latest. I had a visit several days ago from Mary Beth."

"Steve's wife?"

Lara nodded.

"What did she want?" Calle asked, moving to the edge of her chair.

Lara related the story of Mary Beth's visit.

"You aren't actually going to see him, are you?"

"I didn't think so at first, but I've been picturing Mary Beth and her baby, and Steve in jail, and her asking me—pleading with me—to talk to him...."

"If you want my opinion," Calle said, "in jail is where he belongs."

"I know."

"So don't give him a second thought."

"I intend to go through with the trial and testify against him, but maybe Steve needs to talk to me, maybe he deserves a chance."

"He'll just use Mary Beth and the baby to play on your sympathies."

"Maybe so. But I'm thinking I should find out for myself. If the baby has changed him like Mary Beth thinks, he deserves a chance to prove it. If nothing else it might be good for his soul."

"I don't think a man like him changes overnight, and I think you're silly to give him two thoughts."

"We'll see."

"How does Derek feel about it?"

"About like you do."

Calle raised her eyebrows as if to say, "So what else do you need?"

"Maybe I'm a sucker for second wives and babies," Lara said with a smile.

"You know I'll support you in whatever you decide."

"Thanks," she said, patting Calle's hand.

Her friend leaned back then, with an air of resolution. "That's enough on that subject. Let's talk about the good guys for a while. I really think we ought to get these menfolk of ours to take us dancing. What do you say we set it up for Friday?"

"I'll ask Derek."

"Good. I'll put the hammer on Tony when he gets home

from work." Then she winked. "The privilege of marriage."

"I hope there's more to look forward to than that."

"Dirty dishes and squabbles tend to outnumber the bouquets of flowers, Lara. But if you find the right guy you don't have to be the princess at the ball to be happy. That bit of wisdom," she said, snatching a cookie, "is from someone who knows."

WHEN LARA GOT BACK to the cabin she found Derek out on the deck. He'd spread newspapers on the table and was painting the vista down the valley, toward the sea. He turned to her as she approached.

Lara slipped her arm around his waist and looked at the picture with delight. It was lovely. "Derek, why haven't you been painting all these years? You do beautiful work!"

"This is the fourth sheet of watercolor paper I've used. It took me a while to get back the hang of it."

She kissed him on the cheek. "I love it!"

He took her in his arms, kissing her deeply. Then he hugged her. "How about a nude painting? I could do you right out here on the deck."

She slapped his arm. "Do a portrait, or do *me*?"

He laughed. "I can see we've been living together too long. You've already figured out my tricks."

"Yes," she said in mock indifference, "I guess it's time you move on to your next mistress."

He smiled, but it was a sad smile. He loosened his hold of her and pushed the tip of her nose lightly with his finger. Then he sat on the edge of the table. His expression was not angry, but it was definitely studied.

"I shouldn't have said that, should I?" she said.

"The question is what you really meant by it."

"I didn't mean anything."

"Yes, you did. You're not happy, are you?"

"I'm happy, but…"

He folded his arms and gave her a penetrating look. "I haven't been fair to you. I've been imposing my live-for-today philosophy on you, and you've gone along with it. But the decision hasn't really been mutual."

She had been hungering for this conversation, but now that it had come up she was afraid. She didn't want things between them to fall apart. She wanted the love they shared to go on and on.

"I've been thinking it would be nice if we did some things with other people," she said, hoping to switch the tone of the conversation to a more constructive vein. "As a matter of fact, Calle and I thought we'd try to get you and Tony to take us dancing Friday night. There's a disco in Fort Bragg she wants to try. I didn't know whether you like that sort of thing or not."

"It's been years since I've gone dancing, but I used to love it." He smiled. "I know that doesn't seem very professorial, but I did."

"You wouldn't mind then?"

"No, I'd enjoy it."

"I thought maybe we could invite Calle and Tony over for dinner sometime, too. We could play some cards or something afterward."

"I'd like that," he said.

"I don't mean to push, but Calle's my dearest friend. And Tony's not a bad guy."

"No, I like him."

"He's not terribly sophisticated."

Derek put his finger to Lara's lip. "Don't apologize for Tony. My best friend, a guy I grew up with, is an L.A. cop. On the surface we don't have a thing in common, but

I'd hate to think of myself as limited to what I appear to be on the surface.''

She reached up and kissed him. ''I'm glad you've come into my life, Derek.''

He kissed her back. ''So am I. And to think it all started when you dropped a gun at my feet.''

''You must have thought I was a crazy woman.''

He nodded. ''I still do.''

She swung at him playfully. Derek slipped the punch and grabbed her from behind.

''What you doin' this afternoon, kid?'' he asked, hugging her.

''Cleaning house?''

''No.''

''Watching you paint?''

''No.''

''I've run out of guesses.''

''Let me give you a hint.'' He nibbled at the soft skin on her neck and kissed her flesh.

''I should have guessed.''

''I'm at risk of becoming predictable,'' he said.

''That's okay, I don't mind a little predictability,'' she said, starting to get into the spirit of the game. She hugged the arms that hugged her, but his reference to the future brought to mind the dark cloud on the horizon, the storm that wouldn't go away.

LARA DECIDED TO BUY a special dress for Friday night. She and Calle went shopping Thursday to find the right one. The third dress she put on was a supple cream suede, off one shoulder with a low-slung metallic belt. The salesclerk gave her a pair of sandals that went with it to slip on. Lara knew it was the dress she wanted before she even looked in the mirror.

"You're gorgeous!" Calle enthused, as Lara modeled it for her.

Turning in front of the mirror, she had to admit she liked the way she looked. Around the cabin it was mostly jeans and shirts, shorts and T-shirts. Except for the Literary Guild meeting, that night she'd run into Derek at the Mendocino Hotel, and their trip to Ukiah, he hadn't seen her dressed up.

"Derek would have to be blind not to appreciate this," Calle said, reading her thoughts.

Lara wanted him to like it, but she wasn't concerned about him finding her appealing. It was *how* he saw her that mattered. "Do I look like a mistress?" she asked, as she spun around in front of the mirror. Glancing at Calle, she saw her friend had a scowl on her face. "Well, do I?"

"Only in your head. Don't talk that way, Lara."

"Am I spoiling it?"

"You will if you keep that up."

"Maybe you're right," she said, heading for the dressing room. "I shouldn't be a brat."

They stopped for an ice-cream cone on the way home, Calle chastising herself, both before and afterward, for succumbing to temptation. They then went directly to the Biancos'. Tony wasn't home from work yet, but Jodie and Tony Two were playing in the front yard. Theresa was on the porch with the baby-sitter. The kids ran up to the Jeep to greet their mom.

Calle had bought them some ice cream at the store and, when she handed them the package, they whooped with glee and ran into the house to have some. Calle got out of the Jeep. "Thanks," she said to Lara. "Keep smiling, honey."

"I promise to be good."

Derek was working hard when Lara got home. He saw

her carry in the dress, wrapped in a plastic bag, and asked what it was, but Lara wouldn't tell him.

"It's a surprise for tomorrow night."

After kissing him and putting away her things in the closet upstairs, she returned to where he sat at his typewriter.

"How's it going?"

Derek put his hand on the stack of typed sheets. "I'm past the one-quarter point."

"All that and you still have three-quarters to go? I hope they pay by the word."

"Hardly."

Lara rubbed his shoulders, then went over to a chair and curled up with her notepad to write. They worked for a couple of hours, then Derek suggested they go for a walk. Lara agreed and they went up a trail that followed the stream along the valley.

The day was cool, and they wore sweaters. The leaves on the deciduous trees had changed color and were beginning to fall. Indian summer seemed to be over.

Derek took Lara's hand as they walked. After a while they stopped and sat on a log. He still held her hand.

"Are you happy?" he asked.

She nodded, smiled and put her head on his shoulder. "Are you?"

"Very." He stroked her cheek with his fingers. "I should have known you existed, but it's funny how I wasn't in a rush to find you."

"It took a gun dropping on your toe," she joked.

"I guess I had to be ready for you. What a tragedy it would have been if you had come along a few years ago."

"Maybe I've come along a few years too soon."

"No," he said, shaking his head, "that's not what my feelings tell me." He stared at the water tumbling over the rocks in the stream. His tone had been definitive, but there was a far-off look in his eye. It seemed that at last he might be starting to grapple with his dilemma.

Lara wanted to ask what he was feeling, what conclusions he had drawn, but she knew it would sound as though she was pushing. When he was ready to tell her, he would.

THE JUKEBOX WAS on the Coast Highway just outside of Fort Bragg. Lara, Derek and the Biancos arrived in Derek's BMW. Tony Bianco was full of the devil. He had hauled some white buck shoes out of his closet and was wearing a Hawaiian shirt and white duck pants. Calle was a little more sedate in a loose-fitting black dress. Derek wore a white polo shirt and light blue trousers.

But Lara was the belle of the ball in her new dress and sandals. When she had come down from the loft before they left to pick up Calle and Tony, Derek stood for a long time admiring her in silence. For a moment she was worried that something was wrong, but he held out his arms finally and said, "Come here. It's not enough to look. I've go to touch, too."

As they walked toward the door of the disco, Lara took his arm. It was a real date, a double date. She hadn't done that since high school. And she couldn't help feeling a little excited.

There was a lively crowd inside. The men, mostly in their twenties and thirties, all looked at Lara. She felt a special pride, knowing Derek was aware. A month ago she wouldn't have come to the club on a dare, and the obvious attentions of strange men would have been unwelcome, even offensive. But with Derek at her side it became a game, a diversion. She was having fun.

Lara and Derek wasted no time getting onto the crowded

dance floor. The first few songs were fast, and though it had been a while, they soon got the hang of the rhythm.

Watching his face in the dim light, their bodies twisting seductively, Lara could hardly believe how much her life had changed. And it was all because of Derek Gordon.

His hands slid over her narrow waist as he spun her around. When a swing tune came on, he moved into high gear. Her generation had come along well after the swing era, but she had learned the dance as a teenager. Derek was really accomplished, spinning her around the floor.

Calle danced gracefully despite her size. Tony's style was more comic than accomplished. The four of them left the dance floor together. Everybody was out of breath.

"We ought to make a movie," Calle said, fanning herself with her hand.

"What, aerobic dancing?" Tony teased.

Calle made a face at him, then turned to Lara and Derek. "You two dance like you were made for each other."

"Maybe we were," Derek replied.

Lara blushed.

They ordered drinks, and while the cocktail waitress was getting their order, Tony asked Lara to dance. Derek asked Calle and the four of them returned to the dance floor. The record was a current rock hit that Lara couldn't identify, but it was fast. Tony was perspiring heavily by the time it was over.

The next tune was a slow ballad. Calle immediately took her husband by the arm. "Come on lover boy, let's dance." Lara turned to Derek, who gathered her into his arms. It felt like coming home to have him holding her close.

Lara inhaled his cologne and the warm scent of his body, taking genuine joy in the familiarity and the knowledge that they were lovers. She danced very close, telling herself not to think beyond the moment. Nothing mattered now except that they were together and having fun.

They had their drinks, danced for another hour, then decided to go home. Calle had made a cake and invited Lara and Derek to come in for a late dessert and coffee. The four of them sat around the Biancos' kitchen table, exchanging anecdotes about their teen years.

"It's amazing," Lara said, "how unique your life seemed at the time, when in fact everybody in the world has to go through practically the same thing."

"I knew I wasn't the only one with a weight problem," Calle said. "You look around and some things are pretty visible."

"Kids describe their problems differently," Derek said, "but the problems usually relate back to defining just who they are."

"After seeing my father the other day, and having that talk, I can understand your point," Lara said.

Calle offered everybody more coffee, but only Tony accepted. "I'll probably lie awake for hours, but that's okay, I can sleep in."

"You'd better confer with Jodie and Tony Two on that," his wife said.

Tony put his hand over the cup. "On second thought."

Everybody laughed. Lara noticed Derek's admiring looks, and she knew what he was thinking. Dancing with him had put her in an amorous mood. After a while she complained about being tired and suggested they go home.

They were soon on their way. It seemed quiet with just the two of them as they drove along the deserted highway. Tony's laughter and Calle's sharp wit had made for a different and pleasant evening, but Lara was glad to be alone now with Derek. He turned on the radio to a station playing quiet, romantic music. He took her hand.

"I was with the most beautiful girl at the dance," he said.

"You're not very objective, Derek."

"I've certainly never known a more lovely woman, nor can I remember ever seeing one I found more attractive."

"You don't need to flatter me."

"Just telling you what I think."

She pressed his hand to her cheek. "You've made me very happy."

They entered the driveway and drove through the dark woods to her cabin. The only light came from the glow of the living room lamp. Derek parked the car and they got out.

"I've got a silly request," Lara said, as they crossed the porch.

"What's that?"

"This whole evening has been like a date—our first, in a way. Would you mind kissing me good-night at the door?"

"Does that mean I can't come in?"

"No." She laughed. "I just want our first date to be like a first date."

He lifted her chin. "I don't follow your reasoning, but I'm sure I can accommodate you."

Lara shivered from the coolness of the breeze. But his arms were warm and inviting. She luxuriated in the sensation. Lifting her mouth to his, she accepted his kiss, loving the feel of his soft lips, matching the eagerness with which he took her.

They kissed for a long time, their tongues touching and exploring. Then, as Lara felt her heart beginning to race, the phone rang inside. They both were jarred from their dreamlike embrace. Their lips drew apart.

"Who could that be?" Lara said. She opened her purse and fumbled in the dark for her keys.

"Here," Derek said, taking his keys from his pocket, "let me get it."

The phone continued ringing as he struggled to get the right key into the lock. Finally he got the door open, but Lara had only taken a few steps inside when the ringing stopped.

"Darn," she said with exasperation.

"They'll call back if it's important," Derek said, coming up behind her. "It might even have been a wrong number."

MARK GORDON STARED at the phone in the dim light of his father's bedroom in Berkeley for a moment, then went back down the hall to his room. Marcy was sitting at his desk, books and loose sheets of notes everywhere. She turned and looked at him.

"Get him?"

"No. I tried his place again, and the number the sheriff's office gave for Lara. No answer either place."

"Maybe they went somewhere for the weekend."

"Maybe so. I'll try again in a little while, then I guess I'll flick it in for tonight." Mark sat down on the bed, his shoulders slumping. When he glanced up, Marcy was looking at him compassionately.

"I'm so sorry, Mark. I wish there was something I could do."

"I'm sorry this happened the night before you have two midterms. Hope you've been able to study."

"Don't worry about me," she said, stretching and running her ringed fingers back through her spiky hair. "I wish I could have been with you at the hospital."

"There was nothing to do there. It doesn't matter."

"I could have been with you."

Mark smiled weekly. Marcy was really a sweet person. A lot more mature than many girls he'd dated. And best of all, she could show a little compassion and softness without feeling she was giving away anything.

"The one who should be here is Derek," he said bitterly. "He knows Mom is in a fragile state and that something could happen to her at any time. If he's going away, he should let me know about it."

"It might just have been for the evening, Mark. He can't call you every time he goes somewhere for a few hours."

Mark leaned over, resting his head wearily in his hands. "You're probably right. But a decision may have to be made soon, and he's the one with authority."

"They don't need his permission for lifesaving procedures, do they?"

"No, but the doctor said she might have to stay on a respirator until the end, and be fed intravenously from now on." He looked up, his eyes glossy. "That's no way to live."

Marcy got up and went to sit beside Mark on the bed. She put an arm around him and laid her head on his shoulder. "I've got to study for at least an hour or two more. If you want to get some rest, I can dial Derek's and Lara's numbers every fifteen minutes or so."

"No, you've got enough to worry about with your exams. I don't think I could sleep, anyway. I'll just rest here on the bed for a few minutes and try calling again later."

Marcy kissed his cheek and went back to the desk. Mark watched her, knowing he cared for her a lot. He wondered if it might work out that they stayed together, and maybe got married someday. Everyone said you found out what a person's like in a time of crisis. He had to admit Marcy was really good. He couldn't ask for anyone more sympathetic and understanding.

As he lay back on the bed, Mark pictured his mother in the hospital room, tubes and machines all around her, her face a death mask, her body appearing lifeless except for the artificial rise and fall of her chest. A terrible feeling went through him, and he tried to erase the image from his mind.

DEREK LAY BACK on the pillow, feeling contentment, but also expectation. Lara had declined to let him undress her, going instead into the bathroom. In a few minutes she appeared in a filmy negligee with a candle in her hand. She turned off the bedside lamp and put down the candle on the dresser, across the room.

As he watched she smiled at him, her cheeks rosy with girlish innocence. Then, with the candlelight behind her, she unfastened the negligee. Because of the light she was in silhouette. And when the garment fell to the floor, he was able to see the perfect lines of her body. The sight of her excited him, and he felt himself harden under the covers.

Lara slowly moved toward him. She was exquisite— temptress, nymph, sorceress, lover, goddess, all at once. At the side of the bed she leaned over and kissed him lightly on the lips. Derek wanted her so badly, he had done all he could do to keep from pulling her down onto his chest. His teeth gnashed with desire as he stared into her eyes.

Lifting the covers, he invited her into the bed, and she slipped in beside him, her skin cool and smooth as kid leather. He rolled over on top of her, covering her mouth with his lips, tasting her, inhaling her delicate musk.

He began exploring her with his hands when the telephone rang downstairs, shattering the ecstasy of the moment. "Damn," he said through his teeth.

They both turned their heads toward the plaintive sound.

"Shall we ignore it?" he asked.

Lara looked torn. "No," she finally said. "It might be important." She climbed out of the bed and got her terry robe from the closet. After slipping it on, she went down the stairs. The phone continued ringing until he heard her answer.

Lara's voice was muffled, but he did make out a vague tinge of alarm in her tone. He rose on his elbow, watching the shadows on the wall quivering from the dancing flame of the candle.

"Derek!" she called. There was definite alarm in her voice now. He jumped from the bed and went to the top of the stairs. She was standing in the living room, clutching her robe at the neck. "It's Mark," she said, looking up at him. "Margaret has had an attack. She's in the hospital."

CHAPTER FIFTEEN

IT WAS JUST GETTING LIGHT as Derek exited Interstate 80 onto University Avenue. From the center of the campus the campanile rose in the distance, like a blunt needle against the dawn-shrouded hills. The street he drove along was nearly deserted. A lonely bus, lit inside, came down the divided avenue in the other direction. A jogger padded sleepily along the sidewalk.

In just a few minutes Derek was driving up the twisting street leading to his home. The house was dark as he got out of the car and went up onto the porch. He wasn't sure whether to ring the bell to warn Mark of his arrival, or to go on inside quietly so as not to disturb him and Marcy unnecessarily. Finally he rang the bell, then used his key to gain access.

He had only been in the entry hall a moment when Marcy Brandt appeared at the top of the stairs in a flannel nightgown.

"Oh, Professor Gordon," she said, looking surprised and embarrassed. She ran her hand back through her short hair and clutched at the front of her gown.

"Is Mark here?" Derek asked.

She gave a half shrug. "He must have gone to the hospital. I didn't notice him leave."

"I'll go over there, then. Sorry to have awakened you."

The girl stuck a finger in the corner of her mouth. "I've

got two midterms and studied here late, so I just ended up staying over.''

"Don't worry about it. I understand." He turned toward the door. "Good luck on your exams."

Derek went outside, locking the door behind him. Things could certainly change in the course of only a few weeks, he thought. He was practically a stranger in his own house.

Derek got back into the car and within ten minutes he was at Alta Bates Hospital. He found Mark in the waiting room of the intensive care unit. The boy looked up at him, his face haggard.

"How's your mother?"

"Unchanged since last night. She's still in a coma."

Derek went over and put his hand on Mark's shoulder. "How long have you been here?"

"An hour or so. I couldn't sleep, so I came over."

"You look beat. Why don't you go home and get some rest? I'll take over now."

Mark gave him a telling, accusing look, then said, "Thanks but I think I'll stay."

"Is Dr. Duckett here yet?"

"Not yet. And the guy on duty has been tied up. The only one I've been able to talk to is the nurse."

Derek sat down beside Mark. "I'm sorry you had so much trouble reaching me last night."

"I don't suppose I can expect you to sit by the phone, but I would have appreciated knowing you'd moved in with Lara. I'd probably still be calling your place if Marcy hadn't suggested phoning the sheriff to get Lara's number. We couldn't remember her last name."

"You're right. It was stupid of me not to inform you. I wasn't thinking."

"The problem is you've written Mom off—which is your business, if that's what you want to do. But if you feel that way, I should be her guardian. Someone who cares ought to have the authority.''

"Mark, I do care about your mother, and I haven't written her off. My feelings for Margaret haven't changed.''

"Maybe so," Mark replied bitterly, "but she obviously doesn't come first in your life anymore. I'm not complaining about that, but I think you ought to face up to it. I tried to tell you to get a divorce, but you wouldn't listen to me.''

Derek leaned back, sighing deeply. "This isn't the time to discuss that. We've got your mother to think about.''

"Better late than never, I guess.'' With that Mark got up and walked to the drinking fountain up the hall. When he came back, he told Derek he was going to step outside to get some air, and that he'd be back in a little while.

After Mark had gone, Derek found the duty nurse and asked if he could see Margaret. She told him the room number and he went to find his wife. Derek went in and sat beside the bed, his eyes filling immediately. With all the surrounding paraphernalia, it was hard to get a sense of her, except that she was being sustained artificially. The face he saw was Margaret's all right, but she was only a vestige of the woman he had known and loved.

He was holding her hand when Dr. Duckett, a slender man with glasses and thin graying hair, came into the room. Derek got to his feet and they shook hands.

"Come on outside," the doctor said softly, "so that we can talk.''

Mark was waiting in the hall and the three of them went to a small office. The doctor closed the door and they all sat down.

"What's the prognosis?" Derek asked.

"It's very hard to tell. At the moment Mrs. Gordon is being sustained by life-support measures. Whether she will ever be able to function independent of artificial means, we won't know for a while, possibly weeks. The most serious and immediate threat is infection. We've given medication for prophylactic purposes, but much depends upon her resilience. Only time will tell.''

"What are the chances she'll never come out of the coma?" Mark asked.

"It's difficult to specify probabilities," the doctor replied, "but I certainly wouldn't be surprised if she became permanently dependent on artificial life support and never regained consciousness.''

"Then we'd have to decide whether to let her go on that way for the rest of her life, or withdraw life support?" Mark asked.

"We're still quite a ways from any such decision. Today we'll begin tests to ascertain the degree of impairment of brain function, if any. But we feel it's likely there's been at least some.''

"So she won't even be the same as before this attack occurred?" Derek asked.

"It's possible, but unlikely.''

Mark buried his face in his hands. "I think it would be criminal to keep her alive, just to say she isn't dead. I say pull the plug as soon as we know. Mom wouldn't want this.''

Derek swallowed hard, looking first at his stepson, who was hunched over in his chair, then at the doctor. "That's an awfully big step," he said with a tremulous voice. "I'm not sure I could agree to that. Not without conclusive evidence she couldn't recover.''

Mark sat upright. "Even if she regains consciousness, how can we impose this kind of a life on her? She had little enough before. If her mind's gone even more, it wouldn't be right to keep her alive.''

"I'm not sure we have the right to make that kind of a decision, Mark," Derek replied.

The young man's eyes widened in surprise. "You, of all people, Derek! Why keep a woman who's practically a vegetable living? She doesn't need it, and you certainly don't!"

Derek's eyes flashed. "Your mother's life will not be determined by what's convenient for me, or you, or anyone else. I'd never do that!"

Mark got to his feet. "I won't call you a hypocrite, because I know you've meant well. But I swear, Derek, I don't know what it is you really want." He stepped to the door and left the room.

Derek glanced at the doctor. "I'm sorry about that. Mark is feeling resentful that I've gone away on sabbatical...and with some justification. I suppose more of the burden has fallen on him."

"These things are difficult for all concerned," Dr. Duckett said. "But I suggest you don't worry about a decision that may not have to be made. Our first objective is to get Mrs. Gordon through the immediate crisis. We can worry about other considerations later."

They left the office, and Derek found Mark standing down the hall, his hands in his pockets, his head hanging. "Come on," Derek said, taking him by the arm. "Let's go have some breakfast."

They walked in silence for a minute, then Mark said, "I apologize for my outburst. I have no right to take this out on you."

"Forget it. We're facing some tough days. We've got to stick together."

"You know," Mark said, "what I said wasn't just bitterness. There's no reason for you to be selfless for Mom's sake, when keeping her alive really isn't helping her. I'm trying to think of her first. But I'm also thinking of you.''

"Well, maybe we see things differently, Mark. I know what I'm capable of, and what I can't do. I couldn't let Margaret go. Not that way.''

Mark said nothing further, but Derek knew he hadn't heard the last of the subject.

LARA STOOD at the window overlooking her deck. Though everything was wet and the sky was overcast, the rain had finally stopped. The weather had kept her inside her mountain retreat for days, and she was beginning to get cabin fever.

A week had passed, and Derek hadn't returned. He had called from Berkeley the afternoon after he left to say that he'd gotten there all right, Margaret was in stable condition and Mark was having a rough time.

He'd phoned on succeeding nights, and the report didn't change. Margaret hadn't gotten an infection, and she seemed to be getting stronger. The tests showed no significant brain damage as they feared, but the coma persisted.

Then one night Derek didn't call, and it put Lara into a funk. She knew he had his hands full and couldn't worry about her on top of everything else, but she despaired anyway.

The following afternoon, just after she had cleared away her lunch dishes, Derek telephoned to say Margaret had come out of her coma. There was genuine joy in his voice when he told her it looked as though things might return to the way they had been before the attack. The doctor was even looking ahead to the possibility of returning Margaret to the nursing home, though it would be at least a week before that could be decided. Lara was happy for Margaret, for Mark and for Derek, but she couldn't help feeling there was an implication for her in what had happened, a sign of some sort.

"It looks like I'm going to have to stay in Berkeley for a while," Derek said. "I've got to get things on an even keel before I can leave again."

She wasn't sure whether she heard hesitation in his voice, or perhaps doubt. Was he having second thoughts about their relationship? "I understand, Derek. Don't worry about me," she said. "Do what you have to do."

That night she had gone to bed feeling very lonely. Derek had told her that he loved her, but she could tell other things were weighing heavily upon his mind. Perhaps, being home with Margaret and Mark, he was beginning to think of her differently. He'd had a vacation from the painful realities of his life the past few months, but maybe he was ready to go home and reassume the burden he had carried for years.

The next morning Lara was working halfheartedly on a poem when the phone rang. Thinking it would be Derek, she practically ran to the kitchen to get it. But it was Carolyn Buchanan.

"Sorry to bother you," the district attorney said, "but I've been getting some pressure from Steve Adamson's lawyer for an answer to their request for a meeting. What do you want me to tell them?"

"I've been repressing the idea," Lara admitted.

"You don't have to see him if you don't want to."

"No, I think I will. It might do some good. Maybe it will help me to cope. And I feel an obligation not to turn my back on Mary Beth."

"I'll make arrangements at the county jail. Name the day, Lara."

"Let's get it over with."

"How about day after tomorrow, Friday?"

"Fine."

"Ten o'clock okay?"

"Yes, I'll be there."

Lara hung up, not entirely sure why she had agreed to the meeting. She almost felt that having it out with Steve—confronting him—would be the thing to do. And Mary Beth and her baby had been weighing on her, too. Lara wanted to know firsthand how Steve was reacting to that.

It was done, the appointment made. Still, she wished she didn't have to make the trip alone. She would have liked Derek to go with her. He might even come up for the day, if she asked him. But she didn't want to add to his concerns. Anyway, this was something she had to do. Maybe she'd ask Calle to ride up to Ukiah with her, though, just for company on the drive. Lara called her friend to see if she would go.

"Sure, I'll keep you company," Calle said, "as long as I can take Theresa and we're back by the time Jodie and little Tony get home from school."

"It shouldn't take long. I'm sure we could make it back in time."

"Then count me in. How are you doing, by the way? What do you hear from Derek?"

Lara related what had happened. She added her misgivings about Derek's state of mind, simply because she couldn't resist sharing the burden.

"It doesn't mean his feelings for you have changed, just because he's devoting a lot of time to his wife," Calle argued.

"He might not stop loving me, but this can't help but affect him. Imagine seeing his wife every day, watching her suffer. And Mark is having a rough time. Derek has to be thinking what he's doing to them is wrong."

"But *he's* not doing it," Calle had argued. "Derek isn't

responsible for his wife's illness, or his stepson's unhappiness.''

"Calle, he can't play both sides of the street forever!"

"You're getting yourself all worked up. Nothing has changed. There was a family emergency and he went to tend to it."

"Yes, but how can he leave them to come back to me?"

"Because he loves you!"

"Maybe."

"You doubt it?"

"It could just be me, Calle, but somehow I think he wants to stay there. Whether the reason's guilt, doubts about us, second thoughts or whatever. I don't know. I have bad vibrations about it."

Calle didn't say anything for several moments. "Lara, could it be that you're feeling guilty, and you're afraid?"

"Sure. I probably am. But what if it's true?"

She had a sinking feeling. "Do you think it's true?"

"Honey, I'm not in any position to know. I believe Derek loves you and that he'll be coming back to you any day. But if I'm wrong, I know you can handle it. You've been strong and independent your whole life. There's no reason why a love affair should change that."

Lara knew what Calle had said was true. She was getting emotional unnecessarily. Before she started jumping to conclusions, she would wait and see what happened.

Lara decided she was feeling sorry for herself. That made her feel guilty, because she actually had less to complain about than anyone. Wanting Derek back with her was selfish. He and Mark were the ones suffering.

"What if Margaret comes through this all right," Calle said, "and Derek has to go off to look after her every time she has an episode? How will you feel about that?"

"I honestly don't begrudge them that. I wouldn't respect

Derek if he could ignore his family when they were in need. I worry that he's gone, but I'm glad he has the decency to stand by them. Letting him do that is little enough sacrifice on my part, even if it hurts.''

"As long as you feel that way you shouldn't have to worry. I think that's all Derek could ask for.'' She paused for moment, then continued. "Besides, you've got some problems of your own to worry about. There's this business with Steve. And I'm about to give you something else to deal with.''

"What's that?''

"Jodie's birthday is in a couple of days, and Saturday I'm giving a party for her, inviting over several of her friends from school. I'll have my hands full and I'm recruiting a deputy mother. You helped that time a couple of years back, so could I interest you in the job again?''

"Of course, I'd love to help out. I haven't been to a child's birthday party since that last one of Jodie's.''

"Well, dust off your party hat, and come with bells on your toes.''

"I'll mark my calendar.''

They firmed up their plans for the drive to Ukiah and Lara hung up, feeling a lot better. Calle Bianco was the best friend a woman could possibly hope for. She seemed to understand exactly what Lara needed.

THE NIGHT BEFORE her scheduled meeting with Steve Adamson Lara slept badly. Steve was in her dreams, a nefarious presence, frightening her, yet beseeching her to enter his den, his trap. Derek was in her dreams, too. Of course, he was good—a positive force—yet he was somehow always beyond her reach, charming her from afar but never coming close enough to give her the comfort she so desperately needed.

Friday morning Lara awoke exhausted. She showered, dressed and fixed herself breakfast, wondering how she was ever going to get through the day. Whenever she thought of the last time she had seen Steve—when he'd hit her and torn her clothes—she felt ill. Why had she agreed to talk to him? But it was too late to have second thoughts now.

Lara had a little time before she had to drive over to pick up Calle, so she gave in to the temptation to contact Derek. She hadn't called him since he'd gone back to Berkeley, leaving the communication up to him.

Quickly she dialed his number before she was able to talk herself out of it. Mark answered the phone.

"Oh, hi," he said, his tone a bit forced.

"Is Derek there?" she asked, her voice wavering.

"No, he's at the hospital with Mom. An early-morning meeting with the doctor. I have a class, so I couldn't go."

"I see. How's your mother doing, by the way?"

"Better."

"Good. I'm glad to hear it."

"It just puts things back the way they were before, I guess. In a way it's good, in a way it's not so good, depending upon your point of view."

Lara knew Mark was implying something, but she wasn't about to get into it with him. "I know Derek's terribly relieved. He was really worried about your mother. It was evident when he left here how much her attack upset him."

"Derek's been pretty good, I have to admit," Mark said. "I kind of lost my cool when he first got down here. I wanted to pull the plug so Mom wouldn't have to face all the suffering. But Derek wouldn't hear of it. He got pissed off at me for even talking that way. I can see now I was jumping to conclusions. I learned something from him."

"I'm sure he would be pleased to hear that. You should tell him, Mark, if you haven't."

"Yeah, maybe I will. Thanks."

"Well, I'd better let you go. I've got a chore myself this morning. I'm going to Ukiah to see Steve."

"Your ex-husband? What are you going to see him for?"

"Give him a chance to plead for mercy, I guess. It's a long story, so I won't go into it. Maybe I want to set things straight. I've got problems to deal with just like Derek does."

"Yeah."

"Well, take care, Mark. Tell Derek I called, if you will. And I wish you all the very best down there. I hope your mother continues improving."

"Thanks, Lara. That's nice of you. I appreciate it. And I know Derek does, too."

She hung up the phone and almost burst into tears. Mark hadn't said anything to hurt her. In fact, he was rather nice. But the conversation struck her as a eulogy to her dying relationship with Derek. Calle would laugh at the notion, but Lara sensed something had changed. Maybe she had become an embarrassing digression in his life. An error to be forgotten.

Lara drove over to pick up Calle, who was still dressing Theresa when she arrived. Lara watched the little girl fuss as her mother got her into her clothes. Lara reached out to stroke the child's head.

"I know how you feel, angel. I'm not thrilled about going myself."

"Having second thoughts?" Calle asked.

"Of course."

"Nobody says you have to go through with it."

"Yes...I say I have to."

They left. Theresa settled down quietly on Calle's lap in the Jeep. They talked about other things during the drive. Calle was working on a new article, which she hoped to sell to the *San Francisco Chronicle*, and she told Lara about it. They talked a bit about Jodie's birthday party, which Theresa seemed to think was hers.

When they arrived in Ukiah Lara drove straight to the county jail on the edge of town. In the parking lot, after she turned off the engine, she looked at Calle. "What do you want to do while I'm in seeing Steve?" She dangled the car keys in her fingers. "If you want to drive Theresa to a park or something, feel free."

"You won't be that long, will you?"

"I don't know. Probably not."

"We'll just wait inside, then. They must have a reception room of some kind."

The three of them went up the walk.

"This is my first jail," Calle said under her breath as they entered the door.

Lara's nervousness had turned to outright fear. She wasn't sure if she could go through with it or not. She obviously wouldn't be in any physical danger, but even caged animals could be frightening, if you let yourself react to them instead of their circumstances.

The clerk at the reception desk asked her to wait, so she sat with Calle and Theresa. Calle had had the foresight to bring along some books for the little girl and Theresa had one open on her lap. She began recounting aloud the story suggested by the pictures.

Lara was so apprehensive, she almost felt more like the girl who had once been married to Steve than the woman she'd become. She still wasn't sure what would happen once she saw him. If it was simply his intention to plead for mercy, she hadn't figured out how to respond.

She remained angry and bitter toward him, in spite of Mary Beth's visit. But the experience had made her question whether she ought to move beyond her visceral reaction.

"What a crazy thing to be doing,' she mumbled to Calle. Her friend patted her. "You'll be fine."

Lara sat back and tried to calm herself. Calle dealt with Theresa, who was nagging her with a question. Lara took a deep breath. "You know what?" she said to her friend. "I have the strangest urge to call up my father and invite him and Ellen over for dinner or something. Isn't that weird?"

"You're dealing with some of your past garbage, why not all of it?"

"Do you suppose that's it?"

"Could be," Calle replied.

Theresa recited the tale of Little Red Riding Hood in elliptical fashion, punctuating the high points with jabs of her stubby little finger on the pages of her book. Lara cringed at the child's reference to the Big Bad Wolf.

The clerk summoned Lara to the desk. She gave Calle a not-so-brave smile and went over. The clerk sent her through some doors. At the end of a corridor she was directed into a room divided in two by a heavy wooden counter topped by thick acrylic plastic reaching to the ceiling. There was no one else in the room. Lara sat on the wooden chair in front of the speaking port, which was similar to those at the old drive-up teller windows at banks.

After two or three minutes the door on the other side of the room opened and Steve entered, accompanied by a deputy. The face was the same one that haunted her dreams, though his expression was more somber than the angry, arrogant look he'd worn at their last encounter. Steve was still physically imposing, but in prison garb he appeared chastened.

The way he stopped momentarily to stare at her, Lara

felt as though she were encountering a predator on a jungle trail. He seem surprised, as though he didn't quite believe she would be there. But there was no fear on his face at all. Fear was the emotion she seemed to have a monopoly on.

Steve moved to the chair and sat down, looking into her eyes as though he still couldn't believe her presence wasn't a trick. Lara stared at him coldly, perhaps even hatefully. Her heart was rocking with fear. This was the man who had attacked and nearly raped her.

"I didn't think you'd come," he murmured through the glass in a surprisingly timid tone.

"I don't know why I did, unless it was for Mary Beth's sake." Loathing welled inside her as she recalled his offensive touch and the blow that had nearly knocked her unconscious.

The deputy had taken a seat by the door. Steve leaned forward and looked at her through the glass, his eyes sad, his expression cowed, beaten. "I guess it won't mean nothin' to you if I say I'm sorry for what I did."

Lara clasped her trembling hands together. "It won't change anything."

Steve bowed his head. "I won't try to explain it. I felt I had a right when I did it. I was really ticked. So mad I couldn't think straight. But it was wrong. I know that now."

"Why did you want to see me?"

"I had to tell you I'm sorry to your face. I know that don't mean nothin' to you, but it does to me."

Lara's heart was pounding. When she looked into his eyes, she saw the beast that had nearly devoured her. "Is that all?"

"I guess Mary Beth told you what happened," he said, lowering his eyes again.

"You mean that she's pregnant?"

Steve nodded.

"I feel sorry for her."

He glanced up with surprise, as though that thought had never occurred to him. "I know you hate me," he said, "but me and her are still married. And now we're going to have a baby."

"I have a feeling you want to ask me something," Lara said, wanting to get it over with.

"After they arrested me, I sort of gave up on everything," he said. "The only thing I was sorry about was that they didn't beat the hell out of me. I know that sounds funny, but it's true."

Lara could understand that. She had the same regret, though she didn't tell him.

"It's like getting it was almost as good as giving it to somebody else," he continued. "I didn't care what happened to me. Then when Mary Beth came and told me we was going to have a baby, everything sort of changed inside me."

Lara stared into his eyes. For a long time they simply looked at each other. Then she sensed something different in him, as if maybe he had been affected by his wife's pregnancy after all. Steve wasn't capable of acting. She knew that. "It ain't like I found religion, or nothing like that," he said. "Me and Mary Beth talked about babies before. Or she did, anyway. But I never really thought about one. Not like it was real or anything."

"What are you trying to say? That now that you're going to be a father, I ought to take compassion on you and forget what you did? You want me to drop the charges, is that it?"

"Hell, Lara, it ought to be obvious I don't want to do

hard time, especially not now that I'm goin' to be a daddy. I want out of here. What else can I tell you?''

She stared at him blankly. What it boiled down to was Steve's feelings about himself had changed. He had different aspirations now. Something more socially acceptable. But did that mean *he* had changed? And did it matter, even if he had?

"I don't see how I can forget what you did to me," Lara said, trying to keep a tight rein on her emotions. "Mary Beth got pregnant because you took advantage of her for your own gratification. There's no valor in that. It was an accident. What if you'd raped me and I got pregnant? Would that make you some kind of a hero? Getting a woman pregnant is no achievement, Steve. Being a husband and a father is."

"I need a chance," he said weakly.

The adrenaline was flowing so heavily that Lara was trembling. Indignation had slowly replaced her initial fear, and it was on the point of boiling over. "There's no reason you should profit from Mary Beth's misfortune," she snapped.

"She don't want a divorce now," he said almost pleadingly. "I told her I'd try and change. I told her I'd try not to lose my temper the way I do. I told her I'd stop drinkin'."

"It takes more than wanting to change, Steve. You need professional help."

He nodded. "I know."

"So now you want to make Mary Beth and the baby my problem. Is that what this is boiling down to?" Lara knew the answer, had known it even before she agreed to come. Steve wasn't a complex person. What she wasn't sure of was how much he might have been affected by what had happened to his wife, and how much he simply found convenient.

"I don't want to make it your problem, Lara. I just want a chance."

"I figured this was why you wanted to talk to me. And to tell you the truth, I didn't know what I'd do, how I'd feel when you begged for mercy." He waited, watching her sullenly. He seemed to sense it had become futile. She took a deep breath, then continued. "I've decided you shouldn't benefit from a chance event."

"What do you mean?"

"I mean, if you care about Mary Beth and that baby, you'll have to do something about it yourself. Getting out of jail's not the solution, it's only the start."

"Well, I can't do nothin' from in here," he snapped. It was the first overt sign of hostility.

"Steve, I can't stop them from trying you, and I'm not going to ruin their case by refusing to cooperate."

"So you're going to see me hang."

"As far as I'm concerned you've got to pay for what you did. I'm angry still. The truth is, I hate you. Maybe I'll learn to feel sorry for you. Maybe, because of Mary Beth, I feel a little compassion already. But what happens in your life is up to you. You can get through this thing, and if you spend some time in jail, you either come out a changed man, or you can come out bitter. That's up to you."

"But you can help me, Lara. You can make a difference."

"I can scream bloody murder for your scalp, or I can let nature take its course. Those are the only realistic choices."

Steve dropped his head onto his hands. "If you want me to beg you, I will. I'm sorry for what I done to you. Honest I am."

Try as she might, Lara could conjure up no real compassion. She was still shaking with revulsion, even with the Plexiglas between them, even with Steve contrite and begging her forgiveness. "If you want to do yourself some good," she said when he looked up at her, "you can start thinking about Mary Beth and that baby.

"You can convince the psychologists and social workers and the district attorney's office that you're a new man. You can prove you deserve a light sentence, because you're going to be a decent citizen when you get out. You can get some probation time, or an early release from jail. All that's up to you, Steve, not me."

He stared at her dumbly, trying to decide if she was selling him down the river, or giving him hope. His eyes glossed with tears. "Then you're washing your hands of me?"

Lara nodded, feeling his pain despite her hatred, her loathing. Once more he dropped his head. Then, to her surprise, he began sobbing. She watched him cry, noticing the strange effect it had on her. The tension she'd been feeling seemed to drain away. It was almost as if she was the one crying.

After a minute or two, Steve lifted his head. He wiped his eyes and cheeks with his sleeves. He was just a boy in a man's body. Staring at her, he nodded. "Somehow I knew it would turn out this way." A slight smile actually touched his lips. "Maybe it's better. Maybe you're right, Lara."

There was no anger on his face, no desperation. For the first time in her life, Steve Adamson seemed pathetic to her. The conversation had run its course. Lara got to her feet. "I'm going now," she announced in a low voice.

Again he nodded.

But the way he was staring held her gaze. For a moment she couldn't move.

Then he said. "Lara, just forgive me. Will you?"

Tears suddenly flooded her eyes. She'd managed to hold back most every emotion but fear and anger, but now she was overwhelmed with compassion. It was inexplicable, but she felt it. She bit her lip, then whispered, "Yes," and left the room.

By the time she reached the waiting room, tears were streaming down her cheeks. Calle, with Theresa sitting on her lap, looked up as she came through the doors. Calle's expression was questioning, but she said only one thing. "You all right?"

Lara nodded, and Calle gathered up her daughter and the storybooks. Lara was already at the door, holding it open, when Calle got there. They went out into the sunshine and down the walkway toward the Jeep.

"How about if I buy you two a hamburger?" Lara said, her voice unsteady with emotion.

"And french fries?" Theresa chimed in.

"Yes," Lara said with a laugh. "And french fries, too."

CHAPTER SIXTEEN

ON THE WAY BACK to Mendocino Calle admitted she was miffed because Tony had planned a duck-hunting trip for the weekend, having forgotten about his daughter's birthday party. He had promised to leave early, with the intention of getting back in time for the party Saturday afternoon, but Calle told Lara that she was angry anyway.

"His buddies are coming for him after work this evening," she said, "so why don't you spend the night? That way we'll have the house to ourselves. The way I feel, I'd prefer your company anyway."

"I'm sure Tony didn't intend to forget the party. Besides, if he makes it back there's no harm done, is there?"

"It's not just that," Calle said, grousing. "It's the poor ducks. I abhor killing for sport. It's the only thing about Tony I truly don't like."

Lara agreed to spend the night, sensing it would help calm the troubled waters in the Bianco household. Besides, it seemed the least she could do, considering all Calle had done for her.

Tony arrived home an hour after the women got back from Ukiah. Calle turned a cold shoulder to him, which struck Lara as uncharacteristic. She could see the hunting trip was a real problem between them. In the end, it was she who took the kids out on the porch to wave goodbye to their father when his friends arrived. Calle was pretending to be busy in the kitchen. Lara couldn't help feeling a little sorry for Tony as he waved goodbye with a sheepish grin.

Calle turned from the stove when Lara came back into the house. "So, is Bwana gone?"

Lara had trouble keeping a straight face. "Yes."

"I hope a duck poops on his head," Calle fumed.

Lara couldn't help giggling. Her friend turned back to the pot she was stirring on the stove, resting her hand on her ample hip.

"How can such an otherwise decent man be so insensitive to life?"

"Maybe it's genetic, an instinct," Lara said.

"If so, the human race is doomed."

"Each generation of women can try to civilize its sons a little more."

"Yes," Calle agreed, "we are the world's best hope, aren't we?"

Tony Two came running through the kitchen with a yardstick just then, pretending it was a shotgun. Calle groaned and took the stick away from him.

"Why don't you read that Audubon book you got for Christmas last year?" The boy made a face and ran out of the room, shooting imaginary ducks with an imaginary gun. "One step forward and two steps back," Calle said, rolling her eyes. "Does Derek show any of the traditional hunter-warrior traits?"

"He's protective."

"That's the good side, I guess."

"Tony's a wonderful father and husband, Calle. You can't condemn him across the board."

"That's true, but I'm not in a mood to be charitable."

Lara sat at the table, realizing that she was feeling quite sad. Derek seemed so remote just then. How could what they had slip away so easily? Things had been so perfect for a while, at least on the surface. Or had she been deceiving herself all along?

"You're missing Derek, aren't you?" Calle asked.

Her insight was astounding, for its timing at least. "Don't tell me that was written on my face," Lara said.

Calle nodded.

"Some hunters come home, others don't."

Calle came and sat at the table with her. "Why don't you drive down to Berkeley and see him?"

Lara shook her head. "Too desperate. Anyway, if he wanted me there he'd ask me to come. He's got plenty on his mind."

"You're probably right."

"I've got to go on with my life and let the chips fall where they may."

They looked at each other, each propping her chin on her hands. After a moment they both smiled. "Aren't we a sorry pair, though," Calle said.

Little Theresa came into the kitchen, her eyes full of tears over some sibling transgression. Lara picked her up and sat her on her lap, wiping away the tears. Then she pressed her cheek on the tot's head. "Maybe not having one of these is my greatest misfortune. I'm beginning to see why Mary Beth's situation kind of got to me."

Calle got up to return to the stove. "I don't care how negative you're feeling," she said over her shoulder, "I personally think everything is going to work out just great."

Lara, Calle and the three kids had dinner. Afterward Calle read aloud the fairy tale about the Ugly Duckling while Lara listened with sentimental amusement. While Theresa was put to bed, the older children were allowed to watch a television show in the den. Lara was alone in the front room when the phone rang.

"Would you mind getting that?" Calle called from the bathroom. "I'm up to my elbows in soap bubbles."

Lara took the call in the kitchen.

"Just the lady I've been looking for." It was Derek. "I've been trying your place all afternoon and evening. So I took a chance you'd be at Calle's."

"I'm deputy mother for the weekend." She explained about the party for Jodie, and Tony's hunting trip.

"Sounds like you're keeping busy."

"I'm trying." She wondered if she sounded as tentative as she felt.

"Mark told me you called this morning...that you were going to Ukiah to see Steve. I wish I'd known, Lara. I would have come up."

"That's sweet, but I was able to handle it alone."

There was a pause.

"How did it go?"

"It was a bit emotional, but on balance good, I think. I got out some anger and did some forgiving."

"I wish I could have been with you."

"Calle rode up with me. I wasn't alone."

There was another pause.

"Are you all right, Lara?"

"Sure. What do you mean?"

"I sense something."

"I don't know what." She decided she must be a lot more transparent than she thought.

"I miss you."

"I miss you, too." She was sincere all right, but she herself heard the formality in her tone.

"I'm sorry this business is dragging out like this. Margaret seems to be out of danger. The doctors are mystified. She even seemed to recognize me this morning when I visited her."

For the life of her, Lara didn't know what to say.

"I think Mark is more relieved than he lets on," he continued.

"Good. It's been rough for him, I know."

Derek sighed. "But he and I haven't made a lot of progress on where we stand. There's been communication, but not total acceptance. That's my biggest problem at the moment, getting things resolved between us."

"He spoke appreciatively of you this morning," Lara said. "Things may be better than you think."

"He mentioned what you said. Thank you. You've been great through this, Lara. I want you to know how much I appreciate it."

Tears filled her eyes. There it was again, the eulogy. "It's nothing," she managed, in barely a whisper.

"I can't tell you when exactly, but I'll be coming back up."

To say goodbye? she wondered. "Okay."

"I miss you and I love you," Derek said.

A tear rolled down each of her cheeks. "Yeah, me too."

When Calle came into the kitchen several minutes later, Lara was sitting at the table, her head buried in her arms. She was crying softly. Calle didn't ask for the details. It wasn't necessary when Lara told her Derek had called, and he was still struggling to work things out with his family.

MARCY BRANDT HAD FLOWN to San Diego to spend the weekend with her parents. Derek was glad because he wanted the opportunity to spend sometime alone with Mark. Sunday evening he suggested they go to the faculty club for dinner. After driving to the campus, they walked in the moonlight to the rustic wood-and-glass structure nestled under some large oak trees. It was a cool, still evening.

A ring around the moon indicated a weather front was on its way.

They had a prime rib dinner in a quiet corner of the main dining room, dominated at one end by a massive stone fireplace. They drank their coffee after the dishes had been cleared. Mark seemed to sense Derek had something he wanted to say.

"What are you going to do now that Mom's on the road to recovery?" the young man asked, giving Derek his opportunity.

"I wanted to talk to you about that."

"That's what I figured."

"I've done a lot of soul-searching," Derek said. "I don't think it's right to leave things up in the air. It's not fair to you, to Lara or even in a way to your mother."

"What are you saying?"

"That I've come to a decision." Derek paused, looking deeply into his stepson's eyes. "I'm going to see the lawyer tomorrow about filing for divorce and making you Margaret's guardian, if you want and are willing to take the responsibility."

For a moment Mark didn't say anything. "So, you're actually going to do it."

Derek nodded. "It's the most honest thing to do, considering the way I feel."

Mark lowered his eyes, fiddling with his coffee cup. "A month ago it would have torn me up to hear you say that, but it almost comes as a relief now."

"I've worried about putting too much burden on you. That's been my number-one concern."

"The burden is more psychological than anything else. But don't worry. I can handle it, no sweat."

"I don't want you to think I intend to abandon you. As far as I'm concerned you'll always be my son, Mark. And

I'll always be there for you. It's just that it wouldn't be proper for me to remain in a control position if your mother and I are divorced."

"No, and I wouldn't want you to. It's my responsibility."

"I appreciate the way you're taking this," Derek said.

"I was the first one to suggest divorce, remember?"

"Yes, but it wasn't the right thing to do when you brought it up. But the way I feel about Lara now makes it impossible to continue as we have in the past. And I'm also confident about you being able to handle things—with my help and counsel, if you wish it."

Mark nodded. "Have you told Lara?"

"No. I'm going back to Mendocino after I finish with the lawyers tomorrow."

Mark picked up the cup, toying with it. "It's not really fitting to toast your happiness with half a cup of lukewarm coffee, but I don't suppose they'd serve me any champagne at the faculty club."

"We can have a drink when we get home, if you like."

Mark glanced up at him, his eyes a little misty. "So, we've come to a milestone."

"It's not the end for you and me."

"No, but I can't forget Mom. I'm not bitter anymore, but I can't forget her."

"Of course you can't. And I can't forget her, either. This hasn't been an easy decision for me."

"I don't envy you," Mark said.

"I loved your mother," Derek said, leaning back. "I still do in a way. But there is another person in my life. I love Lara now, and I feel every bit for her what I felt for Margaret. And that's not to take anything away from either of them. One's love doesn't change with the tides. If love means anything it builds over time, it defines itself, it develops a life of its own. What's happened with Lara isn't whimsy. It's where I am now."

"You don't have to explain."

"Whether you can fully accept it or not, I want you to know how I feel."

Derek signed the chit, and they went out of the club into the brisk autumn air. They strolled along the meandering walk under the light of the scattered lampposts.

"I hope Lara isn't too angry with me," Mark said. "I didn't feel very charitable toward her at first. She's probably pretty resentful."

"I'm sure she's not. This has been tough for her, too. No woman enjoys a relationship with a married man."

"And dealing with his kid has to be hell."

"She'll be glad to know you're sensitive to the issue."

"Maybe Marcy and I will come up and see you two after things settle down."

"I'd like that. I know Lara would, too." Derek glanced over at Mark. They were nearing the parking lot. He felt as though a tremendous burden had been lifted. But all the talk about Lara had made him very anxious to see her.

She hadn't been far from his thoughts, ever. But Derek had known that their relationship couldn't progress until he settled things in Berkeley, and with Mark.

They came to the car. Derek unlocked it and they climbed in. He glanced over at his stepson in the faint light. Mark was a man now, but Derek couldn't help feeling a bit protective toward him. He put his hand on the young man's arm. "Thanks, Mark."

Mark smiled at him with shining eyes. "Thanks yourself, Dad."

DEREK TURNED OFF Flat Pine Road and went up Lara's drive, his headlights illuminating the muddy track that twisted up the slope. It had rained during practically the entire trip from the Bay Area and, judging by the condition of the drive, the storm had pretty well drenched the Mendocino coast.

He had tried to call Lara Sunday night to tell her he was coming, but got no answer. He tried Calle's but she wasn't there, either. Calle told him Lara had talked about taking a drive on Sunday. "Maybe she decided to get away for a day or two and clear the cobwebs," she said. "I'll tell her you called if I see her."

As he neared the top of the promontory where the cabin was located, Derek spotted the roofline of the building. He was relieved to see light coming from within, but the sight of a strange vehicle parked out front gave him pause. It was an old but well-maintained pickup truck, its shiny paint reflecting the light from the porch.

He couldn't imagine who might be visiting Lara, and was concerned that, because he hadn't been able to reach her, his sudden appearance might be inopportune. But he was so anxious to see her that he wasn't going to be deterred.

The rain began coming down heavily as he parked the BMW next to the truck. Pulling up the collar of his sport coat for protection, Derek dashed up onto the porch and knocked on the door. The faint sound of voices inside stopped. After several moments the door opened, and Lara appeared in a clingy blue knit dress and her hair pulled back in a chignon. She looked beautiful, so beautiful his heart ached.

A surprised expression filled her face. "Derek!"

He stood before her, his skin spattered with raindrops, his collar up, his hair looking particularly dark and shiny from the moisture. He smiled, but there was a touch of concern on his face. "Did I come at a bad time?"

She laughed and pulled him in from the weather. She

had no sooner closed the door than his arms were around her. She lifted her face and he kissed her.

"What are you doing here?" she murmured into his lips. "I thought you were in Berkeley."

"I tried calling you all day yesterday and this morning." He glanced toward the front room, but from where they stood in the entry no one could be seen.

"I went for a drive and ended up at my father and Ellen's place," she said. "I spent the night, and invited them for dinner. They're here now."

"They are?"

"Yes," she said, taking him by the hand. "Come on in."

Derek seemed prepared to protest, but she led him into the front room anyway. The Serenovs were seated at a small table covered with a white cloth. There were flowers in a silver bowl and candles.

"Look who's here," she announced. Glancing at Derek proudly, she squeezed his hand.

Nikolai Serenov, wearing a sport jacket and open-necked shirt, got to his feet. His wife, looking a bit uncomfortable in a print dress, sat expressionless.

"Well, good evening, Professor Gordon," Nikolai said. He stepped around the table and extended his hand.

Derek took it. "Good evening," he said. "Mrs. Serenov," he added, nodding politely at Lara's stepmother. "I'm sorry to walk in on your dinner party like this."

"Glad to see you, son," Nikolai said. "Don't apologize." He grinned broadly. The atmosphere generally was much friendlier than when last Derek saw the family together.

"We were about to have dessert," Lara said, slipping her arm around Derek's waist. "Have you eaten?"

"I had a bite along the way."

"But you'll have some apple pie, won't you?"

He smiled down at her, looking genuinely happy now. "Sure."

Lara realized she didn't know why he'd come back so suddenly, what his state of mind was or even what she should think. The way he'd kissed her when he came in the door told her he was happy to see her. But she needed to know for sure.

"Come on, then," she said, taking his hand again, "you can help me cut the pie."

They went into the kitchen and she closed the door. Then she turned around to find his arms encircling her again. She put a finger to his lips when he leaned forward to kiss her, stopping him.

"Can I interrupt this display of affection with a few questions?"

Derek grinned. "Sure. What do you want to ask?"

"Why are you here? What's happened?"

He touched her nose with his fingertip. "I love you."

She waited expectantly, but he didn't say more. "That's all?"

He shrugged. "I got tired of being apart from you, so I came home."

Home! Did he mean that? Was he building up to something? Derek seemed determined to play things out with agonizing lethargy. "What about Margaret and Mark?"

"I said I would stay in Berkeley until I got things straightened around. And they are now. Margaret was taken back to the nursing home this morning. Yesterday Mark and I had a heart-to-heart talk. We've worked things out."

Lara brushed away the moisture that was still on his cheek with her fingers. She steeled herself for the inevitable. "We go back to the way things were, is that it?"

Derek shook his head, his expression turning somber. "No, we can't go back. Those days are behind us."

She moved a few inches away, searching his eyes, afraid to hope. "So what are we going to do?"

"Get married."

Lara blinked. "What?"

"Before I left I instructed my lawyer to initiate divorce proceedings. I'd been resisting taking the step, but the past weeks convinced me it was the thing to do—for everybody's sake."

"Derek..."

"It'll be a while before it's final, of course. Mark will be twenty-one in a few weeks, and he and I have agreed he should become Margaret's guardian. It's what he wants, and it will resolve things satisfactorily as far as I'm concerned."

Lara reached up and took his face in her hands. "You want to marry me?"

A smile tugged at the corner of his mouth. "You ask like you're surprised."

"I knew you loved me, but I didn't expect this. I wouldn't let myself think about it. I never even mentioned the word to Calle."

"Now you can," he said, sliding her arms around his waist and pulling her against him.

"You're really serious!"

"Of course I am." He searched her eyes. "You *will* marry me, won't you? I didn't rush up here to get a refusal, did I?"

She threw her head back and laughed. "Of course I'll marry you," she said into his lips. "As soon as we can."

Lara closed her eyes and let him kiss her. She gave herself up to his embrace, feeling totally free to love for the first time in her life. The realization brought tears to her eyes. When her lids opened, Derek was gazing at her, as misty-eyed as she.

"I love you," he whispered.

"And I love you."

They kissed again. Then Lara stiffened.

"Derek…"

"What?"

"Do you realize my father and stepmother are sitting in the next room? You just proposed to me, and they're sitting right in there!"

Derek glanced toward the door. "So? Is your father old-fashioned or something?"

Lara started giggling.

"What? Does he expect me to ask for your hand? Is that what you're suggesting?"

"No, but it strikes me as funny to think my dad's right here in the house, and a man just asked me to marry him."

Derek's cheeks colored a little. "Do you think we should tell them?"

Her heart began pounding with excitement as she stared at him. Then she nodded eagerly. "Would you mind?"

"Not if you want to."

"Come on," she said, taking his hand. She gave him a quick peck on the cheek and opened the door.

Nikolai and Ellen looked toward the door. "Damned slow at cuttin' a pie, aren't you, daughter?" her father said mischievously.

"The pie will take a few more minutes, Daddy," Lara said. A few tears, happy tears spilled from her eyes and she wiped them away. "Derek and I have something important to announce first."

"Oh?" Nikolai Serenov's broad smile told Lara exactly what his reaction would be.

"Derek just asked me to marry him!" she said gleefully.

Her father clapped his hands together and shouted his congratulations. Lara turned to Derek then, put her arms around him and hugged him with all her might. She felt his breath in her hair and he whispered his love again.

The words played back in her mind. "I love you. I love you." In the years ahead she would never hear that from him too often. Not for as long as they lived.

EPILOGUE

LARA PEERED INTO the oven at the turkey, then closed the door. She took a deep breath, loving the aroma of roasting fowl and the pungent herbs in the dressing. Outside the cabin she heard the steady thump of the ax, a sound that still brought her contentment.

She went into the living room where the lights of the Christmas tree cast a warm glow into the semidarkness of the room. There was a mountain of presents under the tree, filling nearly half the room. The trunk of the car had been loaded transporting them up from Berkeley. There had hardly been room for their luggage.

The other half of the room was taken up by the long table they'd rented. It was covered with a white cloth and already set, the red candles in the holders ready to be lit as soon as the guests arrived.

Lara moved past the table and peered out at gray sky that looked even colder than it was. She listened to the beat of the ax, then noticed a few snowflakes falling. Her eyes opened wide with delight. Snow! It probably wouldn't amount to much; it rarely snowed that near the coast and almost never stayed long when it did. But the thought of a white Christmas seemed terribly romantic.

As she stared out at the woods she loved so much, the snowfall grew heavier, and it actually began accumulating on the railing of the deck. Smiling happily, Lara slipped down in the chair to watch. On the end table next to her were half a dozen cards and letters they'd picked up in town, mail that hadn't been forwarded to Berkeley.

Idly Lara picked up the top envelope, the card and note from Mary Beth. It was the second time they'd heard from the Adamsons since the trial four years earlier. The card that had come the previous Christmas was a breakthrough, but this one Lara had enjoyed even more. The note was longer and friendlier, and there were pictures not only of Scott, their older child, but of the new baby, too.

Lara slipped out the letter and read it again.

Dear Lara,

It's hard to believe another year has slipped by. This Christmas finds four of us at home. Melissa was born September 27th. I'm sending a picture of both babies.

The lumber business here in Oregon isn't much more predictable than down in California, but we are managing to get by, and when there's layoffs, Steve is one of the last they let go. He worked pretty steady all year, so we bought a little house. Can you believe it?

I was so pleased to get your news. How many women can say they got a master's degree, a baby and a new stepdaughter-in-law in the same month? June must have been interesting in your house. I'm not sure what tenure means, but tell Derek congratulations for that, too.

Last year I told you why I decided to write after all that happened and the time that passed, so I won't say it again. But I wanted you to know Steve and I talked about it this year, and he's started seeing how at this season of the year it's important to ask for forgiveness, and to love. It took me a while to appreciate what you did was right, but I think now Steve does, too. It may not mean anything to you, but I thought you might like to hear it.

Even if I'm the only one who ever says it, I want you to know there's love in our family, Lara. For everyone.

Mary Beth

Lara brushed a tear from her eye and pushed the note back inside the envelope. She looked out the window and saw that a fine dust of snow covered the deck. It was almost time to start on the vegetables, so she got up to return to the kitchen.

As she paused to straighten a fork on the dinner table, Derek came in the front door with an armload of firewood. A rush of icy air came down the hall into the front room before he managed to push the door closed with his foot. He went to the fireplace, a big grin on his face.

"Remind me to chop wood in the summer," he said, dumping the split logs onto the hearth. "It's cold out there!"

"Isn't the snow beautiful, though?" She took him by the arm and led him to the sliding glass door. "Look at it!"

"It's beautiful all right, but not conducive to chopping wood. I would have been smarter to do it yesterday, before we went over to the Biancos.'" He put his arm around her.

Lara shivered at the cool dampness of his coat. "I hope it won't make Mark and Marcy's drive up difficult."

"A couple of kids that ski like they do won't be bothered by a little powder on the pavement." He kissed her on the cheek.

"Still, I thought they would be here by now."

"Mark told me on the phone he wanted to go by the cemetery on the way to put some flowers on Margaret's grave. He did it last year and I think he wants to make a tradition of it, a sort of memorial to his mother. He told me once he missed her most around the holidays."

"He's really a sensitive young man, isn't he? Is that something he inherited, or did he learn it from you?"

Derek grinned. "I've always been willing to take credit for the good traits."

She pinched his chin. "I bet you have."

"Speaking of trouble," Derek said, glancing up toward the loft, "why is my daughter being so quiet?"

"Why is it that she's your daughter when she's sleeping and playing, and she's my daughter the rest of the time?"

"You noticed that, huh?"

Lara cuffed him. "I should be getting her up, actually. Otherwise she'll be awake all night."

"One more load of wood, then I'll build the fire. It'll be nice to have it going when the kids and your parents get here."

He headed back outside and Lara went upstairs to get the baby. She was already awake when Lara got to her crib. Alexandra had Lara's blue-green eyes, but Derek's dark hair. He called her his other beauty queen.

After a quick change of diapers, mother and daughter went down to admire the tree, which had become the baby's principal entertainment since they'd trimmed it a few days earlier. Derek had just gotten the fire going and stood up, beaming at them, as they walked over.

Holding out his arms he took Alexandra, giving her a kiss. She fussed a little because of Derek's cold skin, but the two of them got down near the fire to warm up and observe the dancing flames. Lara proudly watched them together.

She sat in the easy chair nearby and after a minute Derek and Alexandra scooted back to be near her. He leaned his back against her knees. Lara stroked his hair as the three of them stared at the cheery flames. The baby cooed and flailed her arms excitedly, wanting to get closer. But Derek held her tightly.

Lara lightly ran her fingers under his collar at the back of his neck, caressing him affectionately. "Whenever we come up here, I marvel that I actually lived alone in this cabin all those years. It's hard to remember what it was like before we were together."

"It got cold in bed at night. And you didn't have to change any diapers."

She laughed. "Changing diapers isn't a bad trade-off for your warm feet. You aren't completely without redeeming features."

He looked up at her. "Say it isn't so."

Lara leaned over and kissed the top of his head. "I'd rather keep you guessing."

Just then they heard the sound of car doors slamming outside.

"Sounds like guests," Derek said.

The three of them roused themselves. Lara took the baby, and before Derek could get to the door, they heard singing.

"What's going on?" he said with a look at Lara.

They went to the kitchen window and saw Mark and Marcy standing on the porch, bundled up with candles in their hands, singing Christmas carols. Lara held the baby close to the window so she could see. Her little eyes grew round, and the singers, seeing her, smiled.

The lights of Nikolai's truck appeared then, coming up the drive.

"Oh, look," Lara said to the baby, "there's Grandpa and Grandma!"

Alexandra began clapping her plump little hands. They

all laughed and Derek leaned close to Lara, his arm around her. "It looks like the family's home for the holidays," he said into her ear. She beamed at him and he smiled back. "I love you, darling," he whispered. "Merry Christmas."

HARLEQUIN PRESENTS®

HARLEQUIN PRESENTS
men you won't be able to resist
falling in love with...

HARLEQUIN PRESENTS
women who have feelings
just like your own...

HARLEQUIN PRESENTS
powerful passion in
exotic international settings...

HARLEQUIN PRESENTS
intense, dramatic stories that will keep you
turning to the very last page...

HARLEQUIN PRESENTS
The world's bestselling romance series!

Harlequin® Historical

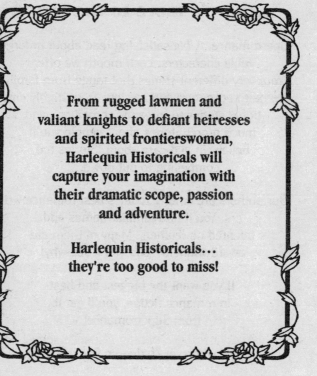

From rugged lawmen and
valiant knights to defiant heiresses
and spirited frontierswomen,
Harlequin Historicals will
capture your imagination with
their dramatic scope, passion
and adventure.

Harlequin Historicals...
they're too good to miss!

HHGENR

HARLEQUIN SUPERROMANCE®

...there's more to the story!

Superromance. A *big* satisfying read about unforget-
table characters. Each month we offer
four very different stories that range from family
drama to adventure and mystery, from highly emotional stories to romantic comedies—and
much more! Stories about people you'll
believe in and care about. Stories too
compelling to put down....

Our authors are among today's *best* romance writers. You'll find familiar names and
talented newcomers. Many of them are
award winners—and you'll see why!

If you want the biggest and best
in romance fiction, you'll get it
from Superromance!

Available wherever Harlequin books are sold.

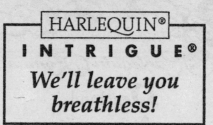

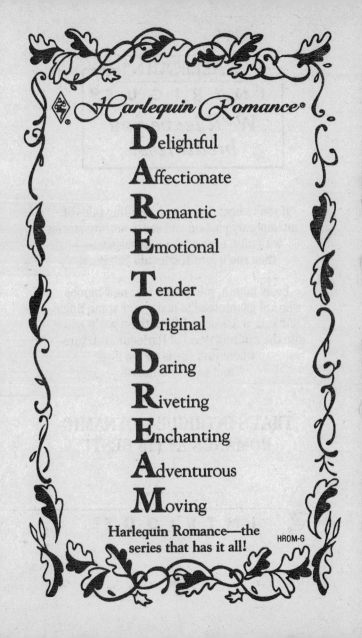

Harlequin Romance®

Delightful

Affectionate

Romantic

Emotional

Tender

Original

Daring

Riveting

Enchanting

Adventurous

Moving

Harlequin Romance—the
series that has it all!

HROM-G